SPIF
WITC..

THE LAZY GIRL'S GUIDE TO MAGIC

BOOK THREE

Copyright © 2017 Helen Harper
All rights reserved.

For Adrianna

Chapter One

Winter was driving me nuts. Stark raving bonkers. While I lay limp on the sofa, like some fainting miss from another century, he was cleaning with a vengeance. Yes, it afforded me an excellent view of his nicely shaped bottom, but the man wouldn't sit still.

Ordinarily, of course, I wouldn't have complained. Having someone do my housework for me should have been manna from heaven. But he'd spent all of yesterday cleaning and the day before that. Not to mention most of the weekend as well. I didn't think there was a single inch of my flat that wasn't sparkly. Apart from the old lady covered in cobwebs and sitting in the far corner staring at me. But she was another story.

Brutus was curled up on the windowsill, his tail twitching. Winter had learned the hard way not to interrupt him while he was sleeping. That corner was about the only safe place; everywhere else was being scrubbed and polished to within an inch of its life.

'Why don't you take a break?' I suggested.

His head jerked up. I'd never get tired of those blue eyes looking at me. 'Are you alright? Do *you* need a break? A cup of tea? A biscuit? More painkillers? How about…'

I held up my hand. 'I'm fine, Rafe,' I said softly. 'I don't need anything. But you need to stop cleaning. There's no more dirt. You've scared it all away.'

'You're right.'

I breathed out a sigh of relief.

'I'll just bleach the grout in the bathroom—'

'Raphael!' I bawled. 'Please, no grout! The grout is fine. It doesn't need bleaching.'

'There's a bit in the corner that looks grubby.'

I didn't think I'd ever had such a long conversation about grout before. In fact, I didn't think the word grout had ever passed my lips. 'Just sit down. Relax. You're like a perpetual-motion machine.'

He gave a brief nod and perched on the sofa beside me. He was hardly relaxed, however. He looked as if he were about to spring up at the first sign of a mote of dust. I pushed myself up towards him, ignoring the flash of pain that rapidly uncoiled deep in my chest and seemed to spring out in all directions. I leaned my chin on his shoulder.

'Chill for a bit,' I whispered. I twirled my fingers into the dark curl that was edging adorably round the nape of his neck and gave it a gentle tug. 'There are other things we can do. You don't have to clean.' I let my fingers trail down the nubs of his spine, seeking out the bare skin just above his belt. Winter groaned slightly – then he pulled away. Arse.

'You know what the doctor said.'

'I really do think I'm feeling better.'

He turned round and met my eyes. 'Good,' he said. 'But we can't take any chances.' He dipped his head and brushed his lips against mine, feather light as if he thought his kiss might break me. What he didn't realise was that the touch of his lips had broken me long ago. I was Winter's, body and soul. I couldn't see a future without him in it and all I wanted to do was to feel him wrapped around me for eternity. I couldn't say exactly when I'd transformed into the sort of soppy sack whom I'd normally slap around the face and truthfully it didn't really matter. Having Winter here with me was about the best thing that could have happened. But, good grief, he needed to learn the art of relaxing.

The old lady cackled and I jumped. Winter frowned at me. 'What's wrong?'

Somehow I didn't think 'I see dead people' would encourage him to chill out. 'Something walked over my grave,' I dismissed. That was truer to the mark than he realised. 'It's nothing.' The old lady scowled at me as if I'd just cursed her firstborn. I passed a hand in front of my eyes. Maybe I really was going mad.

'Do you need another blanket?' Winter asked.

'Nope.'

'Shall I plump your cushions so you're more comfortable?'

'Nope.'

'Do you need…'

'Rafe,' I sighed. 'All I need is you.'

His mouth curved into a smile. 'You've got me, Ivy Wilde. I'm yours.'

I smiled back happily and snuggled deeper against him. 'I know.'

'When I lived here,' the old lady interrupted, 'I always had flowers on this windowsill.' She frowned at Brutus. 'Not a cat. Filthy creatures.'

Brutus opened a slitted eye in her direction. Wait a hallucinatory minute; could he see her too?

'And my lounge chairs faced in the other direction.' The old woman sniffed. 'You have the furniture arranged all wrong.'

Brutus went back to sleep. I wrinkled my nose; I couldn't ask my perpetually hungry familiar about the old lady with Winter here. The last thing I wanted was to worry him with the fact that I was still hallucinating. He'd have the doctor round here in an instant. Or worse, he'd demand that I went back into hospital just to be sure that I wasn't dying. It was lovely having someone so concerned about my health but it could be a bit tiring too.

Princess Parma Periwinkle, Winter's familiar, strolled in and gave him a meaningful glance. He shot to his feet. A heartbeat later, there was a knock on the door. Winter all but ran for it.

I sank down again, hearing a soft murmur of voices. Eve appeared, a hesitant smile on her face. 'Ivy! How's the invalid? Are you alright? Is there anything I can get you?'

I groaned. Death by solicitous concern. 'I'm fine,' I told her. 'Really.' Then I paused. 'Actually if you could get me some gummy bears from the corner shop, that'd be lovely.'

'Gummy bears.' Eve nodded. 'No problem.'

'And maybe some salt-and-vinegar crisps. A multi-pack. The ones with ridges.'

'Sure.'

'A family-sized chocolate bar,' I added for good measure. 'And—'

Winter rolled his eyes. 'How about a cup of tea for you both instead?' he said, heading for the kitchen. I grinned. This was awesome.

Eve sat down, raising an eyebrow in my direction. 'You've got him wrapped around your little finger.'

'I have – although he's driving me a little crazy,' I confided. 'He won't take two minutes to sit back and rest. I don't think unemployment suits him.'

'Have you spoken to him about the Order?'

I sighed. 'I've tried. It's like talking to a brick wall. He doesn't want anything to do with them. But…' My voice trailed away.

'Without the Order, he doesn't know what to do with himself.'

I nodded. Eve understood. The Hallowed Order of Magical Enlightenment might not be my cup of tea but it was what had sustained Winter for many years. Now that he'd abandoned them because of what had happened to me, he was lost. I wanted him to be happy – and being part of the Order made him happy. But now he seemed determined to forget they existed.

'He's missed,' Eve said quietly. 'Not just in Arcane Branch either.'

I could well believe it. Winter's dedication to all things bureaucratic and witchy was the stuff of legend. It didn't matter how many times I told him that what had happened up in Scotland had been entirely voluntary on my part. No one had forced me to half kill myself by absorbing the magic from a teenage necromancer; my eyes were wide open and I knew what I was getting into. When I broached the subject with him, however, Winter always changed it. He was even more stubborn than me – and that took some doing.

As if bored by us, Princess Parma Periwinkle let out a delicate yawn and wandered towards Brutus, giving the old lady a wide berth in the process. I watched her bat in idle boredom at Brutus's tail, which was hanging down from the sill, and considered.

'Actually, Eve,' I said, 'could you do me a favour? And I don't mean shopping for junk food. Could you fetch Harold and bring him round? I'm, um, missing him.'

She looked dubious. I could well understand it – when Brutus, Harold and Princess got together, feline shenanigans always ensued. This was important, though.

'Okay,' she said slowly, obviously unwilling to deny the invalid her request. I could get used to this. 'Give me a minute.'

When she returned with Harold in her arms, Winter reappeared holding two mugs of tea. 'I've brewed it for four and a half minutes,' he announced. 'I think that is the optimum time for the perfect cup.'

I gave him an amused glance. He was clearly prepared to do just about anything to occupy himself. Despite my efforts to teach him, he wouldn't learn the joy of simply doing nothing. Winter had to be busy.

Brutus woke up for long enough to give Harold a glare, while Princess Parma Periwinkle let out a small kittenish miaow of happiness at his appearance. Harold leapt down to the floor, ambled over to Princess and touched his nose to hers. Like her, he avoided going anywhere near the old lady. As far as scientific experiments went, it was hardly watertight but it certainly gave me food for thought.

Ten seconds later, Brutus decided that enough was enough. He charged off the windowsill towards Harold, claws outstretched. Princess fled for cover – and they all made sure they didn't go anywhere near the woman. My flat wasn't tiny but neither was it palatial; it wasn't easy to avoid an entire corner of it unless you were really trying. The fact that none of the cats went near my hallucination had to mean something.

Harold beat a hasty retreat. When Brutus was satisfied that he wasn't returning, he leapt onto the coffee table and gave himself a smug lick. 'Food?' he enquired.

'I'll get you something,' Winter said, bounding into the kitchen. I nibbled my bottom lip. Winter might be driving me nuts but I reckoned I wasn't clinically insane after all. Good to know.

***

I've never quite understood people who aren't good patients. I am an excellent patient. You want to bring me hot lemon with honey? Thank you very much. Mop my brow? Please, go ahead. Spoon-feed me? Well, if you insist. All the same, when I finally felt strong enough to go outside on my own, I felt like I'd been granted a new lease of life. I'd persuaded Winter that it was time for him to head up north and face the music with his own family over his resignation from the Order. As for me, I knew exactly where I was heading and who to ask for answers.

It felt strange arriving at the Order Headquarters and knowing that I wouldn't see Winter while I was here. My skin itched at the thought that I was doing something behind his back by being here. However, I comforted myself that if I told him there was a creepy dead lady hanging around my flat he'd be even more determined to treat me like cut-glass and be even more stressed out. Work relaxed Winter and right now he had no work to do. Relaxing relaxed me. If I came clean, there was also the possibility that he'd lock me up in an insane asylum. Frankly, I wouldn't blame him.

I parked round the back of the library building, hiding my taxi behind a large bus, and skirted the long way round to the main entrance. Normally I would have ignored all the traffic rules and stopped on the yellow lines out front, but I didn't want to bump into anyone who might know me. And, even though the footage of *Enchantment* which involved me had been suppressed by a court order, I knew that virtually every witch in the country would recognise my face. I supposed that was what happened when you saved half of the Highlands of Scotland from zombies. All in a day's work ... or something like that.

I kept my head down, ignoring the people moving around me. Fortunately, the constant drizzle meant that I didn't look out of place; everyone else was rushing to get to their destination rather than looking at passers-by. I dodged out of the way of a group of red robes, narrowly avoided a ginger cat patiently waiting for its owner – and almost smacked into a tall man standing in the middle of the path.

'One should be more circumspect,' he barked.

'Sorry,' I muttered.

'Look at me when I'm talking to you!'

Involuntarily, I raised my head. The oddest-looking man was glaring at me. His irises were a strange yellow colour, more like a cat's than a human's. Perhaps he had a bad case of jaundice. I glanced at his long white bushy beard and his drooping moustache. His eyebrows were so bushy and unkempt that I reckoned I could probably plait them. There was also something familiar about him, as if I'd met him before.

'What are you staring at?' he snapped.

Jeez. One minute he wanted me to look at him and the next he was complaining about it. 'Chill,' I said.

'Pardon?'

'Chill.'

'It seems rather temperate to me, despite the rain.' He folded his arms. 'I need you to listen. This is most important. You…'

The library doors opened and a group of witches came out, giggling among themselves. They were clearly Neophytes who hadn't yet learned that to be part of the Order you have to be serious and sombre at all times and on all occasions. One had purple hair, one had blue hair, while the third was completely bald with a tattooed broomstick on the back of her skull.

The glowering man let out a small shriek. 'Heathens!'

I glanced back at him – but he was no longer there. I spun round. Where the hell had he gone? He'd been right in front of me yet now the path was empty. A shiver descended through my body and a phantom surge of pain rose up to match it. Swallowing hard, I darted round the small group and into the library. This was not looking good at all.

The one saving grace was that at least it was warm and dry inside. I eyed the front desk, not recognising the witch behind it. The easy thing would have been to ask her where Philip Maidmont was; unfortunately, this wasn't a day for taking the easy way out. I avoided her gaze and swerved right, hoping I'd find Maidmont without too much trouble. The library was huge and I didn't want to traipse around it for hours.

I heaved myself up the first set of stairs, scanning round for the nervous librarian. There was a reverent hush across the entire place, as if speaking in a normal tone of voice would invoke untold horrors. I craned my neck upwards, spotting the ceremonial gold sceptre that Winter and I had recovered from the sewer below the basement. Although it was now back in a protective casing and no doubt had several spells round it, I hoped someone had thought to disinfect it thoroughly as well.

I dragged my eyes away and continued to look around. I was pleased to note that there was now a guard outside the heavy door to the Cypher Manuscript room. Yes, he looked beyond bored and, as I watched, he picked his nose, examined whatever sticky green snot he'd snagged then ate it, but at least there was someone there. The Order were proving they could learn from their mistakes. Then I shook myself. What the hell did I care what the Order did?

I was just about to turn left towards the study carrels, in the hope that I might find Maidmont in the quietest part of the quiet library, when a figure carrying a towering stack of books tottered round the far corner. Their face was obscured by the books but something about the shuffling gait made me think I'd found my man. I ambled over and cleared my throat. 'Philip?'

There was a small squeak. Philip Maidmont jerked in

surprise, sending the books flying in all directions. A young woman appeared from nowhere. The skin was peeling off half of her face, revealing charred flesh and the flash of white bone underneath. Oh God. She tutted in irritation while I hastily looked away and focused on Maidmont. 'Hi.'

'Ivy!' He reached over and enveloped me in a warm hug. 'It's so good to see you! But should you be out and about? You look so pale. It's almost as if you've seen a ghost.'

Ha. Ha. Ha. I gave a weak laugh and quickly bent down to pick up the books for him before anyone decided to come and help. Then I took the librarian's elbow and steered him away to a sheltered corner.

'I'm doing well,' I told him. I risked a glance back. The scary half-faced woman had vanished. Breathing deeply, I swallowed and wasted no time in getting to the point. This place was seriously creeping me out. 'But I need a bit of help.'

Maidmont's eyes widened. 'Of course! I'll do anything you want. You've become a bit of a hero around here. It would be my honour to help you. Although,' he added anxiously, 'you don't want me to set fire to anything again, do you?'

I forced a smile. 'No. It's … er…' I scratched my neck awkwardly. 'I could do with some help with research.'

He beamed. In fact, I'd say that he positively glowed. 'Yes. Yes! What in particular? I came across a wonderful old book tucked away just this morning that details the healing properties of rabbit dung when mixed with…'

'Er, no,' I interrupted hastily. The bunnies could keep their poo. 'I need to know about the side-effects of necromancy.'

Maidmont's face immediately dropped.

'Necromancy?' He shook his head in dismay. 'Oh no, Ivy. No, you can't. I know what you did up in Scotland and I know you stopped that boy. But you can't dabble in that kind of magic. It almost destroyed him – and you. You can't think...'

'Hush,' I said. 'I don't want to *perform* necromancy. I don't want anything to do with it. But something weird has been happening to me.' I dropped my gaze. 'I'm seeing strange things and I need to find out if there's something wrong with me. Even better, if there's a way to stop what's happening.'

Maidmont drew himself up. 'Strange things? What kind of strange things?'

I shifted from foot to foot. 'The details aren't important. But any information you have about any side-effects...' I paused and swallowed '...and if I'm liable to become a danger to myself or to anyone around me, would be – helpful.' Understatement of the year.

'Danger?' He shook his head vigorously. 'Unless you're performing necromantic magic, there can be no risk to anyone.' He gave me a searching look as if to ask if that's what I was doing. The trouble was that I didn't know.

'I'm not deliberately performing anything.' My voice sank to a whisper. 'But I might be using necromancy subconsciously. Either that, or I'm going crazy.'

Maidmont seemed relieved. 'That's impossible. You can't *accidentally* cast spells. Look at the boy who did all this in the first place – Alistair, wasn't it? He required blood to do what he did. It's a very deliberate action and takes considerable power.'

'Are you sure?'

'I'm positive.'

'So I'm nuts then.' I wrinkled my nose. I suppose insanity was slightly better than turning evil and being able to destroy the entire country in one fell swoop. Slightly. The costume didn't have the same potential, though.

Maidmont arched an eyebrow. 'Tell me what you're experiencing.'

I pressed my lips together. 'I could tell you,' I said, 'but then I'd have to kill you.'

'Not funny. Ivy, I can't help you look for information until I know what information I should be looking for.'

Damn. I didn't want to drag the poor guy into this but I needed to know. And not just for my own sake. 'I think…' I sighed. I was just going to have to come straight out with it. 'I think I'm seeing ghosts.' There.

Maidmont stared at me. 'Huh?'

Yep. This was kind of how I'd expected the conversation to go. 'I'm seeing ghosts,' I repeated. 'Not like Casper. They're not wearing white sheets or anything like that. They just look like regular people but I think they're – dead. Most of them aren't in the slightest bit friendly. Not that I'd be feeling sociable if I were dead, but I'm just saying. They never ask me how my day is going, they just complain or tut or yell. I wish they wouldn't. I wish they'd go away. So, Philip, you can see why I'm kind of concerned. I absorbed necromantic magic to stop Scotland from exploding and now I'm communing with the dead. I'd like to know if *I'm* going to explode and how I can stop them appearing. Or at the very least from tutting. There's only so much censure a girl can take.'

Maidmont kept on staring at me, his mouth hanging open slightly. There was a shred of green caught in his teeth. It might have been lettuce but I wasn't sure and this probably wasn't the time to point it out. 'Ghosts are tutting at you?' he asked finally.

I shrugged. 'Or tsking. To be honest, I've never been

sure about the difference between a tut and a tsk. I think the last ghost might have been tutting at you for dropping all those books rather than at me.' I hesitated. 'But I kind of made you drop the books by surprising you, so I guess she was getting at me by default.' I forced a smile.

Maidmont still hadn't blinked. Concerned that his eyeballs might dry out and I'd be responsible for him going blind, I reached out and shook his shoulder. 'Hello? Philip?'

'Uh ... let's sit down,' he said weakly. Then his legs gave way and he sank down onto the floor rather than looking around for a chair. I shrugged; it worked for me. I joined him, crossing my legs and resting my chin on my hands while Maidmont tried to recover.

After what seemed an age, he nodded almost imperceptibly and looked at me. 'Sorry,' he said. 'I'm just a bit – surprised. I believe you, though. I've never heard of anything like this before and, working here, I've heard a lot of odd things. Why don't you start from the beginning?'

I gazed into the distance. 'The very beginning? It started in Scotland. Right after I took the kid's magic from him, I saw a floating head. It spoke to me.' I twisted my fingers in my lap. 'It was Benjamin Alberts, the *Enchantment* contestant who'd died. At the time, I was in so much pain that I passed out. Afterwards, I assumed it had just been my imagination or something to do with the trauma of what was happening. Afterwards, though, in the hospital when I woke up...' My voice drifted off.

'Go on,' Maidmont said quietly. There was no censure in his tone and his expression suggested nothing except encouragement.

I heaved in a breath. 'There were lots of them. People, I mean. None of them looked healthy.' Images of gaunt old men and bloodied children flickered through my head. My stomach twisted with sudden nausea and I glanced at Maidmont. 'I was on heavy painkillers,' I said, doing my best to find a rational explanation. 'Morphine and stuff like that, so everything was a bit dreamy. But they kept coming in and talking to me. I thought they were real to begin with, but it didn't take long to work out that no one else could see them.' I gave a short, humourless laugh. 'I asked one woman, who wandered in and demanded to know where her baby was, if she'd spoken to one of the nurses. Winter was there at the time and he answered me. Then he stepped back and passed right through her as if she were nothing more than air. She looked annoyed, then she just vanished. Right in front of my eyes.'

Maidmont cleared his throat. 'And what makes you think they're ghosts and not just hallucinations? Because you had a few of those, didn't you?'

'I had one,' I replied flatly. 'One hallucination caused by the kid's magic. And it was of a bloodstain.' I shuddered. 'What I'm seeing now is nothing like that. I thought maybe they'd disappear if I pretended they weren't there. I thought maybe I was going crazy. But I think cats sense them too.' I told him about Brutus, Princess and Harold and the way they'd avoided Cobweb Lady.

'It's been two months since Scotland and they won't go away. There's a woman who all but lives in my damned flat. There was a red-robed guy outside, with the bushiest beard and moustache that I've seen in my life, who talked like he'd come from another century. His eyes were yellow! Who the hell has yellow eyes? Not to mention the woman here in the library I already mentioned. They're *everywhere*, Philip. And they keep talking to me.' I met his eyes. 'Am I going crazy? Or is the necromancy I absorbed taking me over?'

Maidmont's face was still very pale. 'The man outside, the one with the beard. Can you describe him in more detail?'

I scratched my head and did my best. As Maidmont listened, the young woman with half a face reappeared. She crouched down and stared at him. 'He has something stuck in his teeth,' she declared. 'It's disgusting. In my day, librarians paid far more attention to their personal hygiene. No one likes to be breathed on by someone who still has their lunch hanging out of their mouth.'

I ignored her and continued talking. When I finished, Maidmont nodded and stood up, brushing invisible dirt off his robes. 'We should go,' he said. There was an unusually decisive air about him.

My eyes widened. 'Go where?' I asked.

'The dentist would be a good idea,' the woman said.

Maidmont pursed his lips. 'Just come with me. There's something we should check first.'

I slowly got to my feet. Maybe he was going to drag me off to the loony bin – or stab me in the back before I became an uncontrollable necromancer.

'It'll be fine, Ivy,' he said reassuringly. 'Trust me.'

'You should never trust anyone who doesn't floss,' the woman said.

I nodded to Maidmont. 'Okay. Let's go.' I gave Half Face a fleeting look. She was really creeping me out. 'Quickly.'

Chapter Two

Maidmont led me out of the library. Unfortunately the rain had stopped and there were more witches around than before. I scooted behind him, using his thin frame to try and hide myself. 'What are you doing?' he asked.

'Skulking,' I whispered. 'I can do without someone recognising me and stopping for a chat.'

I could hear the smile in his voice. 'Don't worry,' he assured me. 'We're not going far.' He stepped off the path to avoid the oncoming people and I shuffled gratefully along behind him. Frankly, it was nice to walk with someone who didn't march around as if they were in a competition with Time itself. I started to relax – until I realised where Maidmont was taking me.

'Whoa! I'm not going in there!' I said, shaking my head at the main Order building. I swivelled on my toes and started walking in the opposite direction.

Maidmont trotted to catch up with me. 'Why on earth not?'

'The Ipsissimus will be in there! He's the last person I want to know about this! At least until I have a handle on things.' Or, I added silently, until I'd spoken to Winter first. Going to Maidmont for help was one thing; going to the Ipsissimus behind Winter's back was entirely different.

'We're not going to see him,' Maidmont said. 'There's something in there I want you to look at.'

I shook my head. 'No way. I'm going back home.'

Where I should have stayed in the first place. I pulled away from him and picked up my feet, determined to get as far away from the Order as possible. Then I saw Tarquin ambling out of one of the far buildings and heading towards me. Damn.

I spun around once more. Maidmont squinted, apparently baffled by my repeated changes of direction. Truth be told, I was starting to feel rather dizzy myself. I thought mournfully of my sofa. I should have stayed there. Who cared if I could converse with the dead? If they stuck around long enough, maybe I'd find out something useful from them. Not like who really assassinated JFK or what happened to Lord Lucan; I was thinking more along the lines of how to train them to do my bidding so they could work for me while I stayed at home and conserved my strength.

'The Ipsissimus will be locked away in his study, Ivy. We're just going to the main hall.'

I didn't think Tarquin had seen me; all the same, I felt his presence looming behind me. He was simply too irritating to deal with. I'd managed to avoid bumping into him at home, which was impressive given that he now lived in my apartment building. The last thing I needed now was to listen to him crowing about his heroics. I had a loose enough grip on my own sanity as it was, thank you very much.

'Promise?'

'Cross my heart.'

Maidmont had barely finished speaking when there was a loud caw from a nearby tree. I jumped. Whatever bird it was, I couldn't see it. 'Was that a raven?' I asked suspiciously.

'I'm sure it wasn't.'

I gave him a sidelong look. At least he had the sense to look slightly nervous. Ravens were harbingers of all things doom-related and both of us knew it. Maybe it was a sparrow with a sore throat. All the same, Maidmont and I walked a bit faster and without speaking. It was probably wise to get whatever we were going to do out of the way as quickly as possible.

We entered the building through the main doors, watched by several witches who were in the lobby on security duty. This wasn't the time to continue trying to hide – that would make them more inclined to try and stop us. To make our entry as smooth as possible, I stepped out from behind Maidmont and lifted my head. I have to admit that the looks of respect I received were rather gratifying. Yes, I had saved the country from an influx of zombies. Yes, I had almost martyred myself in the process. Go me.

Maidmont murmured something to the nearest witch and received a small bow in response, then we walked past them and up the first flight of stairs. Despite the guards, we were still on public property; any witch could gain access to this level. When Maidmont veered away from the next set of stairs, I breathed a sigh of relief. He definitely wasn't marching me up to the Ipsissimus.

Maidmont stopped in the middle of the corridor, in front of one of the many old paintings that lined the walls. Pointing at it, he sent me an enquiring glance. I looked at it and for the briefest moment, my heart stopped.

'That's him.' I stared as the yellow-eyed man with too much hair gazed back at me from the portrait. No wonder he looked so familiar – I'd probably passed that damned painting several times. 'That's the man I saw outside the library.'

Maidmont's eyes closed briefly. 'When you mentioned the colour of his eyes, I thought this might be him.'

I read the small card next to the painting. Ipsissimus Grenville, 1742–1803. Well, he was definitely dead then.

'I never liked this painting.'

I jerked and swung round. The man in question was standing next to me. I gave a small shriek and scooted away. It was one thing to *think* I was seeing ghosts; it was another to have that thought confirmed.

Grenville frowned at me. 'Death isn't contagious, you know. I might have died from consumption but I'm reasonably certain that you cannot catch it from my spirit.'

I clutched Maidmont's arm. 'You can't see him, can you?'

The librarian went a shade paler. 'See who?'

'Grenville,' I whispered. 'He's standing right next to me. He doesn't like his picture.'

'Everything I've read suggests it's a very good likeness.'

Grenville's ghost rose up, hovering about a foot off the ground. He lunged for Maidmont, stopping short of his face so he could glower at him. 'It looks nothing like me,' he hissed. 'The nose is out of proportion.'

I swallowed. As far as I could tell, the bulbous end and flaring nostrils were totally accurate but somehow I didn't think it would be wise to say that. 'He didn't mean it,' I said hastily. 'Besides, he's never seen you in person. It's not his fault.'

Maidmont's eyes widened. 'You're not talking to me, are you?' His fingers twitched at his robe. 'I ... I ... could be mistaken about the resemblance. It's a very old painting.' He leaned over to me and lowered his voice. 'Have any of these ghosts ever touched you?'

'No,' I replied, not sure why we were whispering. Grenville could obviously hear every word. 'But, as I said, none of them are very happy.'

Maidmont swallowed and began to back away from me.

'Of course we're not happy, you idiot girl!' Grenville snapped. 'Would you be happy? Instead of enjoying the afterlife, we're stuck here and you're the only person who seems to be able to hear us. I've waited over two hundred years to talk to someone with breath still inside them and when it finally happens I get you. It's bad enough that you're a woman. What on earth are you wearing?'

I folded my arms. 'Hey, buster. You're going to have to start being a bit more polite if you want me to continue listening to you.'

Grenville rolled his eyes then his head jerked up and he looked over my shoulder. 'For goodness' sake,' he tutted. 'Now this idiot is coming.' He wagged his finger at me. 'I need to talk, Missy, and you need to listen. Midnight tonight.' He glared at me with those spooky eyes. 'I expect you to be here.' And with that he vanished from view.

I sagged in relief. Unfortunately it didn't last long. The 'idiot' Grenville referred to strode up to me. The friendly smile on his face didn't make me feel any better. 'Ms Wilde. How lovely to see you.'

I grimaced weakly at Ipsissimus Collings, the living, breathing Ipsissimus Collings. 'Hey.' Then I frowned at Maidmont and he offered a helpless shrug.

'Sorry,' he mouthed.

'I presume you're here to see me,' the Ipsissimus said. 'Has Adeptus Exemptus Winter come to his senses and decided to return to the fold?'

'If he had,' I said, 'then he'd be here himself.'

I received a faint furrowing of the brow in response. 'Indeed. So why *are* you here?'

'She's seeing ghosts!' Maidmont blurted out. 'Ever since she took away the necromantic magic from the boy!

It's obviously a side-effect. Something must be done!' His eyes swung wildly between us. 'I've already offended Grenville. They're going to be after me! I...'

I put what was supposed to be a reassuring hand on Maidmont's arm. He jerked away in fright. So much for a bit of quiet research on the side; my secret was out.

The Ipsissimus raised his eyebrows. 'Ghosts? Are you quite sure, Ms Wilde?'

'Nope, not sure at all. In fact, the more I think about it, the more I'm sure they're just residual hallucinations. I should probably go home and lie down with a cold compress.'

'Let's go to my office.' I knew it wasn't a suggestion. Tough; I wasn't his to order around.

I stepped back. 'No.' I looked at Maidmont, who was beginning to cower. 'It would be helpful if you could find out what exactly is going on and if this means I'm about to become Oxford's next necromancer. But the only place I'm going right now is home.'

The Ipsissimus tightened his mouth. 'Ms Wilde...'

I held up a palm. 'I like you,' I said. 'I think you're a good guy. I think you mean well. But I didn't come here to see you, I came here to get some research done about my current ... condition. You have to understand that my allegiance is to Winter. Until I've spoken to him, I'm not going to speak to you. I don't yet feel the need to drain any sheep of their blood or attempt to raise the undead, so I'm going to assume that I'm not a danger to anyone. For now that will have to be enough.' I turned, half expecting to be body slammed to the ground at any moment.

'Ivy, wait!' It was Maidmont.

Still irritated by his fickleness, I glanced over my shoulder. 'What?'

'Don't try any spells, not until I've had a chance to research what's happening to you. Spells of any sort might be a bad idea if it is necromantic magic in your system.'

I grimaced. Fabulous.

'Alistair has been asking after you,' the Ipsissimus called, referring to the original teenage necromancer.

I couldn't imagine why. All the same, I paused. 'Is he alright?'

'He's doing well, all things considered. His brother Gareth is with him. I believe they are repairing their relationship and coming to terms with everything that has happened. They'd both appreciate seeing a familiar face.'

'I'm sure they would,' I said softly. And then I got the hell out of there while I still could.

***

By the time I got home, Winter was back. He was sitting on the sofa with Brutus and looking deceptively casual. That would be fine for anyone else, but Winter didn't do casual. At least there was no sign of Cobweb Lady.

'You've been out,' he said.

I walked over and planted a sloppy kiss on his lips. 'I have.'

His eyes met mine. Not for the first time, I felt myself being sucked into their deep blue depths. 'I bumped into Villeneuve. He was sure he'd seen you at the Order. But that would be impossible – there's no way you'd be at the Order.' He raised a single questioning eyebrow.

I looked down. 'I was there. I'm sorry.'

Winter reached over and tilted my chin upwards. 'I'm not your keeper, Ivy. You're free to do whatever you want – and I don't think I could stop you from doing something if you put your mind to it. Yes, I would like to know why you were there. And no, I don't think you should be running around Oxford when you're still recovering. But I'm not going to demand answers, not if you don't want to give them.' His voice was soft. 'I trust you. In everything.'

'I trust you too,' I said, even though my actions seemed to belie my words. 'I didn't tell you because I didn't want to worry you.' I ran a hand through my hair, realising how knotted my curls were. 'Some strange things have been happening to me and I thought I might be able to get some answers from the Order.'

He nodded. 'You've been jumping at shadows and staring at things that aren't there. I know you, Ivy Wilde. I know something is up. I wish you'd felt you could confide in me sooner.'

'I don't want you to think that I'm crazy.'

He laughed slightly. 'You're the craziest person I know.' He paused. 'And I love you for it.'

I leaned my forehead against his. I wasn't sure what I'd done to deserve such a divine being. 'I'm being visited by ghosts,' I told him. 'It might be a side-effect of the necromancy. Alternatively, I might be turning evil and, if that's the case, I'll have to be put down.'

Whatever Winter had been expecting, it obviously wasn't that. He drew back and stared at me. 'Are you alright?'

'I think so. I don't actually think I'm evil – for one thing, being a villain would take too much energy. Hopefully Philip Maidmont will find some answers for me.'

Winter relaxed a little. 'That's who you went to see?'

'Yeah. Although,' I added reluctantly, 'now the Ipsissimus knows as well.' I told him everything. To his credit, he simply listened. He didn't question the truth of my words and he didn't tell me off. I'd been right the first time around: he was far too stressed and worried about me than was natural. I'd expected a telling off; I *deserved* a telling off.

'You know the Order aren't going to be able to leave you alone now,' he said once I'd finished. 'You're having conversations with long-dead people. You've met Ipsissimus Grenville, who is credited with turning the Order into what it is today. A lot of witches are going to have a lot of questions.' His expression turned hard. 'And the last thing you should be doing is meeting a ghost during the damned witching hour.'

'It won't be dangerous if you're there to protect me,' I said with a sidelong glance.

Winter snorted. 'Try and stop me from coming.' He hesitated. 'If I'm going to do this though, you need to do something for me.'

I felt a tingle of dread. 'What?'

'You owe me, Ivy Wilde. You've been running around behind my back. Keeping secrets. Potentially throwing yourself into the path of danger yet again…' He pasted on an innocent expression. 'I think I've been very reasonable so far. You need to—'

'Fine,' I interrupted. 'What do you need?'

He grinned, the action lending his face a gorgeously boyish slant. 'You to have dinner with my family on Sunday.'

Uh-oh. 'You're right,' I said quickly. 'I'm putting myself in far too much danger. I'm going to stay under my duvet for the next fortnight at least.'

'Ivy…'

Arse. It was clearly important to him. 'Okay,' I sighed. 'I'll come.' How bad could one meal with a military family be?

Cobweb Lady flashed into existence, cackling away to herself. 'This is priceless!' she gasped. 'I can't wait to see what this man's family makes of you! Hahahahaha!'

I threw her a nasty look. I'd just have to make sure I was on my best behaviour. I might even go all out and brush my hair beforehand. If I could charm the pants off Winter, then his mum and dad would be easy. And those definitely weren't butterflies I was feeling in the pit of my stomach, no sirree. Bring on the in-laws. At least the thought of meeting them made those ghosts seem like fluffy kittens in comparison.

The phone rang and, even though I was closer, Winter sprang up to answer it. Nice. While he spoke to whoever was on the other end, I glanced round. There was a cardboard box sitting beside the coffee table, which didn't look familiar. I crouched down and flipped open the lid, sucking in a breath when I saw what was inside. I reached in and carefully pulled out the delicate apparatus, peering at it from all angles. It was an old herb-purifying system. And when I say old, I mean antique – and probably very, very valuable. No doubt it was a Winter family heirloom. I paused and frowned. Except Winter's family weren't witches.

It was heavier than it looked so, rather than drop it and smash it into smithereens, I placed it on the table. These items were now obsolete. Not long after the Second World War, some Order boffins had put their heads together and worked out that a pinch of salt was more than enough to cleanse magical herbs so they were safe to use in spells. Most witches who use herblore regularly simply add a few salt grains without even thinking about it. It wasn't that big a deal; in fact, even if the salt was forgotten and the herbs were technically impure, it wasn't that big a deal. The worst that could happen was that the herbs would be less effective.

Herblorists enjoyed long-winded arguments about which type of salt was most effective. I had heard that the Order even employed a selmelier, like a sommelier but for salt instead of wine so the end result was far less enjoyable but there was less need for several ibuprofen afterwards. I had a sneaking suspicion that whether you used pink Himalayan rock salt mined by virgins in the foothills of Nepal or table salt from the supermarket shelf, the end results were the same.

'I'm not going to ask her that,' Winter said into the phone in a slightly raised voice. 'You decide. I'm sure it will be fine either way.'

Pulling my attention away from the purifier, I raised an eyebrow. My momentary distraction was long enough for Brutus to take a flying leap towards me. I flung up my hands in front of my face, narrowly avoiding knocking the precious heirloom to the floor. Then I realised that Brutus wasn't aiming for me. He landed on all fours inside the cardboard box with the satisfied expression that I only received from him when I had the weekend off and no plans.

Winter sighed. 'No, Mother. I won't.'

Even more intrigued, I slowly lowered my arms. 'Go on,' I said. 'Ask me.'

Winter's face was expressing abject misery. He cupped his hand over the receiver. 'My mother wants to know if you would mind if the dinner is black tie.' He licked his lips. 'Sorry. She can be a bit of a stickler for propriety.'

I make a point of avoiding dress codes, especially when they are for dinner. What on earth is the point of getting dressed up to eat? I can eat on my sofa in my ancient stained tracksuit with the frayed cuffs and hole in the knee and the food will still taste the same. But this was Winter's family. Having already agreed to attend, I couldn't back out now. If it would make Winter happy, I could make an exception. Once. Especially given that Cobweb Lady was doubled over in hysterics, apparently at the thought of me getting dressed up.

'Fine,' I said.

Winter blinked. 'Are you sure?'

I bit back the sarcastic comment that popped into my head and smiled. 'No problem.'

Confused, but obviously relieved, Winter removed his hand and spoke to his mother again. I glanced down at Brutus who was still inside the box. His whiskers were quivering as if he were trying hard not to laugh. I flipped the lid so he was no longer visible. 'Now we don't know whether you're dead or alive,' I said in a hushed voice. Brutus responded by re-opening the lid in a blur of motion, then a paw with outstretched claws snapped out and scraped down my skin.

'Ouch!' I pulled back and glared. 'Okay, okay, you're alive.'

Winter hung up and glanced at me. 'Sorry.'

I shrugged. There was no point getting upset about it. 'It'll be fun,' I said. 'And now we know that you're not a throwback. Your magic comes from your mum's side.' He stared at me so I explained. 'She knew I'd just agreed to come, that's why she called now. She's probably not even aware of it herself. I know, though, because I'm Ivy Wilde, super-sleuth extraordinaire.'

Winter's eyes flashed in amusement. 'If you say so.'

I gestured to the herb purifier. 'This is pretty darn fancy. I'll scrub the shower grout every day for the next month if it's not been passed down on your mum's side of the family.'

He pressed his lips together. 'Ivy, look at the box again.'

I could hear the faint rumble of a growl from Brutus. 'Er...'

Winter pointed to the side of the box. There was an address label. I craned my head round and read it, taking care this time not to touch the box. I liked all my fingers; I didn't want to lose any to my pissed-off cat.

The address label was neatly printed, using Winter's full name but not his Order title. Judging from the logo in the corner, the box had been sent to him from a company called Multi Multa.

'The purifier's not a family heirloom, Ivy,' Winter told me. 'It's a bribe.'

I sat up. Okay. Now I was interested.

'Word's got round that I'm not in the Order any longer. Multi Multa want me to work for them. They've sent me the purifier as an indicator of their genuine interest. No strings attached.' He snorted. 'As if.'

'But isn't that a good thing? You want to work. They want you to work. They're going to woo you with desirable objects to make it happen.' I shrugged. 'Sounds win-win to me.'

'The only object of my desire around here is you,' Winter said.

My stomach flipped then Brutus growled again from inside the box. I hastily pointed towards it. 'I'm not as desirable as Brutus.'

The growling stopped but I had the feeling that Brutus knew I wasn't being entirely sincere because a paw began to edge out once more. Taking no chances, I backed away.

Winter smiled faintly. 'They're just looking for a highly placed Order witch whose name they can bandy about to make themselves look good. They don't actually want me to do anything. It's a PR exercise, nothing more.'

'You don't know that for sure.'

'The job on offer is Dynamic Magic Configuration Consultant.'

I stared at him. 'Huh?'

'Exactly. The more complicated the job title, the less job there is to do. I'd be wasting my time. I'm going to send the purifier back. The last thing I want to do is have a full-time job that involves nothing more than an hour or two a week of actual work.'

Sometimes it still baffled me how Winter and I had ever got together. My hand shot up in the air and I waved it around. 'Me! I'll take that job! Tell them about me! I'm just as good at magic as you.'

Winter smiled. 'You're better,' he said gently. 'But you weren't Adeptus Exemptus. They only want the title, not the expertise.' He flicked a fingernail against the purifier's base and a high-pitched note rang out. 'This is beautiful but it is going to be returned.'

There was a loud scratching sound from inside the box as Brutus sharpened his claws on the cardboard. A second later a hole appeared in the side, followed by his small, pink, questing nose. Winter looked at me. 'The box might have to stay though.'

I could almost hear the smile in Brutus's slightly muffled voice. 'Fooooooooood.'

Chapter Three

I let out a massive yawn as we pulled up outside the Order headquarters several hours later. Winter immediately turned his gaze to me and frowned. 'Are you alright? We don't have to do this. We can easily go back home.'

As tempting as that suggestion was, there was a light in Winter's eyes that I didn't want to extinguish. He was genuinely excited at having a mission – even if that mission involved sneaking into the Order to watch me talking to thin air. The Multi Multa job offer might not be realistic but he really needed to do something more to occupy himself.

I shook my head and gave a small smile. 'I'm fine.'

'You'll let me know if you start feeling ill.' There was the faintest hint of command in his voice.

My smile grew and I snapped off a salute. 'Yessir!'

'I'm being serious, Ivy. The last thing you need is a relapse. It's already been a long day for you.'

I leaned across and planted a kiss on his lips. 'If I feel anything other than perfect, I promise I will tell you,' I said.

'And if this gets dangerous…'

'I'm here to talk to an insubstantial being who could still be a figment of my imagination. I don't think I'm likely to get hurt.' I raised my eyebrows. 'In fact, you're the one we should be worrying about. We're breaking into the Order. You've not been back here since you signed your release papers. This place was your life, Rafe, and now we're sneaking into it like criminals.

That's gotta sting.'

'It's not a problem.'

Somehow I doubted that but I let it go for now. Dynamic Magic Configuration Consultant jobs aside, I still reckoned it was in Winter's best interests to rejoin the Order. But that was a decision he had to come to on his own and it was really nice having him along with me for backup. More than nice.

'If I forget to say it later,' I told him, 'thank you for watching my back.'

His features finally relaxed into a smile. 'Always.'

We gazed at each other like two lovesick plonkers – hell, we *were* two lovesick plonkers – then I nodded and got out of the car. It was already five to midnight. We had to vamoose.

I might have been able to gain access in the middle of the day with Philip Maidmont by my side but getting in with an ex-Adeptus Exemptus in the middle of the night was entirely different. I snickered softly. 'Ex-Adeptus Exemptus. Try saying that quickly three times in a row.'

Winter rolled his eyes. 'Come on. There are a few lights on towards the back so the main doors will be open.'

If lights were on, that meant people were still working. I shuddered. Winter smirked, as if reading my thoughts, then he took my elbow and steered me up the steps and inside the building.

There weren't as many security witches on guard as there were during the day – which made no sense to me whatsoever – but two of them were still sitting out front and eyeing our approach. Winter hooked his arm through my elbow and we strolled up to them.

'Adeptus Exemptus…' the first one began.

Winter held up his hand. 'Not any longer. As I'm sure you know.'

His buddy was bolder. 'And I'm sure *you* know, sir, that we cannot allow you to enter unless you have an appointment.' He made a show of checking his watch. 'I think visiting hours are over.'

'Of course, of course,' Winter murmured. He showed them an envelope. 'I wanted to leave this for the Ipsissimus. I promised him I'd bring it over.'

The witch's lip curled. 'And you thought you'd drop it off now?' His implication was obvious – Winter was too scared to come by at a sane hour. He wanted to make sure he avoided bumping into any former colleagues. What the witch didn't realise was that Winter didn't suffer from any ego issues.

'I did.' Winter shrugged and stepped back. 'One more thing,' he said, reaching into his pocket.

The witch smirked. 'Yes?'

Winter pulled out a handful of herbs he'd prepared earlier and blew them gently towards the pair of guards. They blinked rapidly several times before their eyes rolled into the back of their heads and they keeled over. I caught the nice quiet one; Winter grabbed Mr Nasty.

'You should have let him fall,' I said.

'He's only doing his job.'

'He didn't have to be a prick about it.'

Winter took my hand. 'Are you angry on my behalf?'

I groaned. 'I guess so. You realise we're turning into the worst kind of couple, right? Making moony eyes at each other and bristling at every perceived slight? It's a slippery slope. Next thing you know we'll be wearing matching T-shirts and getting Winter Luvs Wilde stickers for the car.'

He chuckled. 'I think we're probably safe for now. I don't own many T-shirts.' He had a point. Even when he stayed at home as part of the ranks of the hopelessly unemployed, he wore a perfectly starched shirt.

I grinned and tugged his hand. 'Come on. Grenville's portrait is up this way.'

'What?' he asked in a mocking voice. 'Not up a flight of *stairs*?'

'Ha, ha.' I rolled my eyes. 'Let's go.'

We ambled up together, pausing when we reached the picture. 'Intimidating bugger,' Winter remarked.

'Careful what you say,' I said. 'He's kind of vain.'

'Vain?' Grenville screeched into my ear. 'Vain?'

I winced. 'Sorry.'

Winter gave me a questioning glance. I nodded briefly and turned to face the ghost. 'Hey, chum,' I said cheerily.

Grenville glared. 'Who is this man?'

'A highly talented witch who wanted to meet you for himself.' I smiled.

The ghost snorted. 'He's not that talented then, is he? Only you are capable of that.' He looked me up and down. 'More's the pity.'

I was starting to get a teeny bit fed up of all these dead people deriding me. 'Look,' I said, turning off my friendly expression. 'You're the one who wanted to meet here. I would rather be sleeping. If you prefer that we leave, that can easily be arranged.' I didn't mention that I needed him to tell me if I was turning into an evil necromancer. I'd save that part for when I knew I truly had the ghost in the palm of my hand. I wouldn't exactly call myself a spiritual mastermind but I reckoned I was getting close.

Grenville sniffed loudly. 'As the highest ranking spiritual entity on this plane, I have been nominated to make contact with you and lay out our demands.'

I blinked. 'Demands?' I felt Winter stiffen beside me and put a reassuring hand on his arm but I still stared at Grenville as if he were nuts.

'Indeed.' Grenville rose up so that he towered over me. If he thought that was supposed to be intimidating then he hadn't had to drive hen parties home at three o'clock in the morning. 'What is your name?'

'Ivy.'

'Ha! Figures.'

I narrowed my eyes. 'Why?'

'It's a ground-creeping plant which insinuates itself everywhere and is next to impossible to kill.'

Hmm. I quite liked that analogy. I flashed Grenville a smile. 'Cool.'

'Whatever. Listen very carefully, Ivy.' He bared his teeth. 'I do not wish to repeat myself. First of all, we want a halt put on all future curses. It's getting crowded enough here as it is.'

'What?'

'You are not the brightest witch, are you?' He sighed. 'Why do you think so many of us spirits are still here?'

That one was easy. 'Unfinished business. You need to find the person who killed you, or to look after your family members before you can pass into the light.'

'Pah! I died over two hundred years ago. Do you really think that's an issue? We don't hang around here because we want to, we are here because we are forced to stay. Do you know how common it is for someone to say "rot in hell"? Do you know what happens as a result? All it takes is for the curser to have the faintest smidgen of magic for eternal disaster to ensue.'

'But you're not in hell,' I pointed out. 'You're in limbo.'

He tutted. 'Hell by another name.' He shook his head in disbelief at being faced with such an imbecile. 'Words have power. You're a witch. You should realise that.'

'So any flippant comment can consign someone to eternal damnation?' To say I was dubious about that was putting it mildly.

Grenville sighed. 'What are the marriage vows? To love, honour and obey—'

Whoa. 'None of that obeying crap. We're not living in the nineteenth century. Not any more.'

He was astonished. 'No obedience? How on earth...' He shivered – as much as a ghost could shiver. 'Never mind. That's not what I am referring to. In a Christian ceremony, where it is widely considered that there is life after death, why do the vows state a couple will only last until death us do part?'

'Remarriage.'

'No! You foolish girl!' he bawled.

Taken aback by his vehemence, I flinched.

'Ivy,' Winter said in a warning undertone.

'Don't worry. He's just ... loud.'

Winter glowered. 'We can leave whenever you want.'

'It's not a problem.'

Grenville shook his fist at me. 'Are you even listening?'

'If you stop shouting, then I will,' I replied calmly. 'Right now, it seems like you need me a whole lot more than I need you. Calm yourself down.'

Grenville spluttered but he at least seemed to realise that I was serious. There were plenty of other ghosts I could talk to. They might all be bad tempered but that didn't mean I was going to stand there and be shouted at for no reason.

He took a moment to compose himself before starting again. 'I apologise,' he said stiffly. 'The time I have been like this has not been conducive to good manners. It is not easy spending two centuries watching the country descend into chaos while being unable to do a thing about it. We cannot eat. We cannot touch. We cannot feel.' He paused. 'Not physically anyway.'

'I can see how that would put you in a bad mood.'

Grenville grunted. 'Indeed.' He twitched. 'The point I am trying to make is that vows hold as much meaning in the after-life as they do in life itself. People don't realise what damage can be done by saying the wrong thing or damning someone beyond the grave. We would like something done about it.'

I scratched my head. 'I'm not sure what I can do but I'll give it a shot.'

'I sincerely hope you will do better than that. Besides, I am not finished.'

Genuinely fascinated about what he was going to say next, I gave him my full attention. 'Go on.'

'Other cultures revere their ancestors.'

I nodded. 'You want reverence. Check.' I paused. 'How would you like that?'

'Do you know what the Chinese do?'

'Er…'

'Speak properly, girl! "Er" is not a word! The Chinese provide sustenance for their forebears. They have shrines in their houses. They make offerings and they treat their ancestors with respect! And what do we get? A couple of graveside visits if we're lucky and then we're consigned to history.'

'You want a shrine?' I turned my head to the wall. 'You have a portrait. People pass by it every day. It can't be that bad.'

Grenville's bushy eyebrows drew together. 'This is not just about me!' he barked. 'This is about *every* ghost. I'm speaking on behalf of all of them.'

'All ghosts want shrines? Or portraits?'

'They want to be remembered!'

Ah. That made sense. 'Okay.'

'I'm still not done.' He fixed me with his yellow

stare. 'This part is the most important. We want our descendants to release us from whatever curses or vows are keeping us in this...' his mouth turned down '...place. That way we can move on. We will tell you who to talk to and what they need to do. They will do it and we will pass on to the next plane.'

I was thoroughly confused. 'The next plane? Aeroplane?'

A spasm of anguish crossed Grenville's features. 'Why you? Out of all the people we could have had, why did we get you?'

'I'm starting to ask myself the same question,' I grumbled.

He shook his head in irritation. 'The next plane of existence! The place where we are supposed to be!'

At risk of being shouted at again, I asked another question. Just for clarification, it would be useful to know if Grenville here was destined for the fiery pits of Satan because he was an evil bastard. 'The place you're supposed to be is ... heaven?' I hedged. 'Or hell?'

He sighed. 'It's a much more complicated concept than that. Your tiny brain would not be able to comprehend the truth. In any case, you don't need to know the specifics, you just need to help us move on. We have established a system. Old-timers get priority. They talk to you, you talk to their families. Everybody's happy.'

I passed a hand in front of my eyes while Winter nudged me in the ribs. 'What's going on?'

'In a nutshell,' I said, 'there are a bunch of ghosts trapped here in this existence. They've effectively unionised in order to improve their lot and move onto the next, uh, plane.'

For the first time, Winter looked less wary and more interested. 'So Old Ipsissimus Grenville is the union rep?'

'You could put it like that. The trouble is,' I continued, glancing at the ghost, 'there's only one of me. I have better things to do than spend the rest of my life helping out you lot. I'm not unsympathetic to your cause but there are thousands of you. I can't drop everything and help you out. I don't have the time.'

'Why ever not?'

'Because it would take my lifetime.' Actually, I couldn't abandon them now, any of them, but I needed Grenville to appreciate what a massive undertaking this would be.

'We are not idiots. We will space out our requests.'

'Yeah, but…'

He sighed. 'The living are all the same. They only think of themselves.' He sniffed loudly. 'We expected this. We are prepared to help you in return.'

'Help me how? I asked, cautious now.

'Not you specifically. All of you.' He waved his arms around. 'Come on. Let's be having you.'

I frowned. 'Eh?'

'Not you,' he snapped at me. He gestured at nothing. 'Over here.'

As I watched, the air to the right of me started to shimmer. Bit by bit, the shape of a young girl came into focus. She looked to be round about eleven or twelve years old and her clothes suggested she'd died in the 1940s. Her face was grubby and she was holding a dirty teddy bear by the hand. I swallowed. 'Hi there,' I said quietly.

'Hello.'

Grenville gave her a little shove. 'Go on. Tell her.'

The girl toed the ground. 'There's a place in Dartmoor called Wistman's Wood. You need to go there. You'll find them there.'

'Find who?'

She blinked rapidly as if she were trying to hold back tears. 'The dead witches. They're stuck there. They can't leave. You need to help them.'

'I can do this,' I said. 'But I don't see how helping some ancient witch ghosts is going to do anything for—'

'Shut up,' Grenville said. 'They're not ancient. The last one was placed there last month. Every new moon there is another spirit, another soul cursed in ways that even I can only imagine.' He shuddered.

The blood drained out of my cheeks. 'Someone is killing witches?'

'Help the spirits there and you'll help the living who are yet to be targeted.'

I stared at the pair of them. It didn't make any sense – if witches were being murdered regularly, someone would have noticed. This had to be some kind of ghostly ploy.

'Go there and find them,' Grenville said. 'Then we will talk further. You will see that we can help you and your kind as much as you can help ours.' He bowed his head and started to vanish, his whole body turning transparent.

'Wait! Tell me why I can see you! Am I a necromancer now?'

He didn't answer, he simply disappeared from view. I cursed under my breath. 'Can you tell me?' I asked the girl.

For a long second, she stared at me with limpid brown eyes. 'I don't know what you are,' she whispered. Then she too dissipated.

Chapter Four

The ghost child might not have known what I was but I knew I was hungry, tired and growing more irritable by the second. I hadn't fully appreciated quite how far away Dartmoor was – or how desolate and bleak it could be at this time of year.

'This is a mistake,' Winter said, as we pulled into the car park of a sprawling pub.

'Maybe. But it's taken hours to get here. We can't just turn around and leave.'

'It's probably a trap.'

I shrugged. 'Set by Ipsissimus Grenville? A guy who's been dead for two hundred years? Why would he bother?'

'We don't know anything about him or his agenda.'

'You said he's credited with making the Order a decent organisation.'

Winter snorted. 'Is the Order decent?'

I rolled my eyes. This role reversal, where Winter denigrated them and I was the voice of reason, felt remarkably uncomfortable. 'Rafe,' I chided gently.

His mouth tightened. 'Regardless of what the Order is or isn't, we have no precedent for this situation. Ipsissimus Grenville might have been corrupted by death. Maybe he once was a good guy, but two hundred years of being a ghost could have turned him into something else. We can't trust him.'

'I can't just pretend this isn't happening. Let's see whether Ghost Child and Grenny are right about these dead witches and take things from there. One thing at a time.'

'You're still not entirely yourself, Ivy.'

'I'm okay.' I glanced round. 'Look. There's a sign over there with a map on it. With any luck, it'll include Wistman's Wood. It can't be far.'

Winter strode over towards it while I ambled behind. He pursed his lips and scanned the map. 'It's about three miles from here but the ground will be boggy and steep in places.' He threw me a sidelong glance. 'And there may be some sheep.'

'Three miles?'

He nodded. 'So it's a six-mile round trip.'

'Can't we drive?'

'Even a Sherman tank would struggle across this terrain. We can walk it. There's a path.'

'But there are hills. And – bogs.'

'Yes.' He paused. 'Can you make it?'

I pressed my hand to my forehead. 'Actually, I'm starting to feel a bit weak again. My legs are rubbery. Maybe you should go and check it out and I'll go into the pub and see what the locals know.'

The corners of Winter's mouth twitched. He tried to suppress the broad grin that was slowly spreading across his face but it was clearly beyond him. 'Thank goodness. It's about time,' he said. 'Now I know you're really feeling better.' He sucked in a deep lungful air. 'Perhaps being outdoors will do you good.'

Wait a second. If he could change his mind that quickly about this venture, then I could change mine. Especially when it involved six miles of trudging across moors. 'But I'm still not entirely myself yet.'

'Actually, I think you are.'

'You were right the first time. Ipsissimus Grenville might have been corrupted by all those years as a dead guy. We might be walking into a trap.' I shook my head.

'This is a mistake.'

'Too late, sweetheart.' He put his arm round my shoulders. 'I'm glad you're back to being Ivy again. I've missed your complaining and your laziness.'

'I don't complain!'

Winter laughed. 'Of course you don't.' He held me at arm's length and looked me up and down. 'The pain has gone. I can't see any trace of it.'

Actually, it tended to reappear when I was least expecting it but I wasn't going to tell Winter that. 'Arse,' I said. 'I suppose three miles isn't that far.' I'd barely finished the sentence when the first fat droplet of rain splashed onto my nose. I shivered and turned hopeful eyes to Winter.

'If we want to get there and back before it gets dark,' he said, 'we should go now.'

I grimaced. Another drop of rain fell, this time sliding down the back of my neck. Lovely. 'Let's get going.'

It wasn't too bad to begin with. Despite the rain, which was increasing in ferocity by the second and decreasing the temperature, the path was firm underfoot and clearly marked. There were a couple of stiles to clamber over but I managed. Winter even held himself back from racing across the landscape like a mountain goat and kept pace with me. I tested him by slowing down almost to the point where I was just shuffling along.

He stopped and threw me a look. 'Ivy…'

I smirked. 'I wanted to see how far I could push you.'

He rolled his eyes although he was obviously more amused than annoyed. I had to milk this for all it was worth; Winter's patience wouldn't last forever. I pointed ahead at the next wooden stile.

'That's a kissing gate,' I said, pasting on an innocent

expression. 'I wonder why it's called that. Maybe we should...' My voice faltered as a shadow crossed my path. I looked up to see a grizzled old man leaning on a walking stick and staring at me.

Winter stiffened. 'There's another one, isn't there?'

I nodded, my mouth suddenly dry. 'Wistman's Wood?' I asked. 'It's that way, right?'

The ghost took his time answering. Eventually, he rubbed his cheek and bobbed his head with slow, ponderous movements. 'It is, aye. They're waiting for you. They'll be glad you came.' He turned and trudged up the hill away from us. I watched him as he vanished into the rolling fog that seemed to have appeared from nowhere and was rapidly descending towards us.

'He's gone,' I murmured to Winter, my sense of humour all but vanished along with the old man. 'Let's get a move on.'

'What did he say?'

I pursed my lips. 'That they're waiting for us.'

'Who?'

'The dead witches, I imagine,' I said quietly.

Winter and I exchanged looks. He opened his mouth to speak but I shook my head. I knew what he was going to say. 'No. We should keep going and see what's really going on.'

He didn't argue but he reached across to take my hand and squeeze it. 'Okay.'

As if our combined determination deserved immediate retribution by some vengeful god, the rain increased until it was pelting us. Nervous about what might happen if I attempted a spell, I quickly described a rune I'd developed years ago to Winter. He listened carefully then did as I suggested, using magic to form a shield over our heads. His rune was a bit shaky, which was to be expected for a first-timer, but the end result was enough to keep us dry.

'That's impressive.'

I grinned. 'It's a magical brolly.'

'It's also a clever spell.'

Buoyed up by his praise, I gave a little hop, skip and jump. That was clearly a mistake, as it made me slip on a muddy section of the path. I slid forward, arms flailing and legs out of control, only managing to stop when I reached what was less like a large puddle and more like a deep lake. I narrowly avoided landing face first – but that didn't mean that I was home and dry.

'Aaaaargh!' Up to my thighs in freezing cold muddy water I turned, expecting to see Winter racing towards me to help me out. Instead he was trying very, very hard not to laugh. I folded my arms and glared at him. 'Ha. Ha. Ha.'

He pressed his lips together tightly and walked over, extending a hand to help me out. I ignored it. He'd had his chance. Sniffing loudly, I tried to heave myself out of the gigantic puddle but the mud around the edges was too squelchy and there was nowhere to gain purchase. I scrabbled with my fingers, finding only brown sticky gloop that smelled more like dung than earth. Then I remember what Winter had said about the sheep. Bloody creatures. Since my so-called adventure up in Scotland, I hated those things.

I jumped up, attempting to use momentum to get out. That didn't work either; when I crashed back down, there was a muddy tidal wave and I succeeded in drenching my top half as well.

Winter leaned forward. 'Now would you like me to help you?'

I muttered something under my breath and, avoiding his eye, stuck my hand upwards and waved it around. He grinned and grabbed it, pulling me out. Unfortunately, not all of me wanted to come: my left shoe stayed behind. By the time I got out and faced Winter, I was covered from head to toe in wet mud, with one shoe and one very sodden sock.

Now that he was confident I was fully recovered from my woes and ills, Winter's blue eyes crinkled with amusement. Hmm. I'd show him.

Blinking rapidly, I let my bottom lip jut out slightly and tremble. I couldn't actually cry on demand but I could give it a good shot. I dropped my head and half turned away, as if embarrassed to be caught weeping. Winter immediately reacted, grabbing hold of me and drawing me into a tight hug. Not only was his dry body heat a bonus, so was the fact that he held me close. Only when I was sure that I'd pressed myself fully against his length did I move away. 'Ha!' I stuck out my tongue. 'That will teach you to laugh at me, sirrah!'

Winter was perplexed – until I pointed out the muddy splodges on his body from where I'd touched him. If I was going to look like the creature from the black lagoon, so was he.

'Why you little...'

I raised my eyebrows. 'Little what?'

He shook his head. 'It's probably safer not to say.'

'You betcha it probably is.'

Winter sighed, bending over as if to brush the worst of the mud off his clothes. A heartbeat later, there was a loud splat as he threw a handful of mud at me. The first one missed; the second landed smack bang on my cheek.

I gasped in mock horror. 'You...'

'You what?'

My jaw worked uselessly. I blew out air through my pursed lips and glared. 'It's probably safer not to say.' I paused. 'You black-hearted guttersnipe.'

Winter tilted his head to one side. 'Guttersnipe? If

I'm a guttersnipe, then surely you are a cabbage-headed fribble.'

'I've never heard of a fribble before,' I commented. 'I'm going to assume it doesn't mean supreme being of gorgeousness.'

'That would be a correct assumption.' He eyed me. 'Not bad for a cow-handed gadabout.'

Darn it, he was much better at insults than I was. I was going to have to up my game. 'Why you … you … blue-eyed…' I threw up my hands. 'You win.'

Winter smiled smugly. 'I always win.'

'Oh yeah?'

'Yeah.' His smile softened. 'I got the girl, didn't I?'

I was standing in the middle of nowhere, with civilisation miles away. I was cold. I was wet. I was pretty certain that the dribble running down my cheek was sheep dung. And I couldn't have been happier. The men in white coats would be after me any second now. I actually looked around just in case they were already on their way.

The horizon might have been clear of people but it certainly wasn't clear of rain, which took that moment to splatter down with greater intensity. Winter frowned and raised his hands to re-do the umbrella rune I'd taught him. I shook my head. 'With any luck, it'll wash off the worst of the mud.' I sighed. 'But if you could perhaps retrieve my shoe?'

Winter drew out a quick rune, his elegant fingers dancing through the air. A few seconds later, my poor trainer bobbed to the surface of the evil puddle-cum-sinkhole-cum-deathtrap. I grabbed it and squeezed it back onto my foot, grimacing at the squelch.

'Thank you. Although this is why we need the Order's help,' I said. Winter stiffened. I bit my lip and looked at him. 'I can't rely on you alone to perform magic spells to keep us dry and conserve enough energy to deal whatever might be waiting up ahead. I can't be afraid of using magic.'

'For what it's worth, I'm pretty certain you're not about to go on a zombie-raising rampage. The spirits you're seeing,' he gestured, 'they're probably just a side-effect of the necromantic magic you absorbed. It's not as if anyone else has ever done that before and survived. There's no precedent here to work with.'

'There might be more side-effects to come. We just don't know.' I reached up and brushed away a glop of mud from his cheek. 'About the Order, Rafe. Maybe you should…'

'No.'

I wanted to argue with him. I knew he desperately missed being part of the Order, even if he wouldn't admit it to himself. But if Winter was going to accept all my faults and foibles and daft actions without question, he deserved the same respect from me. I pushed back my hair and nodded.

'Okay.' I wrinkled my nose. 'I'll tell you something for nothing,' I said, changing the subject. 'When we get back home, I am staying put for at least a week. On the sofa, with Brutus and you and absolutely nothing else. I don't care what the ghosts say or do or want. Coming here is already above and beyond. This is probably the spirit equivalent of a daft prank. They're probably watching us and pissing their transparent pants.' I bloody hoped so. When Winter's eyes met mine through the rain, I knew he was thinking the same.

Enough larking around. It was time to get serious.

***

We tramped on as the weather gradually grew worse. It wasn't just the rain, which was mingling with the mud in my hair and on my face and making my eyes sting.

The fog was becoming denser, shrouding everything in a thick veil. Having wet feet didn't make me feel particularly cheery either. I honestly considered casting the spell I needed to dry off but I didn't want to be rash.

Several more times Winter and I slipped, slid and narrowly avoided falling. Dartmoor was supposed to be an area of natural beauty; so far it seemed nothing more than natural disaster. It also seemed a long way to come to dump a body but maybe that was the point. Not that I was a corpse-dropping expert, of course.

I was on the verge of telling Winter that we should turn around and see if the pub had any rooms for the night when, out of nowhere, I spied a wood up ahead. At first I thought it was the heavy mist that made the place appear ethereal and otherworldly but the closer we got, the more I realised that the weather and the circumstances were nothing to do with the atmosphere – or the chilled thrill which was running through my veins. I'd never seen anywhere like Wistman's Wood before.

The area was thick with trees. There were few leaves, which was hardly surprising at this time of year. What was astonishing was the twisty-turny nature of the branches and the heavily gnarled trunks. It was like coming across a wood of cultivated bonsai trees – except these versions were definitely not in miniature. Green moss clung to every surface. The ground wasn't any less strange; heavy boulders and stones lay everywhere, covered in the same moss so that it was almost impossible to tell where the trees began. I gazed round, my mouth hanging open in wonder. Standing here was worth the long, soggy trek.

Winter gave a small shout. 'Bilberry!' he crowed. 'Do you know how difficult it is to get hold of natural-growing bilberry?' He darted over the rocks and wove in front of me.

I smiled. There was very little that could make a herblorist happier than coming across some clumps of fresh weeds. I left him to it and scanned round, searching through the twisted skeletons of the trees for any ghostly movement. There was nothing; the wood was as quiet and eerie as a graveyard. Funnily enough, that thought wasn't the slightest bit comforting. I took a deep breath and tried to force the matter. 'Hello? Is anyone there?'

The wind seemed to pick up in answer, whistling through the bare branches and rustling the loose sections of hanging moss. But no one spoke.

I shrugged. Either the ghosts were shy or they weren't here. I couldn't see any evidence to suggest a body had recently been dumped here, let alone several bodies. Besides, although this place was bleak and chilly it was unusual enough to attract ramblers. No one had noticed anything out of the ordinary. This was a wild-ghost chase.

I picked my way over the rocks to join Winter. He was emitting strange coos of delight and gathering up as much bilberry as he could. 'Having fun?' I enquired.

'There's so much of it! Honestly, Ivy, there are so many applications for this kind of plant. The possibilities are endless. In fact...' he looked up at me, suddenly remembering why we were here. He stilled and searched my face. 'Have you seen any spirits?'

'Nope. It's spooky but there's nothing here that I can see.' I glanced round. 'And I can't see where on earth you'd hide a dead body either. Can you imagine lugging one all the way out here without being noticed?'

'It certainly wouldn't be easy,' Winter agreed. He swung his backpack off his shoulder and stuffed the bilberry inside it before reaching for my hand. 'Come on. I've got something with me that's going to make you squeal.'

I grinned. 'Sounds kinky.'

'Oh,' Winter purred, 'this is better than kinky.' He delved inside the bag and withdrew a flask.

I gasped. 'Is that…?'

He winked at me. 'Hot chocolate.'

Winter was right; I did squeal. 'That's not all,' he said. He reached into his bag of tricks again and pulled out a plastic box. With a flourish, he lifted the lid to reveal two sandwiches, clingfilm-wrapped to within an inch of their lives.

I wrapped my arms round his neck. 'You're brilliant.' And he was. I'd stayed in bed an extra ten minutes and Winter had got up to make snacks.

'Careful!' he warned. 'You'll squash them.'

'I'm sure they'll taste just as good.' All the same I pulled back. There was something suspicious about the sandwiches. I frowned and looked a little closer. 'Winter,' I said, slowly. 'Did you, uh, use a ruler to cut the bread?' It looked oddly perfect.

'Don't be silly,' he said. 'It was a set square.'

His expression was so deadpan that I decided he was serious. Rather than look a gift horse in the mouth – my stomach was rumbling, after all – I gratefully took one of the sandwiches.

'There's a more sheltered spot over there,' I suggested. It wasn't exactly warm or dry, even in the shadow of the great gnarled oak, but there was less wind and the worst of the rain was shielded by the twisted branches overhead.

Winter nodded and we traipsed over. I plonked my bottom on some damp moss and wriggled around to get comfortable. Amused, Winter sat beside me and poured two small cups of steaming hot chocolate. I carefully laid my half-unwrapped sandwich to one side then took the cup from him, curling my fingers round it to get the full benefit of its heat. Then I dipped my head, took a sip and groaned.

'Raphael Winter,' I breathed. 'You might be the best man in the entire world.'

He glanced at me, obviously pleased. 'There's no "might" about it, Ivy Wilde.' He smiled. 'Nice moustache, by the way.'

I ran my tongue round my lips before smacking them loudly. 'Mmm.' I reached for the sandwich again. 'If I ever start taking you for granted, bring me back here and throw me in that puddle again.' Then I took a bite and choked.

The surface of the bread was coated in something dry and dusty which tasted highly unpleasant. 'What are you trying to do?' I asked. 'Poison me?'

He blinked. 'Huh?'

There was a loud tut. I didn't need to look up to know that one of Grenville's ghostly buddies had finally decided to show. Where there was a tut, there was bound to be a spirit waiting to castigate me. It was about time.

'It's not his fault,' a woman said. She was wearing a high-necked white robe with frills that seemed at odds with the barbed-wire tattoo snaking up her neck. 'You're the one who put your lunch in the middle of my remains.'

My mouth stopped working as I looked at where I'd laid the sandwich. There wasn't a large pile of ash but there was enough. I sprang to my feet and spat out what was left. Dead people. I was eating dead people.

Chapter Five

I flung the sandwich away from me. Unsurprisingly, Winter was disturbed. 'What is it? What's wrong?'

'Goodness,' the ghost said, 'he's really rather charming, isn't he? It's been a long time since I had a man of that calibre jumping to my defence.' She pursed her lips. 'Actually, I'm not sure it's ever happened.' She walked over and peered into Winter's face. He, of course, was blithely unaware of her presence.

'Get away from him,' I snarled with more venom than was probably necessary.

Winter jumped. The ghost ignored me. 'Are those contact lenses? He can't possibly have eyes that blue. They're quite extraordinary.' She leaned into him and raised her hand, trailing her fingernails down his chest as if in a caress.

A strange sound emitted from deep in my throat. It took a moment or two for me to realise that I was growling. 'Look,' I said through gritted teeth, 'get away from him or we are walking out of here and leaving you to this place.'

She turned round. 'My, you're a bit touchy, aren't you?' She looked at me more closely. 'It must be a new relationship,' she decided. 'He's not had the chance to let you down yet. Don't worry. He will.'

That was where she was wrong: Winter had already had every chance to let me down and he hadn't taken any of them. I wasn't here to get into a discussion about him though; all I wanted was to ensure that she left him alone and to find out what the hell was going on here. I hadn't met any ghosts yet who were able to touch anyone or anything living – but that didn't mean they didn't exist. I wasn't going to permit even the faintest whisper of danger brush against *my* Winter.

Winter waved his hands curiously in front of him. His fingertips barely grazed the apparition's back. 'Is there a ghost here now?'

She wriggled. 'That tickles.'

I narrowed my eyes. 'You can feel him touch you?' I stepped forward, itching to take a swing at her to find out.

She grinned. 'Nah. Not really.'

Winter tilted his head. 'Is everything okay, Ivy?' he asked softly. 'You look … fierce.'

The ghost laughed. 'He has your measure, hasn't he?'

I glared at her but answered Winter. 'There is a woman here,' I said. 'But I'm not sure she wants our help. She seems more interested in passing judgment on us.'

The ghost held up her hands. 'Hey, there's no need to get upset. I do want your help but you can't blame me for having a little fun. I've been stuck here for ages and the others aren't exactly a laugh a minute. They were bad enough when they were alive. Now they're dead…' She dropped her voice. 'They're mean to me. You wouldn't think a ghost could be bullied but that's what's happening to me.' Her eyes went round. 'It's awful.'

Without warning a man appeared, hovering up the slope behind her. There was a large bloodstain across his chest, although it was clear his pained expression was more to do with his ghostly companion than any lingering physical hurt. 'It's your fault, Karen. Don't start laying the blame on us.'

'How is it my fault? I didn't know what would happen! Besides, would you really be content if that bastard had killed us and got away with it? What about your family? They'd think you'd just run off. They'd never learn the truth. Now we have *her*,' she said, flinging a hand out towards me, 'we have a chance of justice and our families will know what really happened.'

I flicked my gaze from her to him and back again.

'You shouldn't worry about them,' murmured a voice at my back. 'They were even worse when they were alive. I always thought they had the hots for each other and it was suppressed sexual tension but I'm not so sure now. Maybe they just hate each other.' She sighed. 'I do wish they'd give it a rest.'

I spun round, my eyes landing on a young woman. Unlike the other two, she had several painful-looking bruises and open wounds on her body. She caught me staring and explained. 'I woke up and fought back. It would have been easier if I'd been asleep like the rest of them. Although at least I didn't do what Karen did. She woke up at the last moment with no time to do anything except curse our entire coven with her dying breath.'

I must have looked confused because Karen piped up to explain. 'I wasn't cursing us, I was cursing him! I didn't know we'd end up trapped here, did I?' She glanced at me. 'I told him we wouldn't rest until he got what he deserved.'

'And here we are,' the male ghost muttered. 'Not resting.'

Finding my voice, I looked round. 'How many of you are there?'

'Seven.' She looked sad. 'One man killed our entire coven.'

I quashed my rising horror – it wouldn't help any of us right now. I had to focus on the details and find out what had really happened. I looked at the three of them, taking in their matching robes. They were white, not red, and even in ghostly format the material seemed to have a homespun quality.

'You're non-Order witches,' I realised. The fact that their disappearance had gone unremarked was starting to make sense. Not a lot of sense, admittedly, but a little.

The man threw himself down the small hill, ignoring the trees in his path, and planted himself in front of me with a bullish stare. 'You're in the Order? The one person we can communicate with and they're in the bloody Order?' He threw his hands up in disgust. 'She won't help us. We're damned for all eternity.'

I counted to ten in my head. 'First of all,' I said calmly, 'I'm not in the Order. My name is Ivy Wilde.'

Phantom Karen jerked. 'Wait,' she said. 'I've heard of you. You were kicked out for assault.'

'And cheating,' I added. 'Don't forget the cheating.'

'I heard other covens approached you to join them but you told them to sod off.'

I shrugged. What could I say? 'I'm sure it would be lovely having other witches to talk to. But non-Order covens have to work hard and the results are never that...' I paused, trying to think of the right word. This lot were grouchy enough as it was without me insulting their abilities. 'Never that successful. I'm not much of a worker bee.'

She snorted. 'She sounds just like your kind of person, Amy.'

The other female witch, Amy, looked irritated but she didn't rise to the bait. 'And how can you see us?' she asked. 'How can you talk to us?'

'I absorbed the magic from a kid who was playing around with necromancy. By doing that, I stopped half of Scotland from exploding.'

All three jaws dropped simultaneously. 'No way,' the man breathed.

'Yes, way.'

'That's so cool.' He danced around from foot to foot. 'So you must possess necromantic magic now. You can raise us up! You can let us return to our families and—'

Amy cleared her throat. 'There's just one small problem,' she said. 'We've all been cremated.'

For a moment the man's brow furrowed and he stopped moving, then he shrugged as if his lack of a body were a trivial matter and returned to bouncing backwards and forwards. He was making me dizzy. 'I'm sure that won't be a problem. This woman is clearly a strong witch, just like we were. She'll find a way around that.'

I shook my head. 'I can't. And even if you'd been buried, I couldn't raise you up. Necromancy is evil – not to mention impossible to control. The repercussions are potentially catastrophic.'

'But you must be using necromancy now if you're talking to us,' he pointed out.

'I am not.' I was aware that my voice was overly loud.

Bored with the chatter, Karen wandered back to Winter who was watching me like a hawk. It must have been strange for him only hearing half of the conversation. She fell to her knees in front of him and appeared to examine his groin with great interest. 'I'm never going to have sex again,' she said sadly.

I'd just about had enough. 'Karen!' I barked. 'Get over here and sit down. You,' I said to the man, pointing at him as I obviously didn't know his name.

'Paul.'

I nodded. 'Thank you. Paul, you sit next to her. Amy, you go there. I need you all to stop moving around, stop yapping and asking questions, and start telling me exactly who you are and how you ended up here.' I looked around. 'Not to mention where the other four members of your coven are. If they're also dead, where are they? They must be here too, right?'

The three ghosts exchanged glances before Amy piped up, 'We should start at the beginning.' Finally someone was talking sense.

Paul nodded in agreement. 'I was born in June. I was always told it was unseasonably hot for that time of year and my mother—'

'For Pete's sake!' Karen howled. 'Not that beginning, you nincompoop!'

I looked at Winter. 'This might take some time.'

'I was beginning to realise that,' he said drily.

I sat down and stretched out my legs. I might as well get comfy and settle in for the long haul.

***

By the time the three ghosts had finished their tragic story and Winter and I were trudging back towards the car, the sky was darkening and it felt even colder. Now less concerned that he'd need to conserve his magic in case of an emergency, Winter conjured up a heat spell for us but the chill had already settled in my bones.

'All seven of them are dead,' I said. I shivered. Seven was supposed to be a lucky number; that was why there were seven members in their coven in the first place. Unfortunately, it wasn't particularly lucky for them any more. 'However, only three of them are in Wistman's Wood. Every new moon, their killer comes and scatters another witch's ashes. Until they arrive here, the last thing any of the dead remember is the night they were killed.' My mouth flattened. 'And yes, they were all killed at the same time and in the same place. They'd got together to try and perform a concealment spell. They were worried that the Order were after them.'

Winter grimaced. 'Unlikely. Unless they were performing illegal or dangerous spells, I doubt anyone at the Order would care what they were up to.'

'They were sure they were being followed. And if it wasn't the Order tracking them…'

'It was probably the killer.' Winter rubbed his chin.

'That's what I was thinking.' I hunched up my shoulders against the cold wind and plodded on. 'Anyway, the spell exhausted them so they fell asleep after they cast it. At some point the killer appeared and stabbed them all, one after the other. He was – er – adept because only two of them woke up. One had time to mutter a curse. The other tried to fight back but the killer was too strong.'

Winter halted. 'They both saw him?'

'Yep. Karen, the one who made the curse that's keeping them here, described him in great detail. A bushy black beard but no moustache, and a bald head. He had a stud earring of a skull and his skin was a mess, as if he'd had bad acne when he was a kid and the scars had never quite gone away. He was just over six foot and large. Not fat,' I said, repeating verbatim what she'd told me, 'but a large build and fairly muscular.'

Winter nodded approvingly. 'That's good. It gives us a lot to work with.'

'Yep. Not to mention the fact that they were all cremated before they were left in the wood.' I still felt a bit nauseous from the mouthful of Karen I'd eaten with my tuna sandwich. 'The temperatures required to burn a body properly are too high for anyone to do it without professional equipment.'

'Unless they're a witch with a particular propensity for fire,' Winter pointed out.

'True,' I admitted. 'But even in that scenario it can't be common to have that kind of skill. We've still got a good starting point. Whoever our murderer is, he must be keeping the other four bodies back then dumping them one by one when the moon is right. I don't know why the coven members don't remember anything until they're left here, but there's definitely a disturbing ritualistic nature to all this.'

Winter ran a hand through his hair. 'Everything about this is disturbing. Has the killer done something to stop the spirits from moving on? Is that why they're still trapped here?'

'As far as any of them can tell, they're trapped in Wistman's Wood because it's an old pagan site. Magic lingers in the trees and prevents their souls from travelling anywhere else. I don't see how the killer would know that, but at this point almost anything is possible. And the reason the ghosts haven't moved on to the afterlife is because Karen woke up just before he slit her throat to tell him that their coven wouldn't rest until he was brought to justice.'

'They're stuck until he's stopped?'

I nodded. 'Essentially. But he can't know that their spirits are still around and talking to us. How could he? And *we* know exactly where he'll be in less than two weeks' time. He'll return to this spot at the next new moon to scatter another set of ashes. When he does that, we'll find him.' I shook my head. 'I don't understand what his motives are but one thing is very clear.' I gazed morosely into the distance. 'Ipsissimus Grenville wasn't making things up. He wasn't even exaggerating. We're dealing with a serial killer. He's murdered at least seven witches in cold blood and no one has even noticed.'

A muscle jerked in Winter's jaw. I was impressed he was managing to keep his fury at bay; I could virtually feel his body quivering with rage that someone was doing this.

'We have another point in our favour,' he said. He met my eyes. 'He doesn't know that we know. We're on his tail and he doesn't have a clue. This will be over before he even realises it because we have surprise on our side.' He scratched his chin. 'And, no, you don't have to say it. We have to inform the Order. We can't keep this to ourselves.'

I touched his arm. 'They'll want to help – in fact, they'll *have* to help. But they'll also want us to work with them.'

Winter nodded but he didn't say anything else.

Chapter Six

It didn't take much to persuade Winter to book a room in the pub where we'd parked. There weren't many guest rooms – although the bar was packed – and we weren't exactly in a bustling metropolis. This place wouldn't even count as a village. Still, staying here would give us a chance to dry off, sort ourselves out and plan our next move.

The coven had been slaughtered in Dorset, where they were based. Even Winter recognised that traipsing a couple of hundred miles to investigate the exact spot would be better accomplished in daytime.

I called Eve and persuaded her to drop in on Brutus and Princess Parma Periwinkle to feed them and ensure they weren't killing each other. It was tempting to ask Tarquin to do it because I had no doubt that Brutus would make him pay several times over for being a plonker. But the thought of the floppy-haired one pawing through my underwear drawer was too much to cope with.

Although the last thing I was feeling was content or happy, I was impressed with our room. The mattress was comfy – and it wasn't a large bed. We'd have to snuggle very closely together. Perhaps I could pin Winter to one spot and force him to appreciate the joys of a long lie-in before we headed up the coast. It was unlikely but a girl could still try.

While he got on the phone to inform the Ipsissimus about our discoveries, I headed for the shower, turning the dial to super-sexy steaming hot and all but crying out in ecstasy. It was a mystery to me how the mud had managed to invade so many layers of clothing and I wondered idly whether I should inform the Environmental Department so some government-sanctioned scientists could come out to investigate the phenomenon. At least pondering the properties of sludge kept my mind off Blackbeard, as I'd christened the serial killer.

Apart from the shower, the other good thing was that I'd brought a change of clothes with me. My delight was somewhat tempered by the fact that I'd not checked what I was throwing into my bag when we'd left Oxford that morning. This was what happened when I was forced to get out of bed too early: I ended up wearing clothes that made me look like an Eighties pop princess covered in cat hair. At least the clashing neon colours meant I wouldn't get lost in a crowd.

I ran my fingers through my hair, decided I'd done the best I could and went out to check on Winter. I found him sitting on the edge of the bed and staring into space. 'Hey, are you okay?' I perched next to him.

'Mmm.' He sighed. 'You were right. The Ipsissimus does think we should work together. He's prepared to promote me to Third Level if I come back as the prodigal witch.' He grimaced. 'As if he thinks a bribe would make me forget what he's done.'

I ignored the mud still caked on him and leaned against his shoulder. 'Maybe it's not a bribe, maybe it's the Ipsissimus recognising your value. He's not a bad man, Rafe. And no matter what you say, he didn't do a bad thing. There's nothing wrong with swallowing your pride and going back to the Order. In fact, it would be incredibly brave.'

'Then come with me. The Ipsissimus said there would be a place for you too.' Winter arched a sceptical eyebrow. He knew me too well.

'You know the Order's not for me. It doesn't mean it's not for you, though.'

He heaved in a breath. 'I don't know that I can trust them. If it came to it again, if it was the choice between the life of an Order witch or the life of someone like you, I think they'd always choose to save the Order.'

'Life is full of impossible choices, you know that. We do the best we can with the information we have at the time. There's hardly ever a right way and a wrong way, there's just *your* way. I take the lift and you take the stairs but we still meet together at the top, Rafe. And,' I brushed my lips against the stubble along his jaw, 'if I had to make the decision again, it would be the same. It was the best decision to make for everyone.' I met his eyes. 'Deep down you know that. That's why you're still so pissed off.'

Winter stared at me for a long moment. 'Who are you?' he asked finally. 'And what have you done with Ivy?'

I laughed. 'Occasionally I have flashes of intellectual brilliance – but they don't last long.' I gave him a tiny shove. 'You are pretty smelly. Go take a shower and I'll go downstairs and see if I can rustle us up some dinner and a bottle of wine. I think we deserve it.'

He smiled at me. I could live a thousand lives and I'd never feel the same lurch in my chest that Winter's smile provoked. 'That sounds like a plan.' He half turned for the bathroom before pausing. 'Oh,' he said, 'the Ipsissimus is still advising you not to try any spells. Maidmont has found some old tome that discusses an ancient witch who experienced something similar to you, but it's in archaic Latin and is taking some time to translate. He thinks you're probably fine and using magic won't release any latent necromancy which you've absorbed. But to be on the safe side…'

I rolled my eyes. 'Yeah, yeah. I can be a good non-practising witch for a little while longer. Maidmont's going to have to get a move on, though. Once we locate Blackbeard, it's going to be all witches on deck. I'm not staying out of this fight. That bastard is going to get what's coming to him.'

Winter grinned. 'I love you, Ivy Wilde. But, damn, you can be scary.'

I tossed my blonde curls and wiggled my hips with as much sass as my tired body could muster. 'You betcha, honey bun.'

***

There was a pleasant smell of yeasty beer in the bar and, from somewhere further in the depths of the pub, the waft of some kind of meaty stew. Virtually drooling, I went through the crowd and hopped up onto a bar stool. There was no jukebox and no piped music coming through speakers, although the far corner of the room did boast a small stage area that was already set up with a drum kit and microphones. Given the crowd, the warm atmosphere and the hubbub of voices, this was clearly the place to be on Dartmoor on a Thursday night.

I caught the barman's attention and snagged a menu, then ordered two bowls of Lancashire hotpot and two pints of local beer. I almost hoped that Winter would take his time in the shower so I could eat his portion then order another one when he arrived. Maybe there was something to all this fresh air stuff; I felt hungry enough to eat a vat of stew and it seemed unlikely that one bowl would cut it. Maybe part of it was also that I wanted to remind myself that I was alive. There's nothing like chatting with several recently deceased witches to make you realise how important it is to savour every moment. And every mouthful.

I wiggled around to get comfortable and took a large

gulp of beer. Closing my eyes briefly in delight, I smacked my lips. Winter and I were going to catch Blackbeard before he could do any more damage. No one else would die. Winter would return to the Order and be his satisfied, workaholic self. I'd teach him how to binge on box sets; he'd show me all the best gyms within a ten-mile radius and I'd pretend to be interested. Everything was going to work out perfectly.

I opened my eyes to grab my glass and take another glug. It was halfway to my mouth when my eyes fell on a man who'd just made his way to the other end of the bar. A bushy black beard, a bald head, pockmarked skin and a skull-shaped earring. And dead black eyes. Neither Karen nor Amy had mentioned his eyes. I froze, unable to move. He felt my gaze and glanced over, stiffening when he caught my expression.

'The hotpot won't be long,' the barman said cheerfully. 'I've set up a table for you in the corner.'

I put the glass down slowly and tried to look casual but I had the horrible feeling that it was already too late and I'd given myself away. I forced my lips to curve upwards in a smile. 'That's great,' I managed. 'Thank you.'

Arse. Arse. Arse. Keeping Blackbeard in my peripheral vision, I glanced towards the stairs. Come on, Winter. Bloody come on.

'So you walked to Wistman's Wood?' the barman enquired.

'Yes,' I whispered. I couldn't have sounded guiltier if I tried. Summoning every particle of my being, I pulled back my shoulders and smiled harder. 'I love hiking. Especially in the rain. It makes me feel so much closer to nature, you know?'

The barman looked amused but I could still feel Blackbeard watching me. I had to do better. If only I could have cast a spell without worrying about the consequences. Damn Maidmont for not being fluent in archaic bloody Latin. Damn me for not checking out sooner why I was seeing ghosts. Most of all, damn bastard Blackbeard for showing up when I least expected it. It had been a reasonable assumption to think that he didn't live anywhere near here and this was nothing more than a convenient dumping ground because it was so remote. After all, the coven had been killed in Dorset which was a few hours' drive away.

'I don't mean to be rude,' the barman grinned, 'but you don't strike me as the type of person who spends a lot of time in the great outdoors.'

Using the opening to shrug off suspicion, I laughed and raised my voice so that Blackbeard would hear me. 'Well, I'm a taxi driver by trade,' I said. Not a witch. Never a witch. I don't know anything about witches. Only maps and one-way streets. 'I spend more time driving than I do walking. That's why it's so great to be able to have a break somewhere here with my, er, husband.'

Out of the corner of my eye, it seemed like Blackbeard was starting to relax again. My terror slowly dissipated, to be replaced by a sense of euphoria. We were going to nab him two weeks early. Talk about fortuitous. I thought back to see I'd missed any good fortune omens but I couldn't remember any. I was still ecstatic, however. Capturing a serial killer three hours after you learned of their existence is about as good as it gets.

Schooling my face into a careful mask to hide my glee, I babbled away to drive away any last vestiges of suspicion that Blackbeard might possess. 'I'll admit,' I said, 'that we didn't spend very long in the wood itself. The weather was pretty atrocious. It's a lovely place, though. I'd like to come back one day. Preferably in summer.'

'Yeah,' the barman agreed. 'It can be a bit bleak at this time of year.'

I nodded. When Blackbeard crooked his finger at the barman to ask for another drink, I gave a long, silent sigh of relief. There should be plenty of time for Winter to get down here. In fact, what I could do was make noises about nipping up to tell him to get a move on then I could tell him in person before he came down. Not that Winter's expression would give him away as mine almost had; he did stoic and bland better than anyone else I knew.

I was just about to slide off the stool when a fresh-faced young woman with a jauntily swinging ponytail wandered in. 'Jerry,' she said to the barman, 'do you know where the couple in room two are? They have a phone call. I've tried ringing up but there's no answer and I thought they might be here instead.'

He turned and grinned at me. 'One of them is right there.'

The woman smiled at me. 'There's a man on the phone for you. He says he's calling on behalf of the Ipsissimus and that he's looking for Adeptus Exemptus Winter. He's called Tarpaulin Vol-au-vent.' She paused. 'Or something like that.'

I stopped breathing. Blackbeard's head snapped in my direction and his gaze was hard and unyielding. Think, Ivy. Bloody think.

I tried to laugh. 'That's my brother. He's such an idiot. He likes pretending that we're in the Order because my husband knows a couple of card tricks.' The words tripped out of my mouth. That was good, right? That was believable? 'He also likes using stupid names because he thinks it's funny. He's not really called Tarpaulin Vol-au-vent. His name is Joe Smith.'

The smile left her eyes. She clearly thought I either possessed an IQ similar to the temperature outside or I was pulling her leg for my own amusement. 'Yeah, okay. Shall I send the call up to your room or do you want to take it here?'

I couldn't let Blackbeard out of my sight now. 'Here is fine,' I chirped.

She nodded and the barman reached over for an old-fashioned phone, placing it in front of me.

'I'll just go back and press the right button to transfer the call,' she said. 'I should have known the man was joking. He said you were both to be treated like royalty because you were highly talented witches who could commune with the dead and were about to bring down a serial killer.' She laughed politely, albeit without humour. 'It did seem a bit too far-fetched. As if you'd get either witches or serial killers hanging out here!'

Blackbeard was already standing up. He really was immense; he towered over everyone else. I couldn't stop myself from looking at him this time. His fists were curled into tight balls and I could make out the faint lines of a tattoo across his knuckles. No wonder he'd managed to murder the entire Dorset coven with such ease – everything about him suggested brute power. And hatred. The ice-cold venom emanating from his every pore – which was completely directed at me – was utterly terrifying.

I reached for the phone and lifted the receiver to my ear. 'Hello? Joe, are you there?' I don't know why I was continuing with the fiction. It was obviously pointless.

'Hi, Ivy! It's Tarquin, not Joe. I don't know who Joe is.' There was a pause. 'Is he in the Order? Is he someone I should know?'

Blackbeard released the tension in one of his large

hands, flexed his fingers and reached into his back pocket. If he pulled out a knife or, worse, a gun, then I'd have no choice but to cast a spell. I couldn't let this bastard hurt more innocent people. I'd have to pray that I wasn't turning into a necromancer and that, even if there was collateral damage, it could be contained.

'Joe,' I said into the phone, 'are you calling because you have some news for me?' For example, news that I can happily use as much magic as I want to? Because if there was ever a time to let all my witchy skills come to the fore, this was it.

'I told you,' Tarquin said, with confusion colouring his voice, 'it's Tarquin. Tarquin Villeneuve. Your ex-boyfriend and lover. Your current neighbour. The blond-haired boy wonder who's set to become the youngest Order Department Head in history.'

Not if I cut him up into little pieces and fed him to Brutus. I tried very hard not to grit my teeth and appear relaxed. Come on, Winter, I prayed. Bloody come on.

'So you've said,' I murmured into the receiver. 'Why don't you tell me why you're calling? Is Mother alright?'

'Huh?'

Tarquin really wasn't the sharpest witch in the West. I weighed up my options. I could cast a spell – well, several spells – and bring Blackbeard to the floor. He'd kill no more witches, Order or otherwise, and the world would be a far safer place. Not to mention that all those ghosts might live in peace for a while. But if I did that, I might also let loose all that blacker-than-black magic that might be residing deep inside me. Hundreds could suffer, thousands even. But that was the worst-case scenario. Nothing might happen at all.

The alternative was that Blackbeard would be free. Free to kill again. Free to cause disaster and mayhem. The seven witches he'd already murdered would continue to be trapped here. There might even be more than that one coven. I had no way of knowing.

'Forget the drink,' Blackbeard said to the barman in the hoarse, gruff tone you'd expect a serial killer to have. I couldn't hear any particular accent but he might have been trying to disguise his voice. 'I've got to go.' Without waiting for an answer, he pulled his dead eyes away from me and strode towards the door.

I glanced at the stairs one last time. Winter still hadn't appeared. Blast it all – this was the one occasion in his life when he had decided to take his time. If he was down here in my place, he'd know what to do. And he'd have no fear about doing it.

As Blackbeard hefted open the main door and I felt the cold air on the back of my neck, I leaned across the bar. 'Call up to my room. Get my partner down here pronto.'

The barman looked confused; it probably didn't help that Tarquin's tinny voice could still be heard from the phone's receiver. 'Ivy? What's going on? Ivy! Are you there? Do you remember what happened the last time when you couldn't be arsed to listen to me? The Ipsissimus wants…' I hung up and pushed the phone across to the barman with a meaningful glance before running out after Blackbeard. I still didn't know what I was going to do but I couldn't just let him walk away.

It was even colder outside than I expected. Out here on the barren moors there was little shelter. I cast around, searching desperately for my quarry. He couldn't just disappear into the night; I wasn't going to let him.

There was a crunch of heavy footsteps on gravel then Blackbeard's voice came at me from the darkness. I still couldn't see him – for such a large man, he was good at concealing himself. At least he was still here. Right now I'd take every small mercy I could grasp hold of.

'I thought you'd follow me,' he said. 'I don't know who you are or how you know about me – but I do know that you can't stop me.'

I swallowed. My mouth was bone dry. I'd only just recovered from my last near-death experience; I had zero desire to throw myself into that kind of scenario again. Desperate to stall him until Winter showed up, I found my voice. 'You're killing witches,' I said. 'An entire coven. From Dorset. Why?'

His voice drifted through the darkness. 'The more pertinent question is how do you know that?'

'Seriously? That's the most important question? Not who are you, or what's your motive, or what the hell do you think you can gain? Or are you just a deluded psychopath? You think the biggest question is how I know about you? Pah!' I scoffed. 'There's no limit to what I know.' I racked my brains. There had to be something I could do here, some information I could use against him. 'I know that the coven murder wasn't as smooth as you'd have liked,' I said. 'That one of them came round at the last minute and fought you. That made you angry.'

There was silence. Damn it, had he already somehow made his escape? There was nothing around here apart from a quiet country road and mud-filled moors. He could head off in virtually any direction and I wouldn't have a clue where he'd gone, at least until Winter got here and performed a tracking spell. Right now, there was nothing happening which was worth the risk of me being overpowered by necromantic magic.

'Hello?' I called out, my voice carrying across the silent car park. 'Are you still there? Or have I scared you off?' My eyes darted from side to side. Damn, it was dark out here. 'Mr Serial Killer?'

I felt the hot breath against the back of neck and the

cold steel tip nick my skin. 'It'd take a lot more than a blonde woman with dodgy dress sense to scare me,' Blackbeard murmured.

I didn't dare move a muscle. He reached up with his free hand and brushed my hair away from my cheek. His other hand was still gripping the blade – I could feel it pressed against my flesh. One swift movement and he'd slice through my carotid artery. It would be *adios muchachos*. We were too far from any hospital; no matter what Winter did, this time I wouldn't be coming back from the brink.

'You don't want to do this,' I whispered. It was probably about the stupidest thing I'd ever said. Something about being a mere centimetre away from death was hampering my eloquence. Telling a man who was responsible for at least seven murders that he didn't want to round that up to an even eight didn't make the slightest bit of sense.

'Why not, Blondie?' Blackbeard asked. 'Because lover boy is a witch and he'll come after me in revenge?' He laughed softly. 'From what I've gathered, he's already after me. Your death won't change that.'

Arse. Weren't evil villains supposed to be numbskulls with no brain cells to rub together? Why did I get the smart one? I breathed out. I felt strangely calm; every second that I wasn't creating a messy pool of blood was a positive.

Blackbeard moved the blade, scraping it gently against my neck in a caressing motion. 'I should just slit your throat,' he said. 'The fact that you open your legs for a witch should damn you. But I'm not a bastard and I'm not a cold-blooded murderer, either. If you're not a magic freak then you get to live. I can't say the same for lover boy, though. He's already crossed the line. He should be afraid.'

It was the threat to Winter that did it for me. I leapt away and spun round, breathing heavily and glaring at Blackbeard. He didn't look even remotely intimidated. He'd learn.

'You've screwed up,' I said. There was no need to fake the venom in my voice. The dead eyes that glittered back at me told me everything I needed to know about this prick. 'I'm as much a witch as he is – and I'm more powerful than you could ever dream of.'

He laughed, a cold, grating noise like the sound of fingernails scraping down a blackboard. 'If you were a witch, you'd have already tried your magic against me. You should be pleased, Blondie. You're not a witch – it's the only reason you're still living.'

There was a shout from the doorway of the pub. Winter. Finally. Blackbeard's eyes narrowed then he darted to the side. I raised my hands, ready to fling whatever I had at him and damn the consequences.

'Ivy! No!'

The panic in Winter's voice was enough to make me pause. I dropped my hands just as the sound of a revving engine lit the air. A single headlight flicked on, blinding me. 'Winter, it's him!' I screamed. 'We have to stop him!'

'I've got this,' he called, his voice even and calm.

Several people spilled out from the pub behind Winter. 'What's going on? Is there a fight?'

Blackbeard's huge motorbike took off, speeding towards me. As I flung myself to one side, Winter raised his hands to complete a double rune. I hit the ground and rolled, twisting round to watch. Winter's expression was filled with concentration. Not for the first time, genuine awe filled me at his ability to work under pressure. Even from this distance, I could see the spark in his sapphire-blue eyes and the deft way he flicked his fingers to complete the rune. Tough luck, Blackbeard, I thought sardonically. Your time is up.

The motorbike skidded, sending a spray of gravel towards the onlookers. Then it mounted the verge, hit the tarmacked road and sped off into the distance, its red taillight visible only for a few moments until it – and Blackbeard – disappeared round the corner.

I pulled myself up to my feet. Catching a quick glimpse of Winter's frown, I shook out my hair and ran for his car. 'Rafe!' I yelled. 'Car keys!'

The cloud passed and Winter re-focused. He reached into his pocket, his face falling. 'They're still upstairs,' he ground out. He turned and ran inside. Ignoring the rigid tension that made every step jar, I ran after him.

'Hey, are you alright?' the barman asked. 'You're bleeding.'

I touched my neck where Blackbeard had cut me. My fingers came away wet and sticky. I grimaced. 'It's just a flesh wound. I'll live.' But others might not, I hissed under my breath, causing the barman and several others to pull back.

'What's going on?' he asked.

Winter reappeared, the keys jangling in his hand.

'Long story,' I called out, bolting back to the car. We could still catch up to Blackbeard. We could still do this. Winter unlocked the doors and we leapt inside as if the fires of hell were after us. 'I really want to get this bastard.'

Winter nodded. 'You and me both.'

Chapter Seven

When we limped back into the pub after two fruitless hours of driving around narrow, dark roads and scrutinising country tracks and village side streets, a crowd of happy customers turned to stare at us. I wasn't surprised; I was caked in dried blood and Winter looked as if he were about to murder someone. If only. I stalked up to the bar and, without being asked, the barman poured me a shot of vodka. I downed it in one.

'Thanks,' I said.

'You looked like you needed it.' He paused. 'Should I get the kitchen to re-heat your stew?'

The last thing I felt right now was hungry and I was ready to politely decline but Winter was more sensible. 'That would be great,' he said. He took my elbow and drew me over to a small table, away from the rest of the punters.

I flopped down and dropped my head into my hands. 'We had him, Rafe. He was right here. I could have stopped him. If I'd used magic…'

'It was just as well that you didn't,' he growled. 'Anything could have happened. Besides, I had every opportunity, too. I was sure that spell had smacked right into him but…' He ran a hand through his hair. 'I don't get it.'

'Maybe you were tired,' I suggested gently. 'It's been a long day. We drove all the way here from Oxford then tramped across those moors in the driving rain. And you used magic out there to keep us warm.'

He shook his head vehemently. 'No. I know myself

and I know when I've reached the point of exhaustion where my magic will fail. I wasn't anywhere near that point.' He drummed his fingers against the wooden table and cursed loudly enough to upset an elderly couple enjoying a quiet sherry. Winter murmured a brief apology and looked at me. 'Maybe he's a witch too and he'd set up some kind of warding spell. It would have to be a damn powerful one to withstand the magic I flung at him but it wouldn't have been impossible.'

I wrinkled my nose. 'No, I already told you. He hates witches. It was about the only time I saw any emotion in his expression. Anyway, the reason he didn't kill me is because he assumed I wasn't a witch because I didn't use magic against him when I could have.'

'So his motive is that he's a witch-hater. That's why he murdered that coven.' Winter sighed. 'The question is, why did he go for them? Order witches are more establishment. Surely someone who despises magic would be more inclined to hit out at us than at a non-Order group.'

I chose not to comment on his use of the word 'us'. This wasn't really the time. 'Non-Order covens are weak by their very nature. Maybe he was testing the water and he's going to move on to other targets in the future.' I grimaced. It was just a theory; it didn't have to be true.

Winter met my eyes and we shared a moment of quiet horror. 'I can't believe he got away.' His voice was quiet. 'I can't believe that our strongest weapon against him was knowing about him and where he'd be in the future, and we've fucked that up. He won't come back here again.' He sighed. 'I had him, Ivy. I'm sure of it.'

I put my hand over his. 'I believe you.' I paused then said, 'I think there's more going on here than we realise. We'll get to the bottom of it. We won't let this bastard stay free for long.'

Winter's fingers entwined with mine and he squeezed them briefly as if in thanks. 'It'll be my fault if someone else dies. If he kills again, that blood will be on my hands as much as on his.'

'That's not true and you know it. Besides, I was there too. I had more time and I didn't stop him any more than you did. We both screwed up.'

The waitress appeared at the open doorway. I gestured silence to Winter and we both waited while she put two bowls of hotpot in front of us. The fragrant smell reminded me that a while ago I'd been really hungry. My stomach gurgled. There you go. I grabbed a spoon, ready to dive in.

As the waitress smiled, blushing at Winter's murmur of appreciation and the crinkle in his sexy blue eyes, I caught sight of an old man leaning on a stick and looking confused. The waitress passed right through him as she departed. The old man barely noticed; I pretended not to. At the very least I was going to enjoy the return of my appetite. I'd worry about ghosts and witches and serial killers later.

Unfortunately, the old ghost seemed to have other ideas. 'You!' He finally spotted me and stomped over towards us, which was no mean feat considering he was hovering about an inch off the floor. 'What did you do?'

I looked into Winter's face and smiled, then took a slurp of stew. The potato was tender and the faint hint of rosemary, combined with the way the meat almost melted in my mouth, was orgasmic. I was going to enjoy this. I was not going to pay the damn ghost any attention. Not until I'd finished eating.

'I'm talking to you! You did something! I was here and then I wasn't here. It wasn't my choice, something made me leave.' His eyes flicked suspiciously from side to side. 'Except I don't know where I left to.'

I took another mouthful. 'Mmm. This is delicious.'

The ghost snapped his attention back to me, his expression shifting from confusion to hatred. 'You're deliberately taunting me!' he hissed. 'You know I can't eat. You know I can't taste anything. That stew was my grandmother's recipe, it's been passed down for generations and you're using it to make me feel inferior. Well, wait until you've been dead for fifty years, Missy! Wait until you're trapped on this plane and you have to watch idiots treat your family inn like some kind of despicable bawdy establishment. It was bad enough when they used to allow members of the public to get on stage and sing. Now they let people like you inside!'

'I hate karaoke too,' I mumbled through another delicious mouthful.

Winter glanced at me. 'Ghost?'

'Yeah. He's pissed off. They're all pissed off.'

'Pissed off?' the man shrieked. 'Pissed off? I'll show you pissed off.' He leapt onto the table between Winter and myself.

'Go away,' I told him. 'I'll talk to you when I've finished my dinner.' I checked the clock on the wall. 'Twenty minutes. If you've been here for fifty years, I'm sure you've learned something about the art of patience. You can wait that long.'

'Oh, I've learnt plenty about patience, Missy,' the ghost sneered. 'Mostly that it's over-rated. Don't worry though. I know how to get you to finish up quickly.' He started unbuttoning his trousers.

I sighed. 'If you think that mooning at me is going to put me off my food, you underestimate how many hairy bottoms I've seen in my time. The only one that could ever keep me from my food belongs to the man sitting opposite me. Your ugly arse isn't going to work.'

He snorted. 'You lack imagination.' He took out a

flaccid, pale penis, directed in downwards and, with what I could only describe as a contented sigh, began to pee.

I slowly put down my spoon and pushed back my chair. There was a ghost standing on the table in front of me and pissing into my food. Admittedly, it was ghost pee. It wouldn't taste of anything – it probably didn't even exist. Not in any real sense anyway. All the same, the scabby plonker had achieved what he wanted. I no longer wanted to eat a thing.

'What's wrong, Ivy?'

'Nothing.' I crossed my arms and glared at the ghost.

'Why are you looking at me like that?' Winter said.

'It's not you I'm looking at.'

The ghost smiled. 'I've got your attention now, haven't I?'

'Do yourself up,' I snapped. 'If you want to talk, damn well talk.'

His lip curled. 'I'm not here for chit-chat. Why would I want to pass the time of day with you? All I want to know is what you did. Why did I disappear and where did I go?'

'I don't know. You're going to have to give me a little more information.'

'I was here then I was not here.' His eyes narrowed. 'I know who you are. Everyone knows who you are. You must have had something to do with what happened to me. You're the only person on this earth who can both see and talk to us. It cannot be a coincidence that you show up here and I vanish from existence.'

I ran my tongue around my teeth. I was going to have to order some more stew and make up a reason for why I couldn't eat what was in front of me. 'When exactly did you vanish?' I enquired.

'It was a Tuesday. I know it was a Tuesday because that waste of space great-nephew of mine gets all the deliveries on a Tuesday. In my day, we...'

I held up my hand in a bid to get him to stop talking. 'What happened in your day isn't relevant. What *is* relevant is that today is Friday and I only arrived today, so your disappearance obviously has nothing to do with me.'

I rocked forward, using my elbow to nudge the almost full bowl of stew and send it crashing to the floor. 'Oh no!' I gasped. I looked at the barman who was already bustling over with a towel in his hand. 'I'm so sorry! I'm such a klutz.'

'Don't worry about it,' he said. 'It's not a big deal. I'll get this cleaned up in a jiffy.'

The ghost tutted loudly. 'In my day, we'd have made you clean it up yourself.' He jumped soundlessly from the table and eyeballed the poor barman who remained oblivious to his presence. Winter at least knew something strange was going on; he'd stopped eating and was watching me carefully. 'It's difficult to believe,' the ghost continued, 'that I'm related to this idiot at all.'

I got down and tried to help, although I probably just made more of a mess. Then I paused. Hang on a minute. 'That man,' I said slowly. 'The one with the beard who raced out of here.'

'The one you were having the altercation with?' the barman asked.

I scratched my neck, wincing as my fingernails scraped the edge of my wound. 'Er, yeah. Him. When did he arrive?'

'Tuesday. I wasn't expecting him, to be honest. He's here regularly, about once a month, but he doesn't normally stay for more than a night. And it's only been a couple of weeks since his last visit. He gives me the creeps, if I'm honest. I won't be upset if he doesn't come back. There's something about his eyes, you know?'

Oh, I knew. 'So he was supposed to be here tonight? He has a room here?'

'He does.'

I looked over at Winter. He was already getting to his feet. 'Can we see it?'

'I dunno. Maybe we should leave it for the police or until he comes back. I can't just let people wander around guests' rooms.'

I tilted my head to one side. We needed to see that room and I preferred to do it without breaking in. 'We can help you,' I said eventually.

The barman stood up, abandoning the splattered hotpot in favour of looking at me warily. 'How?'

'This pub is haunted.'

He took a step backwards. 'Excuse me?'

I glanced at the ghost. 'What's your name?'

'William.'

'By your great-uncle Willie,' I said to the barman.

'William!' the ghost howled. 'Not Willie!'

'Well then,' I snapped, 'you should have kept your willie inside your damn trousers then, shouldn't you?'

Both Winter and the barman started. 'My great-uncle was known for exposing himself,' the barman said, staring at me.

I raised an eyebrow in Willie's direction. That figured. The ghost pretended to be suddenly fascinated by a stain on the old flocked wallpaper.

'How did you know that?' the barman asked. 'It's supposed to be a family secret.'

'I told you,' I said patiently. 'This place is haunted.'

He looked very pale. 'No wonder the milk keeps going sour.'

'Actually,' William declared loudly, 'that's because the silly woman in the kitchen keeps forgetting to put it in the fridge and she leaves it out next to the oven.'

I focused back on him. 'Why are you here? I'm going to assume it's not just because you want as many people as possible to see your poor excuse for a penis.'

Winter started and, predictably, his expression grew closed and angry. He stayed quiet, though; he knew I was a big girl.

William sniffed. 'The family always hated me. They were jealous. My sister despised me so much that she cursed me to find no rest, not even in death, unless I promised to name her as my sole heir when I died. She was a money-grabbing whore who—'

'Shut up.' I glanced at the barman. I wasn't entirely sure how all this was supposed to work but how hard could it to rescind a generations-old curse that transcended death? 'One of your ancestors cursed ol' Willie to find no rest unless she was given his stuff when he died. I'm presuming that she didn't do that. I guess that to get rid of him and allow him to pass to the next plane, where he's supposed to be, you just need to take back her words.' I shrugged. Maybe. What the hell did I know?

The barman scratched his head. 'Are you trying to fleece me or something?'

'Nope. This is for real. I promise. All I want in return is to get into that room.'

He was obviously still suspicious and on edge. He sidestepped and, in the process, slid in one of the small pools of splattered gravy. Winter reached out and grabbed him just before he went crashing to the floor.

'Ivy is a pain in the arse,' Winter said gruffly.

'Hey!' I protested.

He flicked me a look. 'It's true. You're the laziest person I've ever met. You'll take shortcuts wherever you can and you never do anything the way it's supposed to be done.' He smiled and my heart flip-flopped. 'But you're honest to a fault. You don't lie and you wouldn't deliberately hurt someone.' He paused and I knew he was thinking about what I'd done up in Scotland. 'Not unless you really had to, anyway.'

'So, ridiculous as it sounds, you finally forgive me for sacrificing myself for you?'

Winter's expression was earnest. 'Yes. But don't do it again.'

'I'm not sure I can promise that,' I said with a wry grin.

He leaned towards me. 'Maybe I can make you.'

'How? By tying me up?'

'Perhaps.'

'By flashing those sexy blue eyes at me? By kissing me until…'

Both Willie the ghost and the barman cleared their throats at exactly the same time. Oops. I'd completely forgotten they were there. I coughed. 'Sorry.'

'That's alright.' The barman stared round the room as if expecting Willie to jump out at him at any moment. 'William Barcell. I, er, take back what my ancestor said. She was wrong to want all your money and she shouldn't have cursed you. You are now…' He scratched his nose.

'Free?' I suggested.

He nodded. 'Sure. You are now free.'

Willie's eyes went round. 'Really? I can pass on? I don't have to stay here? Thank you!' He blew me a kiss. He leapt over to the barman and tried to hug him. It didn't really work because the barman couldn't see or feel him but the sentiment was nice.

Willie pulled back and looked around. 'I'm ready to go now!' he called out. 'Where's the light?' He swung his head in every direction. 'I don't see it. Where am I supposed to go?'

'What's happening?' Winter asked.

I considered the matter. 'I think,' I said, 'that Willie has been telling a few porky pies.'

The ghost stared at me. 'What? No, I've not! I'm not a liar!'

'Then why are you still here?'

He appeared momentarily nonplussed. 'I don't know.' Fear crossed his face but was quickly replaced by fury. He jabbed the barman, who was looking perplexed by my one-sided conversation, in the chest. 'You didn't mean what you said! You're the reason I'm still here!'

'You can shout at him until you're blue in the face,' I said calmly. 'He can't hear you. Why don't you go back to the beginning and tell me why you were really cursed?'

'I did tell you!' Willie shrieked.

'Are you absolutely sure?'

He glared at me. 'Fine,' he mumbled. 'His great-grandfather,' he said, without looking at the barman, 'said that if I showed my ... parts to anyone else, I'd be damned for all eternity. It's the only other curse I can think of.'

'And you ignored him and exposed yourself?' I probed.

'Only a few more times.'

I didn't say anything.

Willie sighed. 'Maybe it was a lot more times.'

I folded my arms. 'I'm not sure you should be allowed to pass on. I imagine you caused considerable distress to those poor people who had to see...' I gestured down at his crotch '...that.'

His head drooped. 'I am very sorry.'

There wasn't much else I could do. The offense was generations old and Willie had probably served his time. I shrugged at the barman. 'He has reconsidered,' I said. 'He was actually cursed because he continued to flash himself.'

'By flash, you mean…'

I nodded. 'Yes.'

The barman swallowed. 'Okay. So I forgive him for that and this is over? You crazy people will all leave me alone?'

'After you let us see that room,' I reminded him.

He grimaced. 'Oh yeah.' He sighed. 'Fine. I forgive William Barcell, my ancestor, for exposing himself so he can now stop haunting me and move on to … heaven? Hell? I really don't care.'

Willie's mouth dropped open. 'Hell? It's not like I murdered anyone, you little shit. I…'

There was a sudden flash of light that was so bright I had to cover my eyes. Both Winter and the barman jumped. When I looked round, Willie had gone. 'I think it worked,' I said slowly, hoping I wasn't tempting fate by speaking too soon.

'I felt it,' Winter breathed.

The barman nodded, his face white. 'Like a shadow crossing.' He raised his eyes to mine. 'Wow. Just … wow.'

I smiled, as if helping cantankerous ghosts pass to the other side was something I did on a regular basis. 'No problem. Now if I could get some more stew and the key to that room, in that order, it'd be very much appreciated.'

Chapter Eight

Blackbeard wasn't our serial killer's real name, of course. He'd checked into the pub as Nicholas Remy. That wasn't necessarily his real name either, as I pointed out to Winter when he unlocked the room. 'Until we know for sure, we should just stick to Blackbeard,' I advised.

'Is that because it's catchier?'

I shrugged. 'And I came up with it. I've not achieved much else lately, so I've got to take all the brownie points I can.'

Rather than turn the doorknob and enter, Winter looked at me. 'Ivy,' he said, with a funny look on his face. 'You can communicate with the dead. I've never heard of anyone being able to do anything like that before. You just helped a ghost cross over. Without you, he'd still be stuck here. You did that – Ivy Wilde. Magic or no magic, you can do things no one else can. Face it, we might have temporarily lost him but the only reason we know Remy exists is because of you.'

'Blackbeard,' I said.

A trace of a smile crossed his mouth. 'Fine. Blackbeard it is.'

I bit my lip and looked away. 'He knows your name,' I said quietly. 'He knows who you are.'

He reached out and tilted my face back towards his. 'Well, it's lucky I've got you to protect me then.'

I didn't smile back. 'He's staying in room number four, Rafe.'

'Four is only unlucky in Eastern superstition.'

'Eastern superstition tends to be more accurate than

ours,' I argued. 'And four represents death. That can't be a coincidence.'

'It's just a number,' he soothed.

I sighed and shook my head. 'I have a theory,' I told him. 'You're not going to like it.'

Winter stilled. 'Go on.'

'I don't know very much about the ins and outs of the spirit world so I might be wrong. And I might be committing the cardinal sin of getting the evidence to fit the theory. I know how much you hate that.'

'Ivy, it's okay. You can tell me.'

I sighed. 'William Barcell, the guy haunting this place, vanished on Tuesday. He didn't reappear until this evening.' I tapped lightly on the door. 'Blackbeard arrived on Tuesday.'

'Where did Barcell go?'

'He had no idea. He thought I had something to do with it but he had no memory of where he'd been. It was as if he'd simply been blotted out of existence.'

Winter nodded slowly. 'The coven. They experienced the same thing.'

'Yep. From the moment they died until the moment they were left in Wistman's Wood, they have a blank. And they've all been dumped there at different times. They were all *killed* at the same time, so their lack of awareness is not because it takes a while for phantomly consciousness to seep back in.' I drew in a breath. 'Then there's the spell you threw at Blackbeard. It's like you weren't even trying.'

Winter's expression closed off.

'Sorry, that came out badly. What I mean is that there's no way you could have missed. I saw the rune you used. That was powerful stuff, Rafe. The magic wasn't aimed anywhere other than at our very own serial-killing bastard.' I paused. 'So why didn't it hit him? It didn't even slow him down. You didn't think you'd missed him. I didn't think you'd missed him. So what the hell actually happened?'

He rubbed his chin with the base of his thumb and looked thoughtful. 'I see where you're going with this. You think that magic doesn't work around him. The ghosts cease to exist when he's in the vicinity and spells don't work.'

I bobbed my head. 'It's only a theory.'

He met my eyes. 'It does fit.'

'Maybe it's some kind of amulet. You know, like the one that Tarquin gave Belinda Battenapple to stop her from ageing. Or maybe he is a witch and he hates magic so much that he's cast a spell on himself to avoid it entirely.' I shrugged. 'I don't know. But if we can't use magic against him…'

'Then this is going to be even harder than we thought,' Winter finished for me. 'Let's hold that thought for now. I don't think it's a crazy theory.' He sighed. 'Unfortunately.'

Winter cautiously opened the door to Blackbeard's room and I held my breath. I wasn't sure what I was expecting – some kind of booby trap or explosive device maybe – but nothing happened. A musky scent floated out towards us, as if the room hadn't been aired for days. Other than that, the room was almost identical to the one that Winter and I were sharing.

Winter stepped inside and looked around. I followed. We knew that Blackbeard had left in a hurry but there was little evidence that he'd left behind anything that he would miss. The bed was made, with the sheets neatly smoothed over and the pillow plumped up. There was a duffel bag on the chest of drawers by the window. Winter walked over to it while I headed for the bathroom.

'Oh, I'm sorry!' I said, apologising to the young

woman sitting on the toilet. I quickly pulled back and closed the door. Winter turned towards me with a question in his eyes. I frowned. Hang on a minute.

Re-opening the door, I peered inside again. She was still sitting in the same position. She raised her head slowly and gazed at me, her dark hair hanging limply around her face. 'I'm dead, aren't I?'

I grimaced. 'Yeah. I think so.'

Winter reached into Blackbeard's bag and pulled out an urn. He waved it at me. I gave a brief nod of acknowledgment and returned my attention to the woman. 'You were in a coven. In Dorset.'

She stared at me. 'Were you the one following us?' Before I could reply, she answered her own question. 'No,' she said. 'That would have been him, wouldn't it? The one who did this to me. To us.'

This wasn't an enjoyable conversation but I had to continue. 'You were awake? When he killed you?'

Her fingers went up to her neck where there was an ugly wound. 'I was first,' she whispered, 'and he was clumsy. I came to as my life was ebbing away and I saw what he did to the others.' She looked around. 'Where are they?'

'Three are in a place not far from here called Wistman's Wood. Three are probably still with the man who killed you. He's been dumping your coven's ashes one by one, every time there's a new moon. Wistman's Wood is an old pagan forest and your companions there cannot leave. We don't know whether that's deliberate on the part of your murderer or not.'

I glanced back at Winter. If my theory about Blackbeard's ability to avoid all magic was true, it was certainly possible that he was aware of the strange properties of Wistman's Wood and had chosen it specifically.

'Tonight is a new moon?' she asked.

I shook my head. 'No. We think he was planning to leave your remains in the wood with the others, but we don't know why he's not waited until the moon turns when he always has before.'

'He's bored,' she said softly. 'He needs more.'

I started.

She smiled sadly. 'I wasn't just a witch. I trained as a psychologist too. I didn't work with murderers but they were part of my studies. He has a taste for killing now and he wants to keep going. He's drawn out disposing of our remains because he thought it would prolong his enjoyment, but he's realised it's not enough. He's moved his schedule up. He's going to get rid of all of us as quickly as possible so that he can move on to a new target.'

Her voice was so matter-of-fact that it sent a chill down my spine. 'It's possible that he's targeting witches,' I told her. 'He doesn't seem to like them. And it's possible he can nullify any spells thrown his way.'

She considered this. 'That makes sense,' she nodded. 'Timothy was the second one to die. He had herbs with him for protection because he was more convinced than the rest of us that we were being followed. He used them to set up a ward before we started chanting.' She raised a shoulder. 'Obviously the herbs didn't work.'

I absorbed her words with a faintly sick feeling. 'Why did he think he was being followed?'

'He'd had strange messages. Threats, that kind of thing.'

I sucked in a breath. Timothy hadn't been one of the coven members at Wistman's Wood but if he had evidence that might tell us more about Blackbeard, I had to find out more from him. I swung back to Winter. He was still holding the duffel bag but he'd abandoned rummaging through its contents in favour of watching me. I wasn't sure how much he could glean from what was going on.

'Are there any other urns there?' I asked.

'No. There's just the one. There's a name on it,' he added, 'if that's helpful.'

'I'm Clare Rees,' the woman said.

I checked with Winter. 'Clare Rees?' I asked.

He nodded.

'It was our custom to perform coven spells in ceremonial robes,' Clare said. She gestured at herself and I realised she was wearing exactly the same outfit as the three others from her coven. 'There aren't any pockets. In any case, we tend to leave all real-life objects at home. Karen was convinced that they would interfere with the magic.'

In other words, she didn't have any ID on her when she'd died but Blackbeard had still known exactly who she was.

'She cursed us, didn't she?' Clare said. 'Karen, I mean.'

I tried to demur. 'It wasn't really your coven she was cursing. She just wanted to make sure that your murderer receives the justice he deserves.'

'Funny that we're the ones who are suffering,' Clare commented. 'I can feel it, you know. It's like a block. My body is being tugged away but something's preventing it from going. I can't see it but I can feel it. It's all around me.' Her shoulders drooped. 'It's awful. There was so much I still wanted to do. I never travelled. I always wanted to visit South America but now I'll never get the chance. I was going to tell Mike at work what I really thought of him but I was too scared. I was going to learn how to fly.' Her voice fell to a whisper. 'I'll never do any of that.'

'I'm sorry.' Never had an apology felt so inadequate.

'It's not your fault.'

I watched her for a moment or two. 'We can take your ashes to the wood so you can be with the others. Blackbeard, the man who killed you, cremated you somehow. I guess it made it easier to transport your bodies.'

'Blackbeard?'

I scratched my neck. 'That's what I've christened him. He checked in under the name Nicholas Remy but we don't know if that's his real name. It could—'

'It's not.' I glanced at her askance and she explained. 'Nicholas Remy is the name of an old French witch hunter from the sixteenth century.'

I sucked in a breath. Well, that made a kind of sense.

Clare got to her feet. 'I'd appreciate it if you could give my remains to my parents,' she said. 'I have no desire to be trapped with the others in an ancient forest. They were bad enough when they were alive. I can't begin to imagine how annoying they'll be now they're dead.'

She had a point. 'We can do that,' I promised.

'Thank you. I'm going to leave now. I want to find my family. My real family. I want to find out if they're alright.'

I nodded and watched her dissipate into nothingness. I hoped for her sake that everything *was* alright. It would be torture if her family were suffering and she could do nothing but watch.

Winter strode over and put his arms round me. 'Are you okay? You're shaking all over.'

'I'm fine.' I ran a hand through my hair. 'This is just so hard.' I met his eyes. 'I don't want to be the only person in the world who can talk to ghosts, Rafe. I can't cope with this kind of responsibility. It should be someone else.'

'You're stronger than you know, Ivy Wilde,' he murmured in my ear. 'And I'll be with you every step of the way.'

I leaned into him, taking a moment to enjoy his closeness. I had a horrible feeling I was going to need all the comfort I could get.

Chapter Nine

If this had been a normal kind of day, driving to the arse end of the country to tramp around soggy moorland, converse with dead witches and almost catch a bearded serial killer would have resulted in a good night's sleep. There again, if this had been a normal day, I wouldn't have left my sofa for anything more than a choccie biscuit – and even then I probably could have inveigled Winter into getting it for me. I might have had to put up with him presenting it on a lace doily, followed by him passing judgment when I ate not one biscuit but twenty, but it would still have been better than this.

It was rare that anything prevented me from sleeping; the last time I suffered from a bout of insomnia was around the time Billy Smythe stole my Barbie and set her hair alight and I couldn't decide between turning him into a Barbie himself or making him my personal slave. I think that was when I decided that I was going to do everything I could to avoid letting life's travails stress me out, whether they involved mutilated Barbies or not.

The bed was comfortable and Winter was his usual warm, snuggly self. He didn't snore and he didn't hog the bedcovers. His feet were toasty warm. There weren't any ghosts in the vicinity chatting to me and trying to keep me awake. Brutus wasn't even there, pawing at my face and demanding attention. So why the hell couldn't I sleep?

I sighed heavily and turned over. Maybe counting sheep would help – except that reminded me of what had happened up in Scotland just last month and only exacerbated my sleeplessness. A hot milky drink was supposed to be another helpful remedy – or so I'd heard. Unfortunately, the only milk here was in those little plastic containers designed for tea and coffee. Even if I could work out a way to heat them up without using either a microwave or magic, they'd provide little more than a single mouthful.

If Winter were awake, I'd have asked him to bespell me but he was fast asleep. His jaw was slack and, for once, he was utterly at rest. I screwed up my face. This was ridiculous: Ivy Wilde did not suffer from insomnia. Unless it had something to do with the latent necromancy swirling around my system. That chilling thought had me sitting bolt upright and breaking into a cold sweat.

I got out of bed and padded naked into the bathroom to splash cold water on my face. I was dabbing it dry with a towel when I heard the sound of an engine outside. That couldn't be right; it was three o'clock in the morning and we were in the middle of nowhere. Even farmers wouldn't get up this early.

I checked on Winter, who'd not even stirred, and grabbed my coat, shrugging it on to preserve my modesty. Then, doing what no one should ever do when it's the middle of the night, there is a serial killer on the loose and many, many ghosts to contend with, I slipped out.

The pub was silent inside but I could hear voices outside. Frowning, I walked over to the front door and put my ear against it.

'We should just ring the bell.'

'Or spell it open and find rooms for ourselves. We can settle up with the owners tomorrow.' There was a pause. 'I mean, today.'

'We will do no such thing,' the familiar voice of the Ipsissimus – the living one – said. 'There is plenty of room in the car. Besides, we're not here to sleep.'

'We can't investigate anything while we're out here.'

'Honestly, I never knew witches could whine so much! Villeneuve, get back to the car. You can sleep in the boot. Masters and Houseman can have the back seat. The other two can take the front.'

'What about you, sir?'

'I'm going for a walk. I want to see this wood.'

There were a few audible intakes of breath. 'But it's the middle of the night! It's too dangerous!'

'I rather think,' the Ipsissimus said drily, 'that the only risk will come from stumbling in a pothole. As I can use magic to light the way, that will not be an issue. Go on, you young folks, get your rest. I'll see you in a few hours.'

'I'll go to the wood!' Tarquin burst in. 'I don't mind. I'm not tired anyway.'

'I'm a higher rank than you, Villeneuve,' another voice said. 'I'll go. You stay here with the Ipsissimus. It might not be safe for you.'

'I'm perfectly capable of looking after myself.'

'Hmm,' the Ipsissimus said, staving off the impending argument and sounding for all the world as if he were trying to come up with an amicable solution to suit everyone. I grinned to myself. It appeared that he was a man after my own heart. 'You're right. It probably would be better if more than one person went to the wood. I tell you what, you lot go and investigate then report back to me. I'll stay here.'

There was a moment of brief and, to my mind, sullen silence then the witches acquiesced with a series of quiet mumbles. I listened as their footsteps drew away. I could learn a lot from the Ipsissimus, I decided.

'Are you going to open that door, Ms Wilde?' he enquired.

Startled, I drew back. My smile grew and I unhooked the chain and let him in. The other witches, Tarquin included, had already been swallowed up by the night.

'Don't worry about them,' the Ipsissimus said cheerfully. 'They'll be quite some time before they return. Between their bickering and the fact that none of them can navigate their way around clearly marked roads, they won't be going anywhere fast.'

I couldn't help asking, 'If they're such an annoyance, why bring them?'

The Ipsissimus knitted his fingers together and looked astonished. 'This is the Order, my dear. We work together as a team. Besides,' he added on a grimmer note, 'from what Adeptus Exemptus Winter has told me, there may be serious danger. There are more Order witches on the way. We were caught short in Scotland but I won't let that happen again. Not when there are very real risks to consider.'

'And then some.' I met his eyes. 'There have been some further developments.'

'Excellent,' he replied flatly. 'That's always what I want to hear.'

I drew him over to the deathly silent bar area and we sat down before I filled him in. I have to say this for the Ipsissimus – he knows when to keep quiet and listen. It wasn't until I'd finished talking that he started to ask questions. 'There was no other identification in the room at all?'

I shook my head. 'The Barcells, who own this place, have agreed to seal the room off until the police can get here and dust it down for prints.'

'They'll be here first thing in the morning. It's already arranged.'

I nodded acknowledgment. 'That's good. I just...' I sighed.

'Go on, Ms Wilde.'

My unhappiness was obvious. 'I think that Blackbeard is going to prove a lot more clever than that. He was forced to leave here in a hurry but there are no identifying features anywhere. Not to mention that we only came across his existence by accident. We don't know how long he's been operating for, or how many others he's killed. How can an entire coven vanish and no one think to report them missing or to ask questions? Whether they're in the Order or not, you'd think that someone would have said something.'

'You think that Blackbeard has been covering his tracks.'

'I do.' I grabbed a curl and wound it tightly round my finger, cutting off circulation to the tip and watching absent-mindedly as it turned red. 'This isn't about ego. We weren't supposed to know what he's been doing. He doesn't want fame or notoriety or a following, he's all about the mission.'

'And the mission is to kill witches?'

'So it appears.' I released the curl but the tension still remained.

The Ipsissimus stood up and walked to the window, gazing out at nothing. 'She was right, you know, your ghost. Nicholas Remy was indeed a witch hunter. By all accounts he was a nasty bastard. It cannot be a coincidence that the killer selected that as his name. If we do not find him soon, I have no doubt that there will be more deaths.' He stroked his chin. 'I shall have to reach out to the non-Order covens and tell them to be on the lookout.'

'I think that would be very wise,' I said quietly. 'And as for my theory…'

He turned and faced me. 'If your theory proves to be true and Blackbeard is immune to magic, the situation is incredibly grave. I shall set the librarians to research the matter immediately. If there are amulets to negate the effects of spells or the supernatural, or any precedents for this kind of situation, we shall know about them soon.'

Shifting slightly, I eyed him. I felt guilty for asking about myself considering everything else that was going on but I had to know. 'Speaking of scholarly research,' I said. 'Has Philip Maidmont uncovered anything about my, er, condition?'

'Hmm?' For a brief moment the Ipsissimus looked blank then his expression cleared. 'Ah, yes. You're perfectly safe. Your ability to converse with the dead is indeed a side-effect of the necromantic magic you absorbed from the boy but, as all the energy you displaced is now focused towards the spirits, there is no need to worry. Unless you actually try to raise the dead, you are no danger to either yourself or to others.'

I breathed a sigh of relief. It felt like a massive weight had been taken off my shoulders. An involuntary chortle of glee escaped my lips and I raised my hands, my fingers sketching a rune. The nearby fireplace roared into life, the flames dancing and writhing in an unnatural manner.

'Man, that felt good.' I examined my hands. 'I hadn't realised how much I needed magic until I couldn't use it.'

A faint smile crossed the Ipsissimus's face. 'Yet you did not hesitate to deny yourself that which you so desperately desired. You are to be commended, Ms Wilde.' He looked me up and down. 'Perhaps Adeptus Exemptus Winter is rubbing off on you in ways both seen and unseen. It is obvious that you are affecting him.'

'You keep calling him that,' I said. 'But he's not in the Order, Ipsissimus. He's no longer Adeptus Exemptus.'

'He will change his mind.'

I shook my head. I wasn't so sure about that.

The Ipsissimus leaned towards me. 'We need him to change his mind. He is vital, Ms Wilde. To everything.'

'I don't understand.'

He pursed his lips. 'The recent events in Scotland have forced me to reassess many things. I need to stop pussyfooting around and ensure I have an appropriate successor in place. I did not believe Raphael was ready for that role, but the way he left the Order behind because of his loyalty to you…'

Whoa there. I held up my hands. 'Don't bring me into this. He left on his own terms.'

'Ms Wilde, until you came along he lived, breathed and ate the Order. Many of our witches do. But to be Ipsissimus is to take on board heavy responsibilities. Without a strong and steady network and a life outside work, it is impossible to succeed. The pressure is too great. And that is not all. If one is wholly absorbed in the Order, one can lose sight of the bigger picture. Now that Raphael Winter – Adeptus Exemptus Raphael Winter – has you, he possesses that bigger picture.'

I felt uncomfortable at having this conversation without Winter present. The Ipsissimus kept on dangling juicier and juicier carrots in his bid to get Winter to return but somehow I didn't think Winter would give two hoots about what was on offer. All the same, my curiosity got the better of me. 'But you've said it yourself. He's Adeptus Exemptus and that's only Second Level. There have to be at least a couple of hundred witches who are ranked higher than Rafe.'

'Two hundred and thirty-three, to be exact,' he said. 'Most of whom are tied to their specialisms and who are unable to see the wood for the trees. Adeptus Exemptus Winter has already proved he can manage upwards as well as down. You have more magical talent than he does, after all. His ego doesn't interfere with that fact and he is more than capable of getting the best out of you.'

'I'm one person, Ipsissimus Collings, and I'm in love with him. He gets a lot of leeway as far as I'm concerned. The Order, however, is thousands of people, most of whom probably hate him for being better than they are and for leaving when he could have stayed. Rafe doesn't want it.'

The Ipsissimus's answering gaze was frank and earnest. 'And maybe that's why he should have it. He has already shown he has more integrity than ambition. Besides, I'm hardly at death's door. There is plenty of time for Raphael to take the necessary examinations and move up the hierarchy.'

'Not if Raphael doesn't want to,' said Winter from the doorway. He looked pissed off. I wasn't really surprised. 'What exactly is it going to take for you to leave me alone?'

'Come back,' the Ipsissimus entreated. 'Just think about all the good you could do.' He reached inside his coat pocket and drew out a scroll.

I sucked in a breath. The last time the Ipsissimus had given me a scroll, it had been an incantation which had almost caused my death.

Winter's expression was flat. 'What is that?'

'The paperwork that will bring you back in, Raphael. Your promotion. And more. I've already signed it. All you have to do is add your name and we can forget everything that has happened in the past. It's time to move on.'

Winter crossed his arms. 'No. I don't know how many times you expect me to say the same thing.'

'You belong in the Order. You know you do. You thrive on what we can offer you.'

'I'm doing just fine.'

The Ipsissimus took a step forward. 'As far as this investigation goes, you have no place in it,' he said gently. 'Because you're on the outside. You're not in the Order and you're not in the police. I could force you to stay away from anything related to this Blackbeard fellow.'

'Try it,' Winter growled.

'But that's just it! I don't want to do that. We need your expertise, Raphael. We want you on our side. But you know as well as I do that there will be more doors open if you are in the Order – and more doors slammed in your face now that you are not. There is only so much I can do. Return to the fold and you can take charge of this. You can find Blackbeard and bring him to justice. You can second Ms Wilde to your team and have the might and power of the Order behind you. You know it makes sense.'

Winter crossed his arms over his chest. Despite – or perhaps because of – his anger, he looked incredibly sexy. I'd happily have jumped him right then. Maybe I should have kicked the Ipsissimus back out to his car.

'You need Ivy's ability to talk to the dead,' Winter snapped. 'You don't need me.'

'You're wrong about that. If you think things in the Order should change then tell us and we can look at implementing those changes. You know this is right. You know your place is with us.'

'I'm not staying away from the Order because I'm sulking or because I want you to make me a better offer,' Winter said. 'I can do just as much good on the outside as I can on the inside. Except on the outside there will be less bureaucracy and less chance that innocent people will be hurt in the hunt for your supposed greater good. There's nothing wrong with independence.'

Even I could see that the Ipsissimus was growing

desperate. 'We're all on the same team.'

'Good,' Winter declared. 'So let's work together and find Blackbeard. We'll get justice for the Dorset coven and we can do it by working together. I just won't have that piece of paper stating I'm in the Order.'

The Ipsissimus splayed out his hands in defeat. 'Do I have any choice?'

Winter shrugged his wide shoulders. 'I suppose not.'

'Then that will have to do.' The Ipsissimus gave us both a benevolent smile. But even I could hear the unsaid 'for now', which was tagged on the end of that sentence.

Chapter Ten

Clare Rees lived – or had lived – in a nondescript little terraced house in the picturesque town of Weymouth in Dorset. We found it with no trouble and, even more helpfully, just as we reached the door Clare herself reappeared, gazing morosely at the pavement. 'They don't care,' she said.

I looked at her askance. 'Who?'

'My family,' she said. 'My family don't care that I've gone. They're just getting on with their lives as if nothing's happened. My mum is still helping out at the Salvation Army, my dad is still going to all his local darts matches with his drinking buddies. They're laughing and joking. They don't care. My sister, the person who I was closest to in the whole world, is planning a round-the-world trip for three months. She's not seen me since May and yet she doesn't care. No one's so much as mentioned my name. It's like I don't exist. What the hell is going on?'

By now Winter was getting used to my sudden silences as I listened to my phantom friends. He stopped and waited while I gave Clare a sympathetic look. I could well understand what she was going through. When I die, I expect copious weeping. In fact, not just weeping but renting of clothes and gnashing of teeth. I want my funeral to take place in Westminster Abbey and to include at least two renditions of *Tragedy* – the Steps version and the Bee Gees one. While I lounge back in final rest, everyone else can do the hard work. I will demand elaborate outfits with lacy black veils for both the men and the women. Maybe I'll force my remaining family members to perform a contemporary dance number to express their dismay at my passing. Considering how often I seem to be close to death these days, this is probably something I should sort out. I ought to make a will and make my last wishes clear. Tomorrow. Or maybe the day after. Next week at the absolute latest. It is important to be prepared, after all.

'You could look on the bright side,' I suggested to Clare. 'At least they're getting on with their lives. They're not wallowing in misery or letting grief ruin what's left of their days. In fact, they might not even know that you're dead.'

She wrinkled her nose as if I were spouting nonsense, probably because I was.

'Yeah, screw that,' I said. 'They're bastards who never deserved you in the first place.' At least that raised a small smile.

Winter cleared his throat. 'I'm going to hope that's Clare and that she can tell you there's a spare key hidden somewhere.'

'Under the flowerpot,' she muttered.

I pointed down. Winter bent over and retrieved it. Clare watched him with a downturned expression until he put the key in the lock and sudden fear flashed across her face. 'What is it?' I demanded. 'Clare? What's wrong?'

Winter froze.

'I live alone. I've had other things on my mind and I'd forgotten that I was in a rush before I left for the last time. I think my dirty underwear might be strewn across the floor.'

I gave her a wise nod. 'It's the best place for it,' I agreed. 'You just have to be careful to keep it in localised piles otherwise you can trip on a loose bra strap in the middle of the night, go flying and end up in casualty with several contusions and a broken tibia.' I paused. 'Or so I've heard.'

'I don't want him to see my smalls!' Clare half yelled.

'Huh?' I glanced at Winter. Oh. 'Don't worry. We virtually live together now. He's seen much worse from me.'

'Ivy, please. Just let me check. There has to be something sacred left to me. I have to have some privacy.' Her panic was so palpable that there was nothing I could do but nod.

'Wait, Rafe,' I said softly. Clare stepped through the door, her spectral form passing through its solid oak veneer as if it were air. 'Clare just needs to check on something.'

Winter gave me a confused frown but he did as I asked and took his hand from the door.

'There's not much dignity in death,' I said, doing what I could to explain. 'Clare won't be on a metal table with her body exposed to uncaring eyes. She won't be in a battered locker or jiggled around in a coffin. But that doesn't mean that the next days aren't going to involve strangers rooting through her life and passing judgment.'

'She can't stop that from happening, Ivy,' he said. 'And she can't throw away any embarrassing pornography or secret letters or anything like that. She can't physically touch anything.'

I stroked his arm. 'She knows that. I think she just wants a moment to herself to come to terms with it.' I raised my eyebrows. 'Where are your embarrassing pornography and secret letters? You might as well tell me now before I stumble across them post-mortem.' Winter rolled his eyes and snorted. I grinned. 'You can find mine hidden at the bottom of…'

Clare's head emerged from the door with wide-eyed

alarm. 'Ivy! Something is wrong!'

I whipped round towards her. There was a panicked note to her voice that went beyond anything I'd previously heard from her, something that suggested dire straits and horrendous consequences. Almost unconsciously, my arm shot out in front of Winter as if to protect him from what might be about to happen while I waited for Clare to explain.

'There's something strange attached to the door,' she said. 'I don't know what it is and I definitely didn't put it there. Someone has been inside my house and has messed around.' Her voice rose further. 'In my *home*, Ivy.'

Whatever she was talking about, it didn't sound good. 'Take a deep breath, Clare.' As soon as I said it, I realised how silly it was telling a ghost to breathe but Clare didn't seem to notice. Her hands had now also emerged through the solid door and were fluttering around in increasingly frantic movements. 'Stay calm and tell me exactly what you see.'

'It was that bastard, wasn't it? The one who killed us. He's been here. He's messed with my stuff. He's rooted through my things and seen everything there is to know about me. It wasn't enough that he killed me and my entire coven, he's taken my home and my life too!'

'Clare,' I soothed. 'It's okay. Just tell me what you can see. What's on the door?'

She rubbed her face with both hands. 'A wire.'

I nodded. 'Okay, good. There's a wire,' I repeated aloud for Winter's benefit. 'Where is the wire exactly?'

Clare's head disappeared momentarily as she went to check. 'It starts at the bottom.' She gestured to about a foot off the ground. 'It runs horizontally from here to here,' she said, motioning to either side of the door frame. 'Then it stretches up to the top here.' She indicated with her finger. 'And there's something hanging there. It looks like...' She hesitated and stared at me.

'Looks like what?'

Clare's eyes were wide. 'Like a grenade.'

I did my best to keep my feet planted in one spot and not go sprinting as far away as possible. Turning to Winter, I outlined what Clare had described. He nodded grimly. 'It's a tiger trap. The second we open the door the grenade will fall and—'

'Kaboom,' I finished for him.

'Body parts everywhere,' Clare breathed.

I grimaced. 'I imagine so.'

'You and him will be blasted apart. It'll be impossible to tell which bits belong to you and which bits belong to him. There will be fragments of flesh and blood and bone and—'

'Alright!' I said overly loudly. 'Thank you, Clare.' Winter lifted a questioning eyebrow. I made a point of ignoring it. I already had vivid visuals running through my mind; I didn't need to compound the issue by describing them out loud. 'Is there another way in?' I asked.

'No.' She paused. 'Security is very important to me. I always made sure I lived somewhere with only one entrance. Otherwise someone might have been able to sneak in when I wasn't looking and...' She faltered.

Booby-trap her front door with a damn grenade, perhaps? I shook my head in disbelief. *Enchantment* made more sense than this. It was as if I'd somehow fallen into a Hollywood set – except I was no Sly Stallone.

'I need to tell the police. And the Order,' Winter said. 'If Clare Rees's house is booby-trapped then the others probably will be too.'

I straightened up. 'Yes! Get the bomb squad here to

deal with this. We can check into a hotel and leave them to it.'

'Don't be silly, Ivy,' he said. 'We can go round the back and find another way in.'

Uh-oh. The bad, squirmy feeling caused by the suggestion of blown-apart body bits began to intensify. No doubt Winter was going to suggest some convoluted ninja-esque entry. 'But Clare said there's only one door.'

A smile crooked up the corner of his mouth. 'Ivy Wilde wouldn't let a small thing like a door get in her way.'

You wanna bet? I opened my mouth to argue but Clare's dejected face stopped me. 'Fine,' I grumbled. 'But when my teeth are being picked out of your splattered brain matter, don't come crying to me.'

***

Clare didn't have any garden to speak of but there was a handy alleyway running down the back of the row of houses. It was surprisingly well kept; I guessed that, like her, her neighbours were concerned with appearances and were houseproud. There is nothing wrong with that, of course. Cleanliness is next to godliness, whatever that means. But the trouble with that sort of approach to life is that it never ends. Yes, you can take time to pick the weeds from the pavement outside and scrub your skirting board and make sure there's no dust collecting in any evil corners but you had to keep on doing it. If I had to do it all this week and then again next week and then the week after that, why not just leave it till next month? Or preferably next year?

Winter put his phone away. 'What are you huffing about?'

I did my best to appear innocent. 'Nothing.'

'You have that look in your eyes.'

'I don't know what you're talking about.'

Winter persisted. 'Yes, you do. It's the same look you get when you start thinking about getting off the sofa to do crazy things like answer the door or go out to work in order to pay your bills.'

I drew myself up. 'Well, you have that look in your eyes too. The one that says you just had to speak to the Order and you secretly wish you were still with them so you could feel important and wanted, and had a nice shiny badge to wave at everyone.'

Winter frowned at me. 'The Order don't have badges.'

'I bet you wish they did though. That way, when you went to talk to someone, you could take it out and flip it open.' I mimed doing just that. Then I deepened my voice. '"Raphael Winter. That's Adeptus Exemptus Raphael Winter to you. Arcane Branch. That's Arcane Branch in the Hallowed Order of Magical Enlightenment. I take my coffee black and strong. And I glower at everyone who dares to look at me without receiving permission first. And I enjoy venturing into buildings where there's a good chance I might get blown up."'

Somewhere behind me, Clare snickered.

Winter tilted his head, something dangerous glinting in his blue eyes. Then he let his body sag and his shoulders slump. ' "Ivy,"' he mumbled in a higher-pitched tone than normal. '"Can't be bothered to form sentences or to shake hands with you because it's too much effort."' He froze. '"Wait,"' he said with a sudden toss of his hair, '"do I smell pizza?"'

I put my hands on my hips. 'Ha. Ha. Ha.'

'"I might have to sit down,"' Winter said. '"I've walked at least twenty steps already today and it's been a bit too much."'

I stuck out my tongue and he grinned. 'Actually,' he

said in a low voice as if he were afraid someone would overhear, 'I did want badges. I put in a suggestion to get them for everyone when I first joined Arcane Branch.'

I winced. 'In the shape of witch's hats?'

'Not quite that bad. They needed to look official, not ridiculous.'

'Of course,' I smiled. 'I once put in a suggestion that we pay a teenager to hang around our building and help with deliveries. You know, escort takeaways up to our door, that kind of thing.'

Winter's eyes danced with amusement.

Clare peered at us. 'I don't get it,' she said finally.

I dragged my attention away from Winter and glanced at her. 'What do you mean?'

'That was…' she hesitated as if searching for the right word '…mean. You were mean to him and he was mean to you.'

I tapped the corner of my mouth. We'd needed a moment of levity amid all this serial-killer stuff but I understood what she meant. 'It wasn't mean,' I said finally. 'It was honest. We know each other very well. I suppose what we're really saying is that we know the worst about each other and it doesn't matter. We accept each other for who we are, regardless of our faults.'

Winter reached across and squeezed my hand while Clare stared at me. 'I think I hate you both.'

I beamed back at her cheerfully. 'I would hate us both too.' I lifted my head up. 'Now let's crack on. Which window is going to be the easiest?' I pointed at one on the second floor. 'That looks large enough to wiggle through.'

'It's sealed shut,' Clare said. 'The only one which opens is that one.' She floated upwards until she was hovering in front of the highest – and smallest – window in the house.

Winter followed my eyes. 'The window on the right?' he enquired.

'Apparently it's the only one that will open.' I flicked him a look from under my eyelashes. 'We should definitely wait for the bomb squad.'

'Clare?' Winter said, looking in the wrong direction. 'Can you check whether there are any more booby traps?'

She nodded eagerly and disappeared back through the walls of her house.

'She said she can't,' I told him. 'On account of the fact that her ghostly presence might upset the spiritual atoms and set them off, blowing us all to smithereens.'

Clare's head appeared from the chimney top. 'There's nothing else here!' she called. 'It's only the front door that's been tampered with.'

Winter, reading my expression, smiled. 'Great.' He gestured in front of him. 'Ladies first.'

I stared at him. 'What do you expect me to do? Scale the wall? I'm not Spiderman.' I shifted my body slightly so he couldn't see what I was doing, then I put my hands behind my back and drew out a rune. Ever so slowly, Winter began to rise up. The best part was that, because it happened at such a snail's pace, he didn't even notice until he was at least a foot in the air.

'Ivy!'

I smirked and continued raising him. I had the most amazing view of his arse from here.

Clare's mouth was hanging open in astonishment. 'He can fly?'

'Nope.'

'But...'

'I'm making Winter levitate,' I explained. 'But it takes a lot of energy and I can't hold him for long.' We both watched as he reached the window and began to tug at it, trying to open it up. 'Do you have any wards in place?' I asked. If there were any, they should have been blown when Blackbeard entered but it didn't hurt to ask.

'Oh yes,' Clare said proudly. 'I have several.'

Winter finally managed to open the window and stuck his head inside. A beat later he was violently thrown backwards, somersaulting through the air and down to the ground. In the nick of time I managed to cast a rune to cushion his fall but he still groaned very loudly.

I ran over. 'Are you okay?'

He squinted up at me, pain clouding his gaze. 'We should have waited for the bomb squad.'

Alarmed now, I crouched down, searching for visible wounds. 'That was a bomb? Another grenade?'

'No.' He raised his head then thought better of it and dropped it down again with a thud. 'A ward. Your mate Clare might have been non-Order but she knew her guard magic.'

A huge smile cracked Clare's face, spreading from ear to ear. Almost as quickly as it appeared, it vanished. 'It wasn't really me,' she said, her head hanging. 'It was part of the protective spells the coven put in place when we thought we were being followed. We worked together to set them up on all our homes.'

I sucked on my lip. 'And yet Blackbeard wasn't troubled by them in the slightest.' The magic plot thickened.

She frowned. 'You're right. He's definitely doing something to avoid being affected by magic.'

Of any sort. I sighed. If even latent spells like wards didn't stop him, what would? The fact that he'd managed to gain entry and set up his own entirely non-magical yet death-inducing ward was incredibly worrisome.

I helped Winter up to his feet. 'My turn,' I said grimly.

'You don't want to wait?'

My mouth flattened. 'No. They'll be hours and I've had enough of this place. I want to go home. The faster we do this, the faster that can happen. No serial killer is going to get the better of us.'

I must have sounded determined because Clare looked impressed. 'You go girl.'

'The wards…'

'You can disarm them with the password. Coventastic.'

Coventastic? Good grief. It was probably wise not to say anything aloud. If Winter realised he could have avoided being thrown out of Clare's window at great speed by simply uttering a word, he wouldn't be best pleased. I avoided his eyes. 'Beam me up, Scotty,' I muttered.

Winter used the same rune I had, sending me up smoothly through the air towards the window. All the same, I could feel gravity working against me. The laws of science never enjoy coming up against the laws of magic – it's like oil and water. At least Clare's house was only three-storeys high. It could have been much worse.

When I got to the now-open window, I realised with dismay that it was smaller than I'd thought. Squeezing inside was going to be tough. I grabbed hold of the windowsill, whispered, 'Coventastic,' and started to wiggle through.

To begin with it was fairly straightforward but I was only pushing my arms and head through. My shoulders scraped painfully against the frame and, when I had to push my chest through, it didn't seem that I was going to make it. No amount of holding my breath was going to make my breasts any smaller. Still, I managed to squash in just enough to squeak them past. Now the only worry was my hips. I shuffled forward with the top half of my body hanging into Clare's house and my bottom half hanging out. It bloody hurt. Matters didn't improve when there was a sudden loud shout from outside.

'Oy! What are you doing? I'm calling the polis!'

'It's Pete from down the road,' Clare said, sounding surprised. 'Aw, bless. He was never interested in joining the neighbourhood watch before and now he's looking out for me. That's really sweet. At least someone cares.' She paused. 'Even if he is a scary bastard with facial tattoos and a vicious Chihuahua called Bruiser.'

I wasn't sure whether she was referring to the fact that having a Chihuahua meant he was a scary bastard, or whether it was the Chihuahua's name that created that effect. Either way, this wasn't the time to ask, not with my arse hanging out of her window. It wasn't like I could back out now; the only way was forward, whatever Pete from down the road was doing.

I continued my slow wiggle, growing more and more uncomfortable by the second. Clare kept up a running commentary on the events outside. 'Oooh. Winter has approached Pete and he's looking tough. But I think Pete is tougher. Winter's not acting scared, he's doing that glowery thing that I've seen him do to you. Pete is growling back at him. So is Bruiser.' She clapped her hands. 'This is exciting.'

If she weren't already dead, I'd probably wring her neck. 'Tell Winter,' I said through gritted teeth, 'to get Pete to back off. We don't have time for this.'

'But Winter can't hear me.'

Damn it; I kept forgetting that part. 'Rafe!' I shouted. 'Get Pete to leave! We've got Clare's permission to be here!'

'That was good,' she said.

I wiggled a bit further forward. If I could just shimmy my hips through, I'd manage this. 'So it worked?' I asked her.

Clare laughed. 'Oh no! They can't hear you. Probably because your bottom is in the way and it's blocking out all the sound. But if they could hear you, I'm sure it would make a big difference.'

I cursed to myself. Grabbing hold of the curtains I started to pull, hoping I could yank myself through before I ripped them off the rail. I pushed and I pulled. Come on, Ivy.

'Oh!' Clare said. 'Pete says that my brother told him I'd gone off for an extended holiday. He asked him to keep an eye on the house for me and to call him if there were any problems.'

I grunted loudly. I'd never experienced labour pains but they couldn't be a million miles away from this. Push! Breathe! Push! I threw everything I had into one final effort and my hips finally squeezed past the frame. I popped through, landing on the floor of Clare's upstairs hallway with a loud sigh of relief and what felt like some extensive scrapes and bruises.

As I tried to disentangle my limbs from each other, Clare pursed her lips. 'Of course, I don't actually have a brother so either Pete is lying or Blackbeard spoke to him.'

I staggered upwards and back to the window, peering out. Winter and Tattooed Pete were still facing each other as if squaring off. It looked to me as if things were calming down slightly. That was good – at least until Pete said something and Winter smashed his fist into his nose.

'Rafe!' I yelled. What the hell was he doing? It wasn't like him to grow suddenly violent. He should be doing everything in his power to calm the situation down, not escalate it. There was no way I was clambering out of the window to try and sort things out, though. It had taken far too long to get inside and I didn't think I could do it again.

'We're friends of Clare's,' I shouted.

Pete's fists were tightly bunched. He ignored me and took a swing at Winter, smacking a hefty punch into his jaw.

I yelped, 'Leave him alone!'

Winter and Pete began to circle each other. Good grief, this was about to turn into a full-blown cock fight. I certainly felt like I was watching two cocks, anyway.

'You idiots!' I bellowed. We were hunting a serial killer. There wasn't time for tests of strength or testosterone-fuelled one-upmanship. 'Clare told us about you, Pete. You have a Chihuahua called Bruiser.'

'It has the hots for the cat at number ten,' Clare said helpfully. 'Keeps trying to hump it.'

'Bruiser's in love with one of the cats from this same street!' I shouted.

Pete paused for a moment. Unfortunately, it didn't last as he bounced round and took another shot at Winter from the side. This time Winter managed to duck in time and I prayed that he was keeping at least some of his cool. If he resorted to using magic against this guy, all was lost.

'This is so stupid,' I muttered to myself. 'Winter's been possessed.'

'Nah,' Clare said. 'He's just defending your honour. Pete said he'd never seen a burglar with such a fat arse.' She tilted her head. 'To be fair, it was all he could see of you at the time. He doesn't usually say much at all.'

I should probably have been offended but I actually felt kind of warm and fuzzy that Winter was so worked up on my behalf. But that didn't mean I could allow this to continue.

Until we knew the lay of the land, I didn't want to alert Pete to the fact that Winter and I were witches. I could search for a bucket to throw water over them but in the time it took to find one, both Winter and Pete could end up knocked out. Instead I did about the only other thing I could think of. Pulling down my waistband, I turned round and mooned the pair of them. 'You want a fat arse?' I screeched. 'Here you go!'

'Nice,' Clare said with an approving nod. 'They've both stopped and they're just staring at you.'

I sniffed, returned my clothing to its appropriate position and turned round.

Winter threw me a glare. 'What the hell did you think you were doing?'

'Getting you to stop acting like idiots,' I yelled back. 'This guy is a friend of Clare's. He's only looking out for her. Just because he's a misogynistic bastard doesn't mean you need to hurt him.'

Surprisingly, Tattooed Pete looked rather abashed. He put his hands in his pockets and looked away. 'I'm sorry. But Clare is a nice lady,' he said. 'A really nice lady. She always has a kind word for me. And I promised her brother I'd keep an eye on her place. I didn't mean to be rude but you're breaking in.'

Oh, Pete. Poor guy. 'We're not breaking in.' It was unfortunate that I still had to shout to make myself heard; it didn't exactly ease the situation that I was bellowing out of the window like a fishwife. 'And he wasn't her brother. Clare doesn't have a brother.'

Pete stiffened, his spine rigid. He obviously didn't know whether to trust us or not but either way he was still alarmed. 'Then who was he? Is Clare alright? Where is she then?'

I glanced at Clare. Her head drooped. 'Tell him,' she said, turning away. 'Tell him the truth.' I nodded at Winter. He understood and spoke awkwardly to Pete. His voice was low, so I couldn't hear exactly what he was saying, but the moment that Pete realised that Clare was dead was obvious. His body language said it all.

'I think he really liked you,' I said to Clare.

She wouldn't look up. 'I never knew,' she said. 'I thought he was just a bit rude and bullish. Sometimes he wouldn't even look at me when I said hello in the street. I've been such an idiot.' She sighed. 'About so many things.'

There wasn't very much I could do to comfort her. I couldn't give her a hug; I couldn't tell her that things would look much brighter tomorrow, or that this was just a passing phase. She was dead. That was all there was to it.

I pinched off a headache. When in doubt, be brusque and to the point. I had no words for Clare other than the stark truth. 'I can't make this better for you, Clare. I can't make you undead.' Not without becoming a freaky necromancer who might destroy the entire country in the process. 'All I can do is try to bring the person who did this to justice. That's all I've got.' I gestured downstairs. 'Blackbeard obviously has plans in place. He spoke to Pete and he set up that booby trap. Whatever's going on here, he's nowhere near finished.'

For a beat or two Clare didn't move, then she tilted up her chin. Her jaw was set and her expression firm. 'Then let's see what we can find out.'

Good. That was good. 'You see if he's touched anything, been through any of your stuff or taken anything. Even it's small and inconsequential, it might help.'

She nodded. 'Trophies. Serial killers like trophies.'

I couldn't look her in the eye. 'Yeah, so I've heard.' I licked my lips. 'While you do that, I'll go and check out the booby trap and try not blow myself up.'

Not exploding was always on my daily to-do list. Let's hope today wasn't going to be any different.

Chapter Eleven

In the end, I took various photos of the booby-trapped door with my phone – at a distance, of course – so that I could show it to both Winter and whoever else decided to appear. Clare mooched around, looking for anything out of place. Apart from the door and the precariously balanced grenade, everything else seemed untouched. It felt like I'd gone to considerable effort to get in here but there was actually nothing to be seen or learned. More to the point, it was even harder to wriggle out than it had been to wriggle in.

By the time I was standing with Winter and Pete, who by now had fully abandoned his bid to destroy Winter's good looks and appeared to have transformed into our latest cheerleader, I'd had enough. I didn't think there was any skin left around my hips at all.

'Here,' I said, sulking. I passed the phone to Winter. Both he and Pete were far too eager to see the grenade. Boys and their toys. Frankly, it seemed to me as if it was more like the kind of daft – and very crude – thing a kid would do to annoy a younger sibling. Except a kid would use a cup of water or flour or something, not an explosive device.

'I can't believe it,' Pete breathed. 'What on earth was Clare mixed up in that someone tried to blow her up in her own house? Someone was really desperate to kill her off.'

'The man who put this here knew she was already dead. He killed her. He did this,' I said, pointing to the photo, 'to kill whoever came looking for her.' I glanced at Winter. 'In other words, us.'

Winter scratched his chin. 'We could have been the police or Clare's family or the damned postman. This trap has been here for a while. Blackbeard might be a witch hater but he didn't know for sure that the first person through that door would be a witch. I think this was less to do with killing anyone and more to do with knowing exactly when the coven's disappearance was discovered. We already know he wants to stay anonymous and he's tried to hide what he'd done.' He gestured towards Pete. 'He risked blowing his cover to pretend to be Clare's brother. He was desperate to hide his murders but he was also desperate to know if – when – they'd been found. Setting bombs across a quiet Dorset town would be one way to make sure you hit the national news.'

'Either everyone knows or no one knows.' Pete nodded. 'Makes sense.'

Winter frowned as he thought it through. 'I think the best way to deal with this is to make sure that he doesn't get what he wants. We need to get a media embargo to ensure this is kept quiet. No headlines, no whisper in the papers about serial killers or bombs or missing witches. Effective radio silence. He knows we're onto him but if we don't play the game the way he wants, maybe we can gain some leverage. And he might come back to find out why no one's been to any of the coven's homes to find out where they are.' He paused and looked at me. 'What do you think, Ivy?'

Something Winter had said was gnawing at me. 'Hmm?'

Winter stilled as he clocked my expression. 'You've thought of something.'

'It does happen from time to time.' Not that often, admittedly. I looked at the photo I'd snapped of the door. It included the doorframe and the doormat lying just inside. 'You mentioned the postman. You said that the postman could have been the next person through the door.'

'Well, he wouldn't have had a key but he might have knocked and rattled the doorframe enough to set off the trap.'

I flicked a look at Clare. 'You've not just moved here, have you?'

'No.'

'You don't have a PO box or anything like that?'

She looked confused. 'No. I get post through the door like most regular people. What...' her voice faltered. 'Oh. I see what you mean.'

Pete stared at me. 'Who are you talking to?'

'Clare,' I answered. 'She's here.' He went as white as a ghost, which was kind of funny if you thought about it. I patted him absently on the shoulder. 'She wishes she'd known you liked her before she died,' I said. 'She'd have loved to get to know you better. Maybe go on a date or two. Maybe more. She thinks you're really good looking.'

'I didn't say that!' Clare burst out as Pete's skin almost immediately transformed to bright red. It was an improvement on terrified white.

'Ivy...' Winter said, clearing his throat.

I nodded. 'Sorry. It's quite distracting carrying on two conversations at once. Multi-tasking is not my thing, I tend to have a single-minded focus. Stay on the straight and narrow until a job is done. In fact...'

'Ivy...'

Oh yeah. I got back to the point. 'I once stayed inside for ten days straight. Didn't go out, didn't talk to anyone, just lay on my sofa with my duvet and my cat.' I sighed. 'It was wonderful.' Both Winter and Pete looked at me as if I were mad. I shrugged. 'Anyway, by the time I finally ventured outside again, I had to clear a path to the door. There were bills and junk mail clogging up my doorstep. It took ages to open the door and it had only been ten days. Clare Rees hasn't been home in weeks.' I jabbed at the photo. 'Where is her post? Where are the flyers for the local takeaway? Where are her bills? Or postcards? There's not a single letter lying on her doormat.'

'I know the postman,' Pete argued, momentarily abandoning his bid to wheel round and stare at thin air as if he expected Clare to materialise spookily any second. 'He's a good guy.'

'I'm sure he is. I think Blackbeard has had Clare's post redirected.'

Winter's brow furrowed. 'To what end?'

'Goodness only knows,' I said. 'But if I'm right, we need to find out where her letters are being sent and we'll find him.' I raised my eyebrows. 'It's not just booby traps we need to look for at the other coven members' homes, it's letters as well. As Clare said, serial killers take trophies. Maybe junk mail is the trophy Blackbeard is after.' I wrinkled my nose at Winter's expression. 'I'm not saying it makes any sense. I'm just saying it can't be a coincidence that there aren't any letters waiting for Clare.'

'Are you telling me,' Winter said, 'that you once were too lazy to get up and pick up the post from your own doorstep? For ten days?'

I grinned. 'And look where that attitude has got us! Halfway to solving a series of tragic and brutal murders.' Out of the corner of my eye I spotted Clare wincing. 'We'll get all the way there, Clare. I promise.'

'You shouldn't make promises you can't be certain you'll keep,' she whispered.

'We could still go out on a date,' Pete broke in. 'I could book a table at La Boheme. The lazy blonde one can come and translate for us.'

'I have a serial killer to catch,' I informed him sniffily. 'I don't have time to go on dates so I can act as a conduit between the spirit world and the real world.'

'You mean you're too lazy to do it,' Pete said.

No. I meant yes, kind of, but it was also too damned weird.

Clare smirked. 'This is what you get for suggesting I fancied the pants off him.'

I rolled my eyes. Bloody ghosts.

***

Winter went off to speak to both the police and the Arcane Branch witches who were here to investigate the other coven members. He decided, all on his lonesome, that he'd do a better job persuading them to apply for the media embargo without my help. Apparently I had problems conducting myself in a professional manner and that might discourage them from acceding to our wishes. Pete seemed to agree with this assessment even though he'd only met my front half fifteen minutes earlier. Whatever. My ego could take the hit if it meant that Winter was the one who wasted time answering inane repetitive questions. When it comes to government agencies, whether we are talking about serial killers or rotas for recycling paper clips, the forms and bureaucracy can destroy your psyche in a manner which even Nietzsche couldn't have envisaged. Unless you are Raphael Winter, of course. I secretly suspect he lives for that kind of thing.

Tempted as I was to take advantage of Winter's absence and have forty winks, Clare's obvious unhappiness precluded any naps. Given what neighbourly Pete had told us about the lies Blackbeard had spun him, I reckoned her family had probably been told something similar. Finding out for certain would at least cheer her up; she'd still be dead but she'd know that her family cared about her. Of course, that meant I'd have to be the bearer of bad tidings and tell her family that she'd been murdered. It wasn't exactly my idea of fun by the seaside. Ice cream, yes; lying in the sun, yes. Informing a family that a serial killer had slaughtered their nearest and dearest several weeks ago and they'd not realised anything was wrong … no. It was tempting to sprint in the opposite direction as fast as my chubby little legs would carry me.

Clare's parents lived in a quiet cul-de-sac less than twenty minutes from her house. It was the sort of place where the neighbours all spoke to each other, not just to murmur a hello in the morning but to stop and have a real chat. When someone baked cookies, Tupperware boxes were probably passed around every house on the street. My witchy senses might have never experienced precognition but I foresaw many casseroles in the Rees family's future. I gave a loud sigh.

By my side, Clare was twitchy and nervous. 'What if they really don't care that I'm dead? Blackbeard might never have come here. He might never have spoken to them. They simply might not have noticed that I'm not around.' She wrung her hands and I saw that her fingers were trembling. She might be a ghost but she was still afraid. Apparently you don't lose your emotions or humanity when you lose your life. I wasn't sure whether to be pleased or dismayed by that.

Unable to place a reassuring hand on her arm, I forced a smile in her direction. 'How often did you see your family when you were alive?'

Her expression creased into worried guilt. 'Not as often as I should have. We lived close to each other so I should have been round more often but they were always here, you know? I might have postponed a lot of dinners or days out, but it was only because I thought I could see them any time.' Her voice dropped to a whisper. 'I didn't know. I didn't know I had such little time left. No wonder they don't care that I'm gone – I didn't care when they were here.'

Clare was seriously over-thinking. 'Stop it,' I said, harshly enough to make her glance at me in surprise. 'You were human. You *are* human. You did something that people all over the country do. You can't beat yourself up for living or for making a few mistakes. To err is human, Clare.'

She screwed up her face. 'And to forgive is divine.' She waved a hand around. 'I'm dead and I don't see anyone divine around here. I've even managed to mess that up.'

I was starting to get the impression that nothing I said was going to make any difference. When Clare's family heard what had happened to her and collapsed, devastated, she wasn't going to feel any better about herself. To err was human indeed – I should never have come here. Some things were better left to professionals. What the hell did I know about grief?

I pressed my finger on the doorbell and stepped back. With any luck, no one would be in and the police would come later and do this themselves. I counted to three in my head.

'No one's here! We should go.' I twisted round hurriedly and walked away far faster than I normally did.

'Ivy!' Clare protested immediately. She needn't have bothered – I could already hear the door opening behind me. Arse.

I turned back slowly, my stomach churning and my mouth dry. I'd take on a platoon of zombies over this any day. Hell, I'd take on Tarquin – and that was saying something.

The woman had Clare's face but with a few more careworn lines around her eyes and mouth. She started to smile at me but something about my expression gave her pause because her smile faltered. 'Can I help you?' she asked.

Big fat ghost tears started to roll down Clare's cheeks. 'Mummy.' She ran towards her, arms outstretched, and tried to throw herself into a hug. Of course it didn't work and Clare fell through her mother's body, stumbling to the other side. She let out an anguished sob and slumped down.

I swallowed. 'Mrs Rees.' It wasn't a question.

'Do I know you?'

I shook my head. 'No, but I know your daughter, Clare.' Or should that be *knew* your daughter Clare? I'd not said more than two sentences and this was already one of the hardest things I'd ever done.

'Clare? Where is she? How is she doing?' She pursed her lips. 'Honestly that girl is terrible at keeping in touch! She could be dead for all we know!' She laughed at her weak joke. When I did nothing more than wince slightly, her hand rose to her mouth. 'Wait. What's happened?'

The doorstep was not the place for this conversation. 'Perhaps we should go inside.'

Clare's mum's face went even whiter. 'Tell me. Tell me where she is.'

From behind her mum, Clare pushed herself back up to her feet. She wiped her eyes and looked at me. 'Do it, Ivy.'

I pulled my shoulders back. Woman up, Ivy. This was not the time to hide under the bed and be a wimp. Tell the truth and stop prolonging this woman's misery. 'I'm sorry to tell you,' I said, in a voice that I was relieved to hear was both clear and audible, 'that Clare has been the victim of a terrible crime.'

Her mother gasped. I ploughed on; I had to say this now, before I lost what little gumption I had left. 'She was killed, along with the rest of her coven, by a man we believe to be a serial killer with a grudge against witches.'

Mrs Rees's eyes were wide open. I had to give her credit – she was holding herself together better than I was. Clare stared at her, taking in every nuance of her expression. 'In Iceland?'

What? 'No. On Dartmoor.'

A door opened across the street and a group of laughing children piled out, the occasional delighted scream punctuating the air. Clare's mum didn't even look at them. 'You'd better come in,' she murmured. She led me into the living room and gestured. 'Please. Have a seat.'

I moved to the nearest chair. Clare let out a small shriek. 'Not there!' I sprang up again. 'That's my dad's chair,' she said. 'No one sits in that chair apart from him.'

I edged round to the sofa and did my best to look casual.

'Would you like something to drink?' Mrs Rees asked. 'Tea or coffee or something?'

It should probably be me asking her that. 'No. But I can put the kettle on if you…'

'No.'

Footsteps sounded outside and a man appeared, wiping his hands on an oily rag. He glanced at me, then at Clare's mum. 'What's going on?'

'This is…' Mrs Rees faltered. I hadn't even introduced myself yet.

'Ivy Wilde,' I said. 'I'm…' I'm what? A taxi driver? A medium?

'She's here about Clare,' Mrs Rees said. The note in

her voice said it all.

The man, presumably Clare's father, stiffened. He sat down in the chair, his shoulders slumping. 'Fuck.'

That's pretty much what I was thinking too.

***

It took some time to explain everything. A lot of the conversation had a strange roundabout fashion.

'So you're with the Hallowed Order of Magical Enlightenment?'

'No, but sometimes I work with them.'

'You're not a witch then?'

'I'm a witch.'

'You're in a coven like Clare was?'

'No.'

'So who the hell are you?'

I wasn't sure even *I* knew the answer to that any more. About the only thing that was clear to all of us, even Clare, was just how devastated her parents were. There had been a few quiet tears and very little in the way of hysterics but that was because they had so many questions and, right now, I had very few answers.

'She's here then?' her mother asked. 'She's dead and she's been dead for weeks. Her body has been cremated. But she's here as a ghost and you can talk to her?'

I nodded. 'Pretty much.'

'We don't have any money,' Mr Rees said, with a hard, sceptical look in his eye. 'If you're trying to get us to give you some so that we can talk to Clare then…'

I held up my hands, palms facing outwards. 'I don't want your money. I'm not here for that.'

Clare knelt down beside him. 'He was so proud when my magic first appeared,' she said. 'Even though we all knew there wasn't much of it. There hadn't been a witch in our family for generations. He thought I'd go on to do great things.' She sighed. 'Yeah, right. Tell him that I'm sorry about the money I stole when I was twelve. And that I wish I'd come back to visit more often. And that I'll always be his munchkin, no matter what. Tell my mum that Granny's necklace is in my old jewellery box. There's a false bottom. I only took it because...' Her voice trailed off. 'It doesn't matter now.'

I repeated what she'd said. Both her parents stared at me as if they weren't sure whether to hug me or grab the nearest barge pole with which to prod me out of their house.

'I know this is difficult,' I said. 'Truthfully, I can't begin to imagine how difficult. But the man who did this to Clare and the rest of her coven is still out there. The faster we find him, the less chance there is he'll do this to someone else. I just have a few questions.'

They nodded.

Drawing a deep breath, I tried to prioritise. 'Why did you think she was in Iceland?'

'We got a postcard,' Clare's mum said. She went to the mantelpiece, picked up a pretty card and passed it over to me. 'Here.'

Clare was at my side in an instant. 'I've never been to Iceland,' she said, looking at the photo of a shooting geyser. 'Turn it over.'

Apart from the address, there were only three words scrawled on the back: 'Love you. C.'

'It looks like my handwriting.' Clare's voice started to rise. 'How the hell does he know my handwriting? He copied me. Blackbeard bloody...'

I hushed her while her parents looked on with frozen watchfulness. 'He was inside your house, Clare. It probably wouldn't have been difficult to find an example of your writing and copy it.' I bit down hard on my bottom lip. No, it wouldn't have been difficult. But it did show a level of premeditation that chilled me.

'She didn't write this?' her father probed.

'No. I'm sorry.' I paused. 'Did you ever meet anyone with a black beard and a skull earring who came round and said they knew Clare?'

They exchanged glances. 'No. There's not been anyone,' Mrs Rees said. 'Apart from that Order witch conducting the diligence checks.'

I sat up straight. Clare's gaze shot to her mother as well. 'What?'

She stood up once more and walked over to a bureau, opening a drawer and taking out a business card. 'He left his details.' She passed it over to me. I stared at Tarquin's gold-embossed name and tried very hard not to scream. 'She'd finally given up on that foolish idea of the coven and had applied to become an Order witch.'

Clare's mouth dropped open. 'I didn't! I wouldn't do that! I hate the Order! I'd never join them.' She gave me a sidelong glance. Both of us knew that her magic wasn't strong enough for her to do well in the Order. She'd probably be accepted but she'd never progress beyond Neophyte. She'd been in a seven-strong coven outside the Order for a reason.

'Can I keep this?' I asked.

'Of course. Does it mean something?'

I had a horrible feeling it did. 'No, but it's good to explore every clue.' I stood up. 'I should probably get going.'

Clare's parents also rose to their feet. 'Clare?' her mother asked, almost timidly. 'Will you stay? It will make me feel better knowing you are here.'

Clare sniffed loudly. 'I'll stay. Of course I'll stay.'

I nodded to her mum in acknowledgment.

'We also need to get her remains so we can give them a proper burial,' her father added, in a gruff voice choked by tears.

'The police will be in touch about that,' I said. 'But here's my number as well. Call me any time. I'm so very sorry for your loss.'

They reached for each other, their hands clasping together for comfort. And even though they couldn't see her, Clare leaned in towards them, her head bowed and her hands outstretched towards them for further comfort. I let myself out.

Chapter Twelve

I walked away from the house with a lead-filled soul. I knew speaking to Clare's parents was going to be hard but it had been much worse than I'd anticipated. Taxi driving was a far simpler proposition than all this, even if it meant I had to have the same conversation about the weather twenty times a day.

I trudged away, turning everything over in my mind. The sensible thing to do would be to tell the Ipsissimus, the Order and the police and wash my hands of the entire affair. I'd already done what was required of me.

I'd barely turned the corner when my mobile phone rang. Half expecting it to be Winter, I pulled it out of my pocket. When I realised the number calling me was my home phone, I felt my pulse rate increase.

'Eve?' I asked. 'What's wrong? Is it Brutus? Is everything alright?'

There was no immediate answer. Frowning, I tilted my head and listened harder. Was that heavy breathing? Trepidation building, I tried again. 'Hello? Eve?'

'Fooooooooooooood.'

I frowned. 'Brutus?'

'Fooooooooooooood.'

Since when had he learned to use a damn phone? 'Brutus,' I said slowly. 'Where is Eve?' A horrible thought struck me. 'You've not ... done anything to her, have you?'

'Bitch.' Whether he was referring to me or to Eve wasn't clear. It was probably to both of us for not pandering to his every need. There was a long drawn-out pause. 'Where?'

I was glad no one else was around to realise that I was conducting a phone conversation with my cat. I'd been talking to Brutus for years but even I felt ridiculous doing this. 'I'm in a place called Weymouth, tracking down a serial killer. This is serious stuff, Brutus. I think we'll be back later today but I can't promise anything. This is a fast-moving investigation and I am an integral cog in it.' I hesitated. 'But I really don't want to be. I want to be back at home. And not just because I'd quite like to lie on my sofa with you and a family-sized bar of chocolate. I'm not cut out for this, not because it's work but because it's too emotional. I'm not sure I can cope. But a serial killer is out there and other witches might be in danger.'

'Home,' Brutus said with more than a hint of imperious command. It was more like a smack-you-in-the-face-before-bringing-you-to-your-knees imperious command.

'Believe me, that's what I'm planning to do.'

There was a strange clunking sound in the background then I heard Eve's muffled voice. 'Brutus? Princess? What is that smell?'

My eyes narrowed. What smell?

'Miaow,' Brutus said. Then he hung up.

I ground my teeth. Why, that little... I hissed under my breath. Every moment he got, he complained. Goodness only knew how he was treating Eve or what the smell was that she was referring to. If he thought he was getting his Friday tuna treat now, he was sadly mistaken. Although at least now I was thinking about something other than Clare Rees and her family. I had a sneaking suspicion that Brutus had somehow known how I was feeling and had called me to take my mind off things, but that was crazy. Then the phone rang again and, without looking at the screen, I answered.

'Brutus, how on earth can you get your paws to dial the number?' I asked. 'And what is that smell Eve was talking about? Have you been peeing in the corner?'

'Certainly not,' Winter said. 'I used the toilet and I even put the lid down afterwards.' He paused for a moment. 'Has Brutus been phoning you?' he enquired. 'That cat is bloody amazing.'

That cat is bloody annoying; I think that's why I love him. I shook my head in exasperation and changed the subject. 'I think that Blackbeard sent Clare's parents a postcard and pretended it was from her. He was desperate that no one knew she'd disappeared.'

Winter's answer was grim. 'Unfortunately that's what we're discovering as well. The police have agreed to the embargo, not least because steps have been taken to conceal the disappearance of the other coven members too. And all their houses are booby-trapped in exactly the same manner as Clare's. Blackbeard means serious business.'

I grimaced. 'There's more.' I told him about Tarquin visiting the Rees' family.

Winter drew in a breath. 'How does that boy manage to sneak his way into everything? And why?'

'He has a particularly annoying and peculiar skill set,' I agreed. 'We need to talk to him.'

'Agreed. We should also see if we can get hold of your friend Iqbal. He has proved himself incredibly helpful in the past when it comes to research. The way that Blackbeard is managing to avoid magic concerns me. If anyone knows how he's capable of that, it'll be Iqbal.'

'It sounds like we need to skedaddle back to Oxford.'

Winter agreed. 'The police and Arcane Branch have everything under control here. It'll take some time to defuse all the traps because they're trying to do it quietly so that Blackbeard isn't alerted.'

I ran a hand through my hair. 'He's not just one step ahead of us, Rafe,' I said quietly. 'He's several miles in front. And we both know that I'm no runner.'

'It's not just you on his tail, Ivy, or me. Between the Order, the coven's families and the police, we'll catch this bastard before the week is out.'

Winter was trying to sound confident but I knew him too well. Both of us were feeling the strain – and the doubt. Maybe Blackbeard was just too good. And if his only clear motive was to kill witches, where could we go from here? There were thousands of witches across the country and Blackbeard could be targeting any of them. Talking to the dead was all well and good, but so far the ghosts had only proved helpful in offering glimpses into the past. We were all going to have to step up our game.

***

We made it back home in record time. It was a measure of how seriously Winter was taking things that he didn't comment after I magically encouraged several cars to come to mysterious halts so we could overtake them and get back that little bit quicker. Using magic against vehicles could play havoc with their engines but none of them exploded, so I decided my spells were a resounding success.

Winter wasn't the only one being encouraging. More than one ghost waved enthusiastically as we zipped past. I suppose I should have been cheered by all this support from the dead but I wished they'd leave me in peace.

Winter bounded up the stairs to Tarquin's flat while I waited for the lift, explaining that I should probably make sure that Brutus wasn't gnawing on Eve's cooling corpse. When I stepped out onto my floor, however, I could already hear Winter's barrage of questions from the floor above.

'What were you doing in Weymouth? How did you know the Rees family? Did you speak to Clare? Have you been annoying Ivy again? If you do anything to set back her recovery even slightly, I will serve your head up to my cat on a platter.'

I smiled at the last part. Given the anger rippling through Winter's voice, not to mention Tarquin's propensity for being the most irritating witch this side of the yellow brick road, I decided I should join them and make sure no blood was spilled.

Tarquin, bizarrely, was bare-chested except for a heavily embroidered waistcoat. He was smiling at Winter in a way designed to encourage violence. Before he met me, Raphael Winter always managed to present himself as a slightly standoffish and occasionally offensive witch – and one with absolute control over his emotions. I wasn't the same person I had been back then and neither was he. Usually that was a good thing – but not always.

Rather than answering any of the questions, Tarquin's gaze switched to me as I came up the stairs. He loped towards me and stretched out his arms, trying to draw me into a tight embrace. What he didn't yet know was that I could perform magic safely again. I flicked out a surreptitious rune that I doubted even Winter would notice.

Tarquin drew in a sharp breath and stepped back, dropping his arms; otherwise he didn't react. 'What's the problem?' he asked. There was a faint squeak in his voice.

'You were in Dorset recently,' Winter said, folding his arms. 'Weymouth, to be exact.'

Tarquin suddenly looked bored. 'I've been in a lot of places recently. The folks in Human Resources can't seem to let go of the fact that I'm now in Arcane Branch and they keep demanding my time.' He shrugged and examined his fingernails. 'I can't help it if every other witch in HR is incompetent and they need me to do their work for them.'

More like Arcane Branch had quickly realised Tarquin was incompetent and were trying to palm him back on his original bosses. Rather than say that, I focused on what was important. Go me – I could be the bigger witch after all. 'What work are you doing exactly?'

'Pre-entrance interviews for mature non-Order witches who wish to gain entrance to our esteemed establishment,' he said. He looked at me archly. 'If you want to join the Order, Ivy, I promise to treat you fairly and in the same manner as the others. I won't automatically turn you down just because I know how to make you scream in the sack.' Beside me, Winter stiffened. I nudged him with my elbow. I was by his side, not Tarquin's.

My floppy-haired foe continued. 'And I won't automatically add you to our ranks either. We are a merit-based organisation, as I'm sure you know. If you can prove yourself to me, I'll consider your application.'

From anyone else it would have sounded as if they were taking the piss, but Tarquin managed to sound sincere. It took everything I had for me not to burst into giggles. Insults would slide off his glossy exterior; laughing at him meant he'd refuse to talk to me for a month. Normally that would be a good thing but, with Winter no longer in the Order, we needed Tarquin on our side if we were going to find out the information we wanted.

Winter, speaking through gritted teeth, stared at him. 'You make the decision whether new witches are allowed into the Order?'

'New old witches,' Tarquin said. 'And yes, that responsibility is mine. It is a heavy burden, I admit, but someone has to step up to the proverbial plate and take charge.'

I tilted my head. 'Let me guess,' I said drily. 'You talk to the applicants and make notes, which are then passed to someone else. Someone who makes the final decision.'

Tarquin frowned and held up his index finger. 'First of all, I don't talk to the applicants themselves. My task is far more important than that. I talk to their families, that way one can get to the heart of the matter whether they have enough talent to join the Hallowed Order of Magical Enlightenment.'

I pressed my lips together. Don't smirk. Don't smirk. Don't smirk.

'Secondly,' he said, 'the notes I pass on are taken very seriously. I have been told that, if it were not for my recommendations, Human Resources would not have the faintest idea whether to allow entrance or not.'

Tarquin had never really understood sarcasm. I nodded as if to agree with him; I could keep a straight face if the situation demanded it. 'So you visited the Rees family in Weymouth in Dorset to find out about Clare and whether she had the ability to become an Order witch?'

'Yep. Her and the other members of her coven. Seven of them. It took bloody ages but,' he said with a sidelong look at Winter, 'when it comes to the Order, there's nothing I'm not prepared to do. I am now, and will for ever be, fully motivated and dedicated to the Order's cause. Only the worthiest and most hard-working witches are like that.'

'Indeed,' Winter murmured. 'And only the worthiest and most hard-working witches avoid pointless self-aggrandisement.'

Tarquin frowned. 'Self what?'

I interrupted hastily. 'Never mind. So if I have this right,' I said, 'Clare Rees and the rest of her coven applied to become Order witches and it was your job to vet them.'

'Yes.'

'And,' I pressed, 'if your recommendation is positive, what happens next? What's the next step?'

'They enter the Order, of course.'

Winter's lip curled. 'Just like that?'

'Yes.'

'The applicants aren't interviewed or tested or anything?'

'Oh. Sure, yeah, that happens.'

I could hear Winter's teeth grinding from a foot away. He obviously never worked anywhere near HR when he was in the Order. 'Go on. Explain how that works.'

Tarquin looked confused. 'I don't know. That's not my remit.'

'You have no interest in or curiosity about the rest of the process?' Winter's voice dripped with disdain.

Tarquin leaned over. 'Not. My. Job.'

I put a hand on Winter's arm. Just because he wanted to know everything about the Order Departments he'd been in didn't mean everyone was like that.

'Anyway,' Tarquin continued, 'I should get on. I'm a very busy and important person these days. It's lucky you caught me, to be honest. I don't always have time for conversations with civilians.' As he glanced at Winter, his implication was clear. Where Tarquin once did everything he could to bow and scrape and get into Winter's good books, now that Winter wasn't in the Order Tarquin couldn't care less what he thought.

Because I could, I repeated my earlier rune and this time I put a little more effort into it. Tarquin's eyes widened and his hands dropped, scrabbling at his trousers. His cheeks began to turn red. 'I have to go,' he said in a high-pitched rush. He spun round and headed back into his flat as if hell itself were after him.

As soon as Tarquin's door closed, Winter turned to me. 'What exactly did you do to him?'

I shrugged. 'Nothing.'

'Ivy.'

I grinned. 'Okay, I may have performed a small spell which I developed for some of the more gropey taxi customers.'

Winter's eyes darkened at the idea that I'd been forced to drive around men whose octopus arms and pinching fingers had caused me grief. 'What's the spell?' he asked, his jaw tight.

My smile grew. 'Let's just say that it can make you feel rather uncomfortable in the groin area.' Winter frowned so I elaborated. 'It constricts your underwear until…'

He held up his hands and winced. 'I get the picture.' He glanced at me. 'Don't ever do that to me.'

'I won't. But I've developed other spells that are less uncomfortable and more – pleasurable. I've never really had cause to practise them on anyone. Perhaps you would be willing to be a guinea pig?'

A deep growl emanated from Winter's chest and he reached for my hand, squeezing my fingers. 'That sounds like the sort of test I would enjoy.'

I snorted. 'You're Raphael Winter. Is there any kind of test you don't enjoy?'

He considered. 'My sister used to make me take tests to find out what kind of fairy-tale prince I was most like, or how many children and wives I would end up with. I didn't enjoy those very much.'

Tarquin's door re-opened and he stuck his head out. 'I'm Prince Charming,' he yelled. 'You can't have that one.' The door closed again.

Winter and I exchanged looks. 'I beg to differ,' I whispered.

He smiled. Unfortunately, the moment had passed and both of us knew it. 'Let's try out those spells some other time,' he said.

'It's a date.' I sighed. A future date, when we didn't have serial killers to worry about. 'Just what the hell is going on? Clare was adamant that she didn't want anything to do with the Order and neither did her coven. If the others had put in an application to join up, she would have mentioned it. She made a point of saying that her magic wasn't strong enough and that she hated the Order. This has got to be Blackbeard's doing. But to what end? What is he really up to? Is he…' My voice trailed off.

'Trying to find a way to sneak into the Order himself?' Winter finished for me. 'It does sound like it, doesn't it?'

'We know he hates witches,' I said softly. 'If that's what he's trying to do, it's not because he wants to make new friends.'

We shared a look of mutual dismay. 'No,' Winter agreed. 'It's definitely not.'

Chapter Thirteen

It didn't take a genius to realise that Eve hadn't imagined the smell. I didn't even have to open my front door to notice the reek – and there was no denying what it was.

Winter glanced at me. 'Is that…?'

'Cat pee?' I opened the door to fully appreciate the eye-watering effect. 'Oh, yes.'

He looked embarrassed. 'I'm so sorry. Princess Parma Periwinkle is never normally like that.'

'Don't apologise. I'd lay money on this all being down to Brutus.'

For a moment Winter looked puzzled then his face cleared. 'The phone call earlier. This is what you were on about.'

I nodded grimly. Yeah. Talk about rubbing your nose in it.

Princess was nowhere to be seen. Brutus, however, was sitting on the windowsill and staring outside. I marched over. 'What gives?'

He didn't so much as twitch.

'Brutus,' I said, in my best stern voice, 'why have you been peeing in here?'

'I'm so sorry, Ivy!' Eve appeared in the doorway. She was dressed in overalls and holding a spray bottle. 'I've gone through a litre of this stuff trying to get rid of the smell and clean it all up but I can't seem to find it all. Poor Brutus has really gone to town.'

My eyebrows flew up. Poor Brutus? 'Oh,' I said, 'I wouldn't feel too sorry for him. He knew exactly what he was doing.' I glared at his back. He still didn't turn around but I was fairly certain that there was a whisker quiver. He was probably suppressing a feline belly laugh.

'He obviously missed you.'

'We were only away for one night,' I pointed out. 'And he had you.'

'And Princess Parma Periwinkle,' Winter added.

'All the same…'

'Don't worry about it, Eve,' I told her. 'It was very kind of you to try and clean up but I'll sort this out.' I looked around. 'You could have used magic, you know.'

She seemed taken aback. 'But that would have been a waste of energy.'

My mouth dropped open in astonishment. Winter looked away, trying not to laugh. 'Elbow grease never did anyone any harm, Ivy,' he said, with barely suppressed mirth.

I took the spray bottle from Eve and passed it to him. 'Go on, then. You are really into your cleaning, you can sort this out.'

'I can't. I have to call the Order and warn them about what's going on. If Blackbeard is trying to gain entry, they need to know straight away.' He hurried out of the room.

I sighed. 'Two days ago all he wanted to do was clean. I should have stayed ill for a bit longer.'

Eve looked almost as amused as Winter had. 'Who's Blackbeard?' she asked.

I grimaced. 'Long story.'

Brutus got to his feet and stretched out before turning towards us and yawning pointedly. 'Bitch,' he hissed.

'I'm going home,' Eve said hastily.

I waved a hand at her. 'Yeah, that's probably a good idea.'

She flashed me a quick smile then departed almost as quickly as Winter. I glared at Brutus. 'You made everyone run away.'

I could swear he shrugged. Jumping down from the windowsill, he padded towards me, coiling himself around my legs. 'Bitch,' he said again.

I crouched down and scratched him behind his ears. 'I'm sorry,' I said. 'I didn't mean to leave you behind. I didn't think we'd be away overnight. I did miss you a lot.'

Brutus sniffed and gave me a head butt. He let out the tiniest purr.

'You shouldn't have done that in here, though. We all live here. It's not just your home.' Remembering how my old geography teacher had managed to make me feel guilty when I'd used to magic instead of brain power to complete my earthquake project, and had got not just the entire school but the entire town evacuated because of dangerous tremors, I pasted on a suitably serious but sad expression. 'I expected more from you. It's not that I'm surprised, Brutus. It's that I'm disappointed.'

His head drooped as if in apology. 'Miaow.'

I wiggled a finger in my ear. 'Pardon?'

Brutus slowly looked up at me, his yellow eyes wide and limpid. 'Brutus sorry.' He rubbed himself against my leg once again, although this time there was a hint of desperation to the action. I nodded, satisfied. Brutus understood that what he'd done was wrong and that he shouldn't do it again. It was the best I could ask for. He tilted his head to one side and blinked slowly at me. For a big cat, he could do cute when he wanted to.

'I wouldn't have stayed away if it wasn't important,' I told him. 'And you had Eve. You like her. And Princess Parma Periwinkle.'

His tail began to flick dangerously from side to side. 'Love *Ivy*,' he said.

My heart melted. Eve was right, he'd missed me.

Abandoning all pretence that I wasn't his slave, I did the one thing that I'd promised myself I wouldn't. 'Before I go looking for the pee which you've left behind, would you like some food? Some tuna treats?'

Brutus purred. Yeah, no surprise there then.

I got him what I'd promised and, while he gobbled the treats down at breakneck speed, I flicked out a quick rune to dim the natural light in my flat. With my other hand, I created a rune for blacklight. It was the fastest way to locate where exactly Brutus had peed. There were probably just a few spatters somewhere in the corner. I just had to... My mouth dropped open.

Winter, wandering back in, stopped in his tracks and stared at the wall. 'Is that...?'

I folded my arms and nodded grimly. The little shit. 'Brutus!' I yelled.

He came sauntering back in, having finished his treats in record time. No wonder; if I'd seen this, I'd have denied him tuna until his next life. He sat down in the middle of the floor, washed his face then glanced up to admire his handiwork. There, across my entire wall, sprayed in cat pee was the word 'bitch'.

In the corner, the old cobweb-covered woman appeared. She craned her neck, took in the full effect of what Brutus had achieved and started to cackle loudly. I sighed. I was being driven out of my home by ghosts and cat piss.

'Screw this,' I said to Winter. 'Let's go catch ourselves a serial killer.'

***

Although I was still pissed off at him – and making sure he knew it – Brutus appeared determined to come with us. Rather than leave him to destroy my flat completely, I let him. Winter seemed more amused than anything. When Iqbal beamed delightedly at the sight of my furry frenemy and made a fuss over him, I glared, Winter smiled and Brutus purred.

'You're not going to believe this,' my old friend said. 'But I've finished my first draft.' He twirled in delight. 'Sixty-three thousand words.'

Impressed, I reached across a tottering pile of books and gave him a hug. 'That's brilliant!'

He nodded. 'Yes, I am brilliant. I will accept any and all accolades.' He bowed.

'I don't know why he's making such a big deal about it,' sniffed a white-coated man with crazy hair springing out in all directions. 'It's not very good.'

I flicked the ghost a look. 'Don't be mean,' I said sternly. After seeing what Brutus had achieved, I wasn't in the mood for dissenters.

Iqbal stared at me. 'Who are you talking to?'

'Well,' I said, 'while you've been busy writing, I've been busy having conversations with the dead.' In a loud stage whisper, I added, 'They're not very interesting. And they don't know as much as they think they do.'

The Einstein-esque ghost scoffed loudly. 'Oh yeah? Well you didn't know there was a mass murderer on the loose, did you? We told you that. He'd have carried on without any of you realising, if it wasn't for us.'

'You're dead,' I said. 'You can see everything and go everywhere. There are thousands of you – and yet none of you can tell me who the killer is or where I can find him.'

'We're dead, not omniscient. Anyway,' he sniffed, 'I'm supposed to tell you that Ipsissimus Grenville wants to see you.'

'He'll have to wait,' I growled.

Iqbal glanced at Winter. 'Has this been happening a lot?'

'You get used to it,' Winter said. 'And it's not all that

bad. It keeps her occupied and makes her feel wanted.'

'Oi!'

He grinned.

Iqbal's hands rose to his cheeks and he gazed at the pair of us. 'Look at you. It's like you've just discovered your first spell.' He sighed happily. 'Young love.' The ghost pretended to vomit and I was pretty certain that Brutus rolled his eyes. 'When do I get my wedding invite?' Iqbal enquired.

I laughed. 'Hold your horses.'

'Have you met your future in-laws?'

'No,' I shot back. 'I haven't.'

He visibly deflated. Winter jumped right in. 'But she will tomorrow. We're all having dinner together.'

Iqbal lit up all over again. 'See? One minute you're lounging on your own sofa eating cold pizza in your knickers, and the next you'll be wearing pearls and baking cupcakes to bring to your mother-in-law.'

Fear widened my eyes. 'Baking cupcakes? Do I really have to do that?'

'Of course not,' Winter said. I began to relax. 'My mother despises cupcakes. She prefers old-fashioned Victoria sponge cakes.'

I half choked. Domestic goddess I am not. Hastily changing the subject to the reason why we were here, I picked up Brutus to prevent him sending the pile of papers that he was batting at from falling to the floor. I looked at Iqbal. 'We're not here to banter about my culinary skills,' I said. 'We're here because—'

'You need my help,' he finished for me. 'Of course. Now that I've finished sixty-three thousand thesis words, I will be happy to oblige. It's either that or I have to start editing the damn thing. I got a lot of leeway from my supervisor because I helped you save Scotland from zombies. Any more world-rescuing operations I can sidle into are very welcome.'

I frowned. 'Did you help us save Scotland?'

'I got you information.'

'Information that in the end had nothing to do with zombies.'

He shrugged. 'That wasn't my fault.'

True. 'Well,' I said, 'this time it's witches we are hoping to save.' My light-hearted tone dropped several notches. 'Seven are already dead and we expect there will be more if we don't catch the bastard who's doing it.'

Iqbal's humour and banter vanished in an instant. 'Go on.'

I disentangled Brutus's claws from several of my curls while Winter explained. 'Right now,' he said, 'we're playing the waiting game.' The frustration in his voice made it clear how annoying he found that. 'We're waiting on the police telling us where the coven members' post is being re-directed to. We're waiting on the Order working through their files to find out what happened with the coven's application to become Order witches. And, unfortunately, we're waiting on Blackbeard making another move.'

'What?' shrieked the ghost in my ear. 'That's your plan? To wait until he kills more witches? That's ridiculous! That's not a plan!'

I winced and stepped away. Even if I secretly agreed with him, technically there was more to it than waiting for further deaths.

Brutus hissed loudly and wriggled out of my arms so he could dart into the corner where it was apparently safer. 'Why didn't you tell me you could see ghosts?' I asked him as he shot behind another dusty pile of books.

Brutus bobbed his head up from behind the literary parapet and flicked me a look as if to say I was being stupid and that I'd never have believed him. I sighed.

Yeah, he was probably right; it wasn't worth getting into now.

Iqbal coughed pointedly. 'Well,' he said, 'there is definitely one thing I can help with. It came up in my research for my thesis. If you're going to explore the history of magic in the British Isles then you also need to explore the *absence* of magic too.'

Both Winter and I leaned in. 'Go on.'

'Nulls,' he said. 'People who are entirely unaffected by magic. It doesn't matter what you throw at them or how powerful a witch you are, they're immune.'

'Immune to magic?' I said slowly. How on earth was that even possible? I looked at Winter; he seemed just as baffled as I was. 'Have you ever heard of a null?'

'No.' He ran a hand through his hair. 'But if that's what our Blackbeard is, it makes a lot of sense.'

'If it makes you feel any better,' Iqbal said, 'they're incredibly rare. We're talking about maybe one person in a million who's affected, so it stands to reason that you don't often hear about them.'

I grimaced. 'Better odds than being a serial killer,' I said. 'Probably.'

'Well,' Iqbal demurred, 'your guy is not a serial killer, he's a mass murderer. Until he's actually killed more than three people on separate occasions, he doesn't count as a serial killer.' He scratched his head. 'So, uh, there's that.'

Whoop-de-do.

'This could be good news,' Winter said. I glanced at him askance. I couldn't possibly see how. 'Someone somewhere must have noticed that Blackbeard is a null. It might have been a schoolteacher or a friend or a doctor. But whoever it was or whenever it happened, nulls are rare enough that there must be a record of who he really is. It might not lead us right to him but it could teach us a great deal about him.'

Okay, that kind of made sense. 'So, as the Arcane Branch expert among us,' I said, 'how would you search the records for him?'

'I'd put in a bi-request for Order and police records. For something as vital as this, it would be a rush job so it would take two or three days. Obviously, I can't request it in my current position.'

I was getting a headache. 'We need to go back to the Ipsissimus and get him to do it.' Winter nodded. He really didn't look happy about it. 'Maybe you should re-join...' I began. His expression stopped me from finishing my sentence.

'Is there anything else about nulls that you can tell us?' he asked Iqbal. 'Anything at all?'

My friend shrugged. 'There's not much to tell. They're just the same as any ordinary person. They don't have magic and magic can't affect them. To stop a null you need to use other means.' He paused. 'You two are smart. You can work it out.'

Judging by the expression on Winter's face, he felt as doubtful as I did. Magic was what we did; it was in our blood and in our DNA. If we couldn't rely on it, I didn't know what we could do. It felt like our chances of catching Blackbeard and bringing him to justice had gone from slim to none.

The ghost frowned at me. 'Give me a break,' he complained. 'You think that just because you've found someone who you can't bespell it's the end of the world.'

I glared at him. 'It was the end of Clare Rees's world.' And Karen's. And Paul's. And Amy's. Not to mention the other three whom I had yet to meet but who I knew were out there somewhere.

'Death isn't so bad,' the ghost went on. 'It's the hanging around that sucks. All this waiting for something to happen and nothing ever does. Being here is like being stuck at the dentist and waiting to have your teeth pulled without anaesthetic. Except you don't know when it's going to happen. Or if it's ever going to happen. You just know that you can't do anything apart from wait.'

Damn. 'I'm … sorry,' I said. It was inane but true.

Crazy Hair sighed. 'It's not your fault.'

'Who is it, Ivy?' Iqbal asked. 'Who's the ghost? Why are they here haunting me?'

I raised my eyebrows in question. Crazy Hair shrugged. 'I'm not haunting him. I used to work here. It's a good place. I normally hang around the canteen because that's where you get all the best gossip but I got word that Grenville wanted me here. He really does want to talk to you.'

It was my turn to shrug. 'I'll try to drop in when we go to see the Ipsissimus.' The current Ipsissimus. Man, this could get confusing. 'How can I help you?' I asked. 'How can I help you move on? Who do I need to talk to?'

A calculating look flitted across his expression. 'You'd do that?'

I blinked. 'Of course.'

'It's not a person who can free me,' he said. 'It's a plaque.'

'I thought you guys wanted things like plaques.' And shrines and paintings and whatever.

'You guys?' he snorted. 'You'll be dead one day too, you know. Then you'll see.'

Iqbal reached forward and touched my elbow. 'I can only hear a bit of what's going on,' he said, 'but if it's a plaque you're looking for, I might know what you mean.' An expression of reverence crossed his face. 'Is the ghost you're talking to male, with frizzy hair that looks like yours? You know, like it's been electrocuted?'

'Electrocuted?' the spirit spat. 'Just because I had

better things to do than worry about my appearance! I'll have you know that I was the one who discovered the gene that is responsible for determining magic ability. Hundreds, no, thousands of witches have been discovered because of my work, instead of being left to languish in anonymity!'

I felt a sudden kinship with the phantom. After all, I also had better things to do than worry about my appearance. My better things weren't amazing scientific breakthroughs, however; they were amazing days snuggled up underneath my duvet. I decided I probably shouldn't say that.

'That's him,' I said to Iqbal instead.

He fixed his gaze on a point over the ghost's shoulder. 'Professor Wiggins,' he breathed. 'It's a genuine pleasure.'

Crazy Hair – or rather Professor Wiggins – looked slightly embarrassed. 'That's okay,' he said gruffly. He glanced at me. 'You should tell your friend that he needs to have another look at the third chapter. He's got his sums wrong.'

I relayed this information to Iqbal, who didn't look exactly thrilled. I suspected that he already knew that but hadn't got around to fixing it. Or maybe he'd hoped no one would notice.

'Thanks,' he muttered. 'I appreciate the help.'

'Why don't you take us to the plaque, Iqqy?' I suggested, before he gave himself away completely.

'Sure, yes.' He bobbed his head vigorously. 'I did wonder about it, you know. There's something about the wording that always makes me feel uncomfortable and now I know why.'

'What does it say?' Winter asked.

It was Wiggins himself who answered. '"It was on this spot in 1989 that Professor Horace Wiggins changed the course of biological magic study for decades. May his zest for science and his soul endure here for eternity, affecting all these walls and all who study within them.'"

I winced. That was a pretty definitive curse, even if it was nicely worded.

'Of course,' Wiggins continued, 'it wasn't on that spot at all. I was trying to get the Dean's secretary into the stationery cupboard when the real breakthrough actually came to me. You see, she had these massive—'

'Professor,' I said in an overly loud voice, 'if you want my help, then you should probably stop talking now.'

He paused. 'Uh, okay. Yes. Good idea.'

Brutus sighed. I shrugged at him. 'You could have stayed at home, you know. There are plenty of corners to sulk in there. You don't have to do it here.'

He raised a paw as if examining it, then extended his claws one by one.

'Come on, Iqbal!' Winter said cheerfully, with as much haste as he could muster. 'Let's go!'

And with that, we all barrelled out of the room.

Chapter Fourteen

One minor act of vandalism and a short journey later, we arrived at the Order Headquarters. Winter couldn't wipe the guilty expression off his face, as if he were about to be carted away to complete ten years' hard labour for prising an old plaque from a wall. He'd never make much of a criminal, I thought fondly.

'You know,' I said, as we got out of the taxi, 'maybe this ghost business isn't so bad after all. I'm starting to feel like I'm getting the hang of it. That's two spirits I've already helped cross over. I realise there are problems with Clare and her coven but that's different. All I need is to set up an office where the ghosts can come to me, and hire an assistant to sort out the curses, and I reckon I could be on to a winner. I'd miss taxi driving but I'd be prepared to give it up to be altruistic and help out all those lost souls.' I paused. 'And work for only twenty minutes or so a day.'

'Who would pay you?' Winter asked.

Hmm. Good question. I pocketed the keys and we walked towards the main building in search of the Ipsissimus. Brutus fell in beside us, although he seemed rather distracted by the new environment and kept stopping to sniff suspiciously at scary objects. He appeared convinced that the empty packet of crisps tumbling in the breeze was out to get him.

'I could get the families to pay me,' I said finally. 'You know, the descendants of the ghosts or whoever it is who cursed their souls in the first place. I'm doing them a favour – they should pay for the privilege of no longer being haunted.'

'Except,' Winter said, bending over to grab the crisp packet and drop it in a nearby bin, 'they don't *know* they're being haunted. So why would they be grateful?'

I rubbed my chin. 'Maybe before the curses are cleared, we get the spirits to tell us where all the ancient family heirlooms are buried.'

'Because every family must have buried heirlooms?'

Brutus leapt onto the top of the bin and peered inside before pawing for the crisp packet. He obviously didn't get out enough.

'Of course,' I said. 'For a start, in the corner of my parents' garden there's the head of a Barbie doll that I buried when I was a kid. Goodness only knows what else is there.'

'The head of Barbie doll? Treasure indeed.' Winter smiled.

'For all you know,' I said, 'it could be a collector's item.'

A small group of red-robed witches appeared from round the corner. When they caught sight of us, one of them immediately peeled away and raised a hand in greeting. 'Adeptus Exemptus Winter!'

Winter let out a hiss of irritation but he stopped and waited for the witch to catch up to us. 'Magister Templi Kirk,' he said formally.

I stood to one side, watching with interest as Kirk, a Third Level witch and therefore higher in the Order hierarchy than Winter, all but bowed to him.

'You're back!' he exclaimed. 'I'm so pleased! We've missed you hugely. I cannot wait to get your opinion on my latest project. It's really suffering for not having your input. You see I'm trying to combine—'

Winter held up a hand, interrupting the flood of words. 'I'm not back. I'm just here with my partner to see the Ipsissimus.'

I smiled and waved. 'That's me. I'm his partner. Me. Ivy Wilde.'

Magister Templi Kirk threw me a distracted glance. 'Oh yes. You're the one who stopped the teenage necromancer. Well done.'

I beamed. A beat later, however, Kirk returned his full attention to Winter. 'Why aren't you back?' he demanded. 'We need you.' His words could have sounded petulant but instead he came across as confused – and more than a little desperate.

'I don't belong here any more,' Winter said. 'The Order is not the place for me.'

'Of course it's the place for you!' Kirk protested.

Winter smiled. 'We should get going.'

'Wait! Can you tell me if you think I'm doing the right thing? I've been using catnip and hibiscus to work on a spell to alleviate depression but every time I test it, it creates a terrible skin rash.'

Winter frowned. 'How are you purifying the catnip?'

'The usual way, with a pinch of salt.'

He shook his head. 'No. That won't work. Catnip has unusual properties. Stick with the salt but try adding some dried sage. That should clear up your problems.'

Kirk's expression transformed in an instant. 'Sage,' he breathed. 'Of course, I should have thought of that. I asked several other herblore experts and none of them mentioned it but the purifying properties will definitely make a difference. You're a genius, Adeptus Exemptus. Thank you so much.'

Winter forced a smile. 'It's just Rafe. I'm not an Adeptus Exemptus any longer.'

'You always will be in my eyes,' Kirk said, without a trace of irony. I glanced round, half expecting to see a full orchestra playing a stirring soundtrack. Honestly, the situation really called for it.

'I have to go now, Magister,' Winter said.

Kirk's eyes widened in apology. 'Yes, yes! I'm so sorry to have kept you. You must be very busy.' He hesitated. 'Please reconsider your decision to return.'

Winter half grimaced and half smiled and turned away. I shot Kirk a quick smile of my own and joined him. 'I thought I was the only person in the world who could possibly be in love with you,' I said. 'Now I realise I have a lot of competition.'

Winter looked exasperated. 'Don't be ridiculous.'

'I'm not. Seriously, Rafe, that witch was ready to prostrate himself at your feet.'

'He's like that with everyone,' Winter dismissed.

Actually, I didn't think he was. In fact, I didn't think Winter had any idea just how much people around here wanted him. I understood it because I wanted him too. The trouble for the Order was that I had him and they didn't.

'Let's focus on the matter in hand, shall we?' he grunted. 'Look, there's the Ipsissimus. We can talk to him here without going up to his office. That'll please you.'

I glanced over, following his finger. He was right: Ipsissimus Collings was strolling along a well-kept path round the corner of the Runic Magic building. He wasn't alone; Philip Maidmont, handily, was with him. The pair of them were deep in conversation, their serious expressions and stiff body language suggesting that they weren't discussing what was on television last night. I bet that their topic of conversation started with the letter 'B' and ended with 'beard'. I opened my mouth to shout to them. That was when I realised what they were walking towards.

'No!' I shrieked.

Both the Ipsissimus and Maidmont glanced up. They saw us – but they also carried on walking. No, no, no, no, no! Round the corner of the building and out of their sight – but visible to me – was a ladder. If the pair of them took just four or five more steps they'd walk right underneath it. If there is an omen that is destined to screw up your day, your week, your month and quite possibly your entire life, it is walking under a ladder.

Freaking out in a manner most unusual for me, I flapped my arms. Winter stopped and stared at me, mystified. But then he'd never understood superstitions and the power they really held.

Realising that something was wrong, the Ipsissimus did exactly the opposite to what I wanted and sped up to find out what the problem was. Time slowed around me, like in a Hollywood movie when you know the hero is in mortal danger. Reminding myself to breathe, I lifted both hands and concentrated. This needed to be one of the fastest spells I'd ever cast but I couldn't afford for it to be sloppy.

'Ivy?' Winter began.

From behind, Brutus let out a yowl and barrelled towards the two men. At least he recognised the danger. As I flicked out a double-handed rune, Brutus bounded towards the ladder. Almost simultaneously, my spell toppled it as Brutus also smashed into it. There was a loud clatter as the offending object hit the path. Praise be – that was a close-run thing. I doubled over, breathing hard.

Maidmont spotted the ladder and started to hyperventilate whilst the Ipsissimus definitely appeared concerned. Winter just looked a bit puzzled. 'What's wrong? Is someone there? Is there a problem?' he asked.

Jeez. I gasped, trying to catch my breath. 'Ladder,' I wheezed.

'Huh?' There was a pause. 'Oh.'

I twisted my head towards him in time to catch his beautiful blue eyes rolling in amusement and exasperation. 'It's just a superstition.'

I managed to straighten up, although my breathing still wasn't back to normal. 'It's not just a superstition, Rafe!' I shook my head and jogged over to Maidmont and the Ipsissimus. At this rate, I'd give myself an aneurysm.

'How can you let ladders onto this campus?' I yelled, admonishing the Ipsissimus. 'And who the hell would leave one lying around like this?' I swung my head from side to side as if expecting a ninja assassin to appear at any second.

Ipsissimus Collings didn't look particularly happy but he wasn't panicking either. 'There are renovations taking place. We've recruited a non-witch construction firm. One of them must have left the ladder here by accident. I'll have words with them. It won't happen again.'

I was tempted to continue yelling at him to press home the potential consequences of such death traps in the Order headquarters. Given the circumstances of our visit, however, there were probably more important things to talk about. Brutus, almost as shaken as I was, leapt into my arms. I stroked him, as much to calm myself as to calm my cat.

'We need to talk about Blackbeard,' Winter said. 'There have been some developments with our investigation.'

The Ipsissimus nodded. 'Excellent. We have some new information too, although I'm not sure how helpful it will be. We should move inside for some privacy.' He looked around. 'And so that we're not in any further danger from construction equipment cursing us to eternity.'

Maidmont looked ready to turn tail and run screaming for the hills. I didn't blame him; I was tempted to jump on his back and demand a piggyback to the same place. Instead, I stroked Brutus a bit more and remembered to breathe.

'Sure,' I said, the epitome of casual behaviour. In fact, if anyone looked up 'relaxed' in the dictionary, my photo would be right there. Nobody would be able to tell that I was actually quaking in my boots. 'That sounds fabulous.'

Winter patted my hand. 'Don't worry,' he said. 'The nasty ladder has fallen down and can't hurt you any more. We're all perfectly safe. You don't have to panic.'

Darn it.

Rather than take us up to his office, the Ipsissimus led us towards a small room on the ground floor of his building. No wonder renovations were underway around the Order; we were in the room that time forgot. It was cramped and, quite possibly, dustier than the top shelf in my bedroom that I couldn't see over so I never cleaned it. One side of the room was crammed full of books, most of which probably hadn't been opened in decades. The other side was filled with the strangest examples of taxidermy I'd ever seen.

'Is that a stuffed deer?' I asked.

The Ipsissimus didn't look up. 'Yes.'

'With floppy rabbit ears?'

'Hare,' Winter interjected helpfully.

'My favourite is the cat,' Maidmont said.

I looked round. 'The one with the horn?'

He nodded cheerfully.

I stared at the three of them. Still in my arms, Brutus growled. 'What the hell is this place? Have you lot been experimenting with magically spliced animals?'

The Ipsissimus waved a hand dismissively. 'Don't be ridiculous. These were all completed post-mortem, and not even by a witch.'

'They were donated,' Maidmont said. 'Along with a generous annual stipend on the proviso that the collection is on display.'

I didn't care how generous the stipend was, these things were damned creepy. 'That winged bear is staring at me.' I bent down to Brutus. 'Kill,' I whispered to him. 'Kill the bear.' I released him onto the floor with a gentle nudge in the bear's direction. Brutus threw me a baleful look and darted under the table to avoid the creature's glassy-eyed gaze. I shuffled over to Winter and hunkered down next to him. He was a bigger target.

'So,' the Ipsissimus said, settling back into an ornate mahogany chair with flea-ridden velvet cushions. 'What exactly have you discovered?'

Winter spoke clearly and succinctly, outlining everything we'd found out so far from Clare Rees, her family and Professor Wiggins. As he spoke, it occurred to me that none of it was good.

The Ipsissimus pursed his lips. 'I've been back here for several hours. I've had reports from Human Resources regarding Rees and her coven's application for admission to the Order. I have to say, there's not much information. Their application was received two months ago and background checks and initial interviews with friends and family members were started.'

Two months ago. By that point they were all already dead.

'Is there any record of the coven's interviews?' Winter asked.

'That's the only interesting part. They were due to take part next week. They've been delayed because apparently the coven is away on a meditation holiday to improve their magic.'

'How do you know that?'

'About the holiday? We received a letter from them. It is how we usually communicate, Ms Wilde. Email and telephone are too unreliable and dangerous with all the magic around here, so we rely on the old-fashioned methods of posted letters or face-to-face communication. It's why so many people consider us dinosaurs. But you can learn so much more from someone's facial expressions or penmanship than you can from an emoticon.'

I raised an eyebrow. 'Really? And what did you learn from the penmanship of seven dead witches?'

He grimaced. 'Alas, all the letters we received were typed. The police have taken them away to check for fingerprints but the only prints that have appeared so far belong to our own staff.'

That figured. 'Well,' I said, 'I guess all you Order geeks are kind of screwed.'

Winter winced at my turn of phrase but the Ipsissimus seemed amused. 'Why do you say that?'

I shrugged. 'It's obvious, isn't it? Blackbeard hates witches but loves killing. He massacred an entire coven but has drawn out the process of disposing of their remains so that he can savour each and every death. But the coven's murders are still only a means to an end. That's why he's stepped up his timetable for scattering their ashes – he has a date.'

I jabbed a finger at the Ipsissimus. 'He's coming here. His end game is to come to the Order and murder again and he's used Clare's coven to gain admittance. That's why he's had all their letters redirected. He doesn't want their postcards as trophies, he wants to use their identities to sneak into the Order. He's honed his skills with a group of weak, non-Order witches so he can step up and make a move against the big boys.' I paused. 'In other words you. It's why he's kept his murders so quiet. He's saving up everything for one grand finale.'

The Ipsissimus drew in a breath. 'That's quite some theory.'

Maybe, but it felt right. I knew it in my bones.

'He wouldn't get very far,' Maidmont protested. 'Even if he is some kind of magical null, as you say, there are thousands of witches and only one of him. We wouldn't need to use magic to stop him.'

'But,' Winter said, with a troubled expression, 'how many would die before we got to that point?'

I sat up straight. 'Fewer now that we have regained the element of surprise. He doesn't know that we know what his plans are. We lost the upper hand by accident when we were in Dartmoor. We need to make damn sure we don't lose it again.'

'The media embargo is in place,' the Ipsissimus said.

I shook my head. 'Even with the best will in the world, someone will end up blabbing something. The police need to back off from the coven's homes. Everyone needs to lay low. Then, when Blackbeard arrives for his supposed interview, we take him down before he so much as shakes anyone's hand. We don't need magic, we just need a baseball bat to whack him over the head with. Job done.'

A fleeting smile crossed Winter's lips. 'You make it sound very easy. It will be even easier if we can find out his real identity and get to him before he gets close to the Order.'

The Ipsissimus sighed. 'The police have been looking at crematoria but there are a lot of them and they operate under very strict guidelines, as you would imagine. So far there's been no one who meets the description of our killer. Whatever he's been doing to burn the bodies of coven members, we haven't found it yet.'

'Maybe he works somewhere with industrial fires that get to the required temperatures to cremate bone,' Winter suggested.

'He may do – but bear in mind that the police are trying to conduct their enquiries without tipping him off. With more time, we might get somewhere. If we broadcast a photofit of the man, we certainly would.'

I sighed. 'But if we do that, we could well be unleashing hell. What about the mail redirection? All the coven's post has to be going somewhere. It can't just disappear into thin air.'

'All the letters have been sent to a PO box. The police have discovered that it's registered under a fake identity.' The Ipsissimus looked grim. 'A Mr Ripper.'

I rolled my eyes. 'He's not very imaginative, is he?'

Winter cocked his head. 'You named him Blackbeard because he has a … black beard.' Touché.

'I'm here,' Maidmont said helpfully, 'because I've been researching nulls. I've managed to trace several historical figures who may or may not have been nulls in the past. It's quite interesting, really.'

I raised my eyebrows. 'There are bloodlines we can follow?'

He slumped into his chair. 'No. It appears to be a condition that just occurs at random. Truthfully, there haven't been enough nulls for us to conclude any definitive evidence about them. That's probably why we didn't know anything about them. The trouble is that absence of evidence doesn't equate to evidence of absence.'

We lapsed into silence. There had to be some way of working through the problem of Blackbeard's real identity. Winter, Maidmont and the Ipsissimus were super-clever; If they thought hard enough, I was confident they'd come up with an answer.

Rather than tax my brain pointlessly when there were others around who could do it for me, I leaned back in my chair and yawned. The past few days had been considerably more energetic than I liked. If it weren't for the creepy stuffed animals, I'd probably have asked the Ipsissimus if I could bed down for a quiet nap but, with all those dead eyes staring at me, I wouldn't manage to sleep – and, for me, that was saying something.

Brutus, slightly braver now that none of the stuffed creatures had twitched, ventured out towards the horned cat, sniffing warily. He raised a paw and struck it sharply on the head then backed away again, as if more disturbed by the stuffed cat's lack of response than that it looked like Dr Frankenstein's favourite pet. Why anyone ever thought that taxidermy was a good thing was beyond me. I loved Brutus to bits but if he died before me, he was either going in a hole in the ground or…

I shot to my feet. 'Pets!'

The others stared at me in alarm. Winter's eyes flicked from side to side. 'Who are you talking to this time, Ivy?'

'You! I'm talking to you! Look,' I said, feeling an ecstasy of urgency flood my veins that was most unusual. 'The police have investigated the crematoria, yes?'

'All the ones with a reasonable radius of Dorset and Dartmoor,' the Ipsissimus answered.

'All the crematoria?' I pressed. 'Or just the human ones?'

Maidmont looked confused but Winter immediately grasped my meaning. 'Pet crematoria,' he said. 'The temperatures to cremate the body of a dog must be the same as those required to burn a human's.'

I nodded. 'And while I'm sure they have strict rules, they're probably not as rigorously inspected as human crematoria.'

'There won't be that many of them,' the Ipsissimus said. 'It wouldn't take long to pinpoint any which Blackbeard might have used.'

'How would he sneak a human corpse into a pet funeral service?'

I shook my head. 'Maybe he works in one. Maybe he lives next to one.' I shrugged. 'I don't know. But it has to be worth checking out.'

Maidmont got to his feet. 'Give me fifteen minutes,' he promised. 'I'll find out if there are any around that area.'

'They probably won't be in Weymouth or on Dartmoor,' Winter said. 'He'll be using different locations to avoid detection.'

'But,' I added, 'he won't want to travel too far for the same reason.'

Maidmont frowned. 'You do know I'm a librarian? Research like this is my bread and butter. I know what to look for.'

I grinned. 'Sorry. We trust you, Phil!' He raised his eyes to the heavens and left.

The Ipsissimus knitted his fingers under his chin and watched me. 'Are you sure, Ms Wilde, that you wouldn't like to return to the Order? I really do think you might fit in better than you realise.'

'She's sure,' Winter snapped. Then he looked apologetic. 'I'm not trying to speak for you,' he muttered to me.

I gave him a quick, reassuring smile. 'I know.'

'Pfffft!'

I jumped as Ipsissimus Grenville's head appeared next to the stuffed bear's. Brutus hissed and darted away again. 'He *should* speak for you,' the ghost said. 'He's a man. He has a far better understanding of Order matters than you ever could.'

I gritted my teeth. 'Yes, he does, but only because he used to be in the Order. Not because he happens to be a man.'

Grenville frowned. 'What do you mean *used to be* in the Order? Has he been expelled? Did you conspire to have this good man thrown out?'

I didn't deign to answer that question. I'd already had words once with Grenville about his rudeness and I wasn't going to repeat myself. Frankly, at this point in time he needed me a great deal more than I needed him.

Ipsissimus Collings looked fascinated. 'Is that Ipsissimus Grenville?' He clapped his hands. 'How wonderful! I've been reading his old journals. They're quite fascinating.'

Grenville harrumphed loudly and floated down from the bear to the Ipsissimus's face. 'You've been reading my journals? Those are private, sir! In my day a gentleman would never stoop to such an act.'

'I've just reached the part where you went back and perused the diaries of one of your predecessors,' Ipsissimus Collings burbled happily. 'And you realised that there was a lot you could learn from the past. Now we can communicate with each other through Ms Wilde, we can learn from you. This is truly a fortuitous opportunity.'

I snorted at Grenville's expression. His face contorted further and he whipped round. 'Shut up, woman!' he thundered. 'This is all your fault,! Do you have any idea what a mess you've created? Just as things finally seemed to be looking up, I'm getting spirits from all over the damn country complaining to me because of what you've done!' His voice was still rising. Whether that was a special gift granted to all ghosts, or whether he'd managed to achieve similar decibels when he was alive, I didn't know but it was an impressive sound.

I leaned back further in my chair and lifted my legs, propping my feet on the table. Both Ipsissimus Collings and Winter frowned but they were too intrigued by what Grenville might be saying to admonish me. I made a show of inspecting my fingernails; out of the corner of my eye, I could see that steam was almost coming out of Grenville's ears.

'Ivy,' Winter said, 'does Ipsissimus Grenville have any insights to offer about Blackbeard? Could he perhaps send some ghosts to search for him? They could prove to be our salvation.'

Grenville didn't react to Winter's suggestion. His attention remained wholly on me. 'Don't you want to know what you've done?' he demanded.

I started to pick at a hangnail as Grenville started to stamp his feet. Perhaps we all regressed into childhood after we died. Spending the afterlife throwing temper tantrums didn't seem like the best use of a phantom's time, but maybe with eternity to contemplate there wasn't much else to do. What did I know?

'Maybe he could speak to Clare Rees and the other coven ghosts again,' Ipsissimus Collings suggested. 'Ask them if they noticed anything to do with animals, or if they had any pets that died recently. If they used a pet crematorium to dispose of their pet's remains, that might be how Blackbeard targeted them in the first place.'

I looked up. 'That's a really good idea.'

'I can't talk to anyone else!' Grenville yelled in my face. 'They won't talk to me any more! And it's all your fault! Because you've screwed everything up, the others all want a new representative! We've spent a long time working out a schedule. There is a hierarchy and some people have been waiting here for generations. The queue has been established for over a century and you leapfrog it willy-nilly! That last spirit whose curse you smashed had only been here for a decade or two. He was number 22,633 and you put him at the front of the line! And that idiot who couldn't keep his penis in his clothes wasn't much higher. This is what happens when women are given a bit of freedom. They mess everything up!' He held up his palms towards me. 'I can't even bear to look at you. You have no understanding of anything.' He shook his head and vanished.

Winter raised his eyebrows. 'Well?'

I bit my lip. 'I don't think Ipsissimus Grenville is in a good mood. We might be on our own for a while.'

The door banged open and Maidmont reappeared, clutching a piece of paper. His face was shining. 'I think I have the place,' he said. 'I think this might be where Blackbeard is burning his victims.'

There was a brief mutter from underneath the table. 'Thank fuck,' Brutus said. 'We need to depart this hellhole *tout suite*.'

I started and looked down at him. Had I really just heard that? He blinked innocently and started to lick his paws.

Chapter Fifteen

'We should call the police and get them to visit the place,' Ipsissimus Collings said.

Winter pursed his lips. 'They don't know what they should be looking for. It'll be like sending in a barber to do the work of a plumber. It's not about using magic, it's about having the knowledge to follow the right clues and find the right person.'

'There are Arcane Branch witches nearby, some very talented ones. We could send them in.'

'But they haven't seen Blackbeard in person. Ivy has. She'll recognise him faster than anyone else. Besides, if one of the Arcane Branch witches gets twitchy and uses magic by accident, they could ruin everything.'

The Ipsissimus grimaced. 'But if Blackbeard is there because he works there, he'll recognise you both and the game will be up.'

Winter drew back his shoulders. 'If Blackbeard happens to be there, he won't be walking out of that building unless he's in our custody or a body bag.'

Even I sucked in a breath at that one. Winter had a way of saying things that could send serious shivers of fear down your spine. It was probably the military blood in him, and the way he managed to be so sincere and yet completely matter-of-fact whilst discussing killing another human being.

The Ipsissimus was prepared to continue arguing. 'You are both civilians. You have no place…'

'When you put Ivy on Dead Man's Hill with an

incantation to draw a necromancer's magic and martyr herself, she was a civilian.' Winter stared at his old boss, his eyes like chips of blue ice. The moment of silence that followed was one of the most uncomfortable of my life.

'Fine,' the Ipsissimus finally said. 'But don't screw this up.'

Winter was very still. 'You forget who you're talking to.' With that, he turned on his heel and stalked out, Brutus and I close behind him.

It was fascinating to see Winter transform into icy action. It was if he shut down part of himself so he could focus on only one thing. As a testament to his witchy commando mode (and if only he really would go commando under those well-tailored trousers) I even gave him the keys so he could drive. Then the three of us piled into my trusty taxi.

'Put your seatbelt on, Ivy,' he instructed.

'This pet crematorium is only a guess, Rafe. Blackbeard might have nothing to do with the place.'

'He has to be burning the coven witches somewhere.'

'True.'

'And he doesn't appear to be involved with, or have visited, any other crematoria.'

'True.'

'And this place, Dignity Valley, is in the ideal location with transport links to both Dorset and Dartmoor.' He paused. 'Not to mention Oxford.'

'True.' I scratched my head. 'Far be it from me to be the voice of reason and to suggest that our evidence isn't concrete, but there's still no definitive proof that this is the place. It's all circumstantial.'

Winter's eyes met mine. 'I know,' he said quietly. 'But you feel it, don't you? As if we're on the right track.' He shook his head slowly. 'I've never put much faith in instinct before, it's always been about cold, hard facts. You're affecting me in more ways than either of us realise.'

My mouth suddenly felt dry. 'I hope that's a good thing.'

'It couldn't be better.' His gaze held me. 'You don't have to be afraid of me, Ivy. I would never hurt you or put in you in harm's way.'

'I'm not afraid of you, Rafe,' I answered honestly. 'Sometimes the things you say can come across as a little scary but I'll never be scared of you as a person.' I gave a crooked smile. 'Besides, I can look after myself.'

'If you could look after yourself, you would eat healthily, go to the gym and sort out your own damned grout,' he said.

I smirked. 'Love you too, baby.' I leaned across and planted a kiss on his lips. From the back seat, Brutus sighed loudly. Yeah, alright. 'Time to go and catch a killer.' Or so I hoped.

***

It was early evening by the time we pulled up outside Dignity Valley. Considering its business was effectively death – and I had yet to meet a ghost who wasn't a ball of tension – it looked remarkably peaceful and serene. It wasn't just the lush green surroundings or the clean modern lines of the buildings, which somehow fitted the country landscape. There was an overall atmosphere that felt wholly relaxing. Perhaps animals were simply more accepting of their fate than humans, though I hadn't met any ghostly dogs or cats yet so I couldn't say for sure. In any case, Dignity Valley, despite the nature of its everyday events, did not seem a likely venue for a serial killer. Or mass murderer. Whatever.

Brutus opened a lazy eye then closed it again, immediately going back to sleep. Winter and I climbed out of the taxi and walked up to the main entrance.

'Maybe I should be wearing a disguise,' I suggested. 'You know, in case we bump into Blackbeard.'

'Good disguises take a lot of time and effort.'

I considered this. 'It wouldn't have to be a *good* disguise. I could dress up as a clown and pretend to be looking for a children's party. That wouldn't be hard to do.'

'A clown? At a pet crematorium?'

I shrugged. 'A bit *avant garde*, I admit.' I glanced at him. 'Blackbeard would recognise you too, so you should wear a disguise as well.'

'I am not dressing up as a clown, Ivy.'

I wrinkled my nose. 'No, a clown wouldn't suit you. I was thinking of something more distracting. Tarzan, perhaps. That would be easy to manage. You just need to strip off and I'll fashion you a quick loincloth to wear.'

'Don't be ridiculous.'

I kept my expression blank. 'You can go starkers, if you'd prefer.'

Winter pressed his lips together. 'You know we're here tracking down a vicious, evil bastard who has destroyed at least seven lives and who would destroy many more given half the chance?'

'This is what we humans do. We have a sense of humour and we make the best of everything. If you can't laugh, what's the point of living?'

Winter's eyes travelled slowly up and down my body, heat flaring in his gaze. 'I can think of one or two things.'

Beaten at my own game, I swallowed and looked away. If I looked directly at Winter much longer, I'd be tempted to jump him right here in the car park. 'Let's find that vicious, evil bastard, shall we?' I said instead.

A smile tugged at Winter's mouth but he nodded in agreement.

The glass-fronted façade of Dignity Valley was nondescript. It could have been the front of any office or business. Perhaps there was a factory somewhere churning out identical buildings so that everywhere in the land leisure centres, police stations, DIY depots and dead-pet disposal services looked exactly the same.

This particular establishment was closed. There were no lights on inside and the doors didn't swoosh open as we approached. That was a shame – I love electronic doors. What's better than not having to expend the effort to turn a door handle yourself? They are almost on a par with robot vacuum cleaners and the moving walkways you get at airports.

Winter searched around for a doorbell or comms box. I tilted my head to one side and pulled back my hair, drawing a quick rune to temporarily extend my hearing. There was only so much magic could do but I was certain I could hear the faint strains of what apparently passed for music in these parts. I tapped Winter's shoulder and gestured round towards the back of the building. He nodded and we carefully edged down a well-worn path.

The music, some godawful screeching with a heavy bass line that was totally at odds with the peaceful surroundings, was coming from a fire door that had been propped open round the back. Winter and I exchanged glances and immediately snuck in.

Avoiding the source of the music, we veered left, following a drab beige corridor round a corner and into an enormous room stacked full of urns and boxes. Suddenly I was glad that Brutus had chosen to stay sleeping in the taxi rather than come with us. He'd never struck me as the kind of cat who would enjoy picking out his own urn, although no doubt if he did he'd demand the top-of-the-range, gold-plated version just to enjoy emptying my bank account. In reality, when it was time to use the thing, he'd be dead and he wouldn't care what kind of vessel his remains ended up in. Of all the things the ghosts had complained about, none of them had mentioned being irritated by their physical holding arrangements.

Turning around again, Winter headed for a closed door halfway back down the corridor. The difference as we entered this new area was marked: these walls weren't a dull, dirty colour but a calming light purple. There were three small offices to the right, none of which were locked. Winter stepped into the first one and lifted a photo frame from the small wooden desk. He glanced at it, returned it to its place then shook his head.

I headed into the second office. There weren't any helpful family photographs in this one but there was the lingering scent of heavy perfume. Unless Blackbeard had a penchant for sickly florals with lilac undertones, this room had nothing to do with him either.

Winter checked the final room, exiting almost as quickly as he entered with a gruff, albeit muted, denial. If Blackbeard did work here, he didn't have anything to do with the management team.

We headed towards the front and the deserted reception area. The name tag on the desk was for an Alison Hibbert. No luck there, then. We continued, popping into family rooms no doubt designed for heartbroken pet owners to wait in. Apart from tastefully placed fake flowers, and leaflets to help people through the grieving process, there was nothing here. Maybe instinct didn't count for much after all.

Winter beckoned me over. 'There's nothing here that's of any use,' he whispered.

I nodded. 'We should look for filing cabinets and personnel files. Maybe we'll get lucky and there'll be photographs of the employees.'

'As a last resort, we'll have to confront whoever is still here playing that music in the back. But until we know more about who Blackbeard is and who his friends are, I don't really want to do that.'

I gave him a sloppy salute. He was used to this kind of gig and knew what he was doing. 'Maybe we should search the smaller outbuildings,' I suggested. With any luck, we'd bypass the furnaces. The thought of them gave me the creeps.

We went back the way we'd come, taking as much care to stay quiet and remain unobtrusive as we could. The music now had a more muffled quality, as if the sound had been turned down. Relaxing a little, I picked up my feet and moved a faster. That was my first mistake.

Slightly ahead of Winter, I turned the corner towards the back door entrance and froze. Silhouetted against the darkening sky was a large man, standing at the threshold and smoking. I barely had a second to take him in before I pulled back and grabbed Winter's arm, gesturing frantically. Because of the light and the fact that he'd been turned away I hadn't seen the man's face clearly – but there was definitely a shiny bald head and a bushy black beard.

Winter's eyes darkened to a stormy blue and he dipped his head forward to look. Almost immediately he drew back in, his features and his body tense. We shared a glance of grim determination – coupled with a tiny edge of satisfaction. Although I'd felt the same as Winter and my gut had been telling me that Blackbeard's trail would lead here, I hadn't expected to find the man himself.

Winter tugged at my sleeve, pulling me further back into the main building. He didn't speak until we were out of earshot. 'He's wearing a uniform,' he whispered so quietly that I had to strain to hear. 'He must be a security guard.'

I agreed. 'And on the night shift, no less.' It was perfect – if you wanted to secretly cremate bodies without being observed. 'How do we do this? We can't use magic against him because it won't work. And if he's a security guard, he's probably armed.' Not with a gun – this was middle England, after all – but there was a chance he had a Taser or a knife. Even a baton used by someone who knew what they were doing could cause us problems. Hell, for all we knew he could have a bloody submachine gun with him. It was unlikely, but nothing was impossible where Blackbeard was concerned. Besides, I was a plump woman of less than average height and rather dubious fitness. Winter, naturally, was in a better position to attack Blackbeard without a spell to back him up but even he would find it tough. The man was built like an oak tree.

'You stay here,' Winter said. 'Call the police, the Ipsissimus and whoever you can get hold of at Arcane Branch. Tell them to advance here on the double. I'll make sure Blackbeard doesn't get away.'

'You're fit, Winter, but he has to be twice your size.'

'I can do this.'

He was an idiot. 'Actually,' I said, 'I don't think you can. Look, just because we can't use magic directly *against* him doesn't mean we can't use magic *around* him.'

'What do you mean?'

'We could weaken the building's foundations to the point of collapse. I know a few spells for that. We bring several tonnes of concrete down onto his head, then he'll stop moving. He'll be as flat as a pancake.'

Winter nodded gravely, as if he were taking my suggestion seriously. 'There's just one tiny problem with that scenario, Ivy.' He waved a hand. 'We're inside the same building and the only way out is the exit where Blackbeard is standing.'

Ah. Okay. I could concede that point. 'Fine. But there must be a way.'

'Well, I suppose we could—'

'Who the fuck are you?'

Winter and I sprang backwards in shock. Then, without thinking, I let out a war cry and ran headfirst towards Blackbeard. My head smacked into his not-inconsiderable belly and he let out a loud oomph of surprise. He reached down, grabbed a hank of my hair and dragged me upwards. It felt like my scalp was being ripped out. I shrieked in pain and writhed, trying to kick my way to freedom. My feet connected with solid flesh several times but Blackbeard wasn't letting go of my hair for anything.

While I swung ineffectually round like a doll being held by a giant, Winter leapt towards the pair of us with his fists raised. Blackbeard let out a guttural, inarticulate yell of rage, confusion and fear. The sound reverberated round my skull while I stared dumbly at his face. Arse. Double arse. Triple arse. Arsing hell with an arsing cherry on top for effort. This was very bad.

Unfortunately, before I got the chance to say or do anything, he flung me to the side so he was free to face Winter's onslaught. I both felt and heard my head crack against the concrete wall. Pain shot through my body, rippling through me in waves that made it difficult to think coherently. I was dimly aware of Winter letting out a howl of rage of his own. I opened my mouth to speak but all that came out was a strange grunt. Blinking several times, I tried to focus but it was no good. My vision was blurred and two Winters and two bearded men were hovering and wobbling in front of me.

Winter threw the first punch, slamming into

Blackbeard's face. His jowls juddered and blood spurted out from his nose, splattering onto the floor in front of me.

'Wait,' I tried to croak. 'Stop.'

Neither of them heard me – and even if they had, I doubt they would have paid any attention. I tried to stagger to my feet but I didn't even make it to a crouching position before I collapsed again. 'Rafe,' I said.

Both versions of him ducked away from two swinging fists. I squeezed my eyes shut and tried to clear my vision. It was making me incredibly nauseous but that was nothing compared to how I'd feel if either of these two got seriously hurt.

'It's not him.'

Blackbeard's doppelganger reached down to his belt to unclip whatever weapon he was carrying. Winter was determined not to give him the chance, however, and shoulder-slammed him, knocking him to the ground. Unfortunately Winter fell with him and both men rolled around on the floor, grabbing, kicking and trying to hit each other. From this angle, it looked like they were making love rather than war but the grunts and yelps of pain told a different story.

My head felt like it was going to explode. It wasn't a throbbing ache, it was an all-out, searing pain that made it difficult to think. And I was definitely going to throw up at any moment. I sucked in a breath and concentrated. I had to do something before these two killed each other and I should probably do it now before I passed out.

My rune was sloppy; truth be told, it would barely pass muster in the weakest non-Order coven. As long as it did what I needed it to do, though, that didn't matter. I intended to douse them in icy water. A good drenching, as Winter well knew because he'd done the same to me in the past, was more than enough to jolt anyone back to reality.

Unfortunately, the blow to my head meant I was thrown off my game. From out of nowhere, a shower of ice cubes rained down not just on Winter and the security guard but across the whole room. Within seconds there were four inches of ice cubes carpeting the floor and I was shivering violently.

Winter managed to extricate himself from the fight and rushed over to me. 'What are you doing? What's wrong?'

Thank goodness. I raised my eyes to his, an action that took a lot of effort and energy, particularly as I still didn't know which was the real Winter. 'It's not him,' I croaked. 'That's not Blackbeard.'

He frowned. 'What?'

I opened my mouth again but it was too late. The security guard raised his hand and thumped Winter on the back of the neck. Winter collapsed, his body sprawled heavily against mine.

'I'll try again,' the guard said, blood streaming from his nose and into his beard. 'Who the hell are you?'

I'd have answered him if I could. I really wanted to answer him but consciousness was too difficult to sustain and the lights dancing in front of my eyes were taking over. Another surge of nausea rippled through me then I passed out too.

***

I returned slowly to the world of the living. For the first few seconds nothing hurt and I wondered if I were still alive or if I'd joined the ranks of all those angry spirits. It didn't take long, though, for the pain to make a comeback – and when it did, it was like being hit with a ten-ton truck.

I could have played dead and used the opportunity to

learn more about the situation I was now in; that's what a Hollywood heroine would have done. Instead I moaned loudly, then I threw up. Thanks to the fact that I was now trussed up like a chicken, the vomit ended up all down my front instead of anywhere moppable. I groaned again.

The security's guard face loomed in front of me. At least there was now only one of him and I was no longer seeing double – but I still blinked rapidly. His resemblance to Blackbeard was quite uncanny but, now I was close to him, it was obvious that this was a different man. He didn't have an earring for one thing, and his ear didn't have the tell-tale hole where an earring might once have been. His face was older, with laughter lines around his eyes and mouth, and his dark beard was speckled with grey. The real giveaway was the expression in his eyes; it was brimming with suspicion, worry and more than a little fear. It certainly was nothing like the dead emotion in Blackbeard's gaze.

'Ivy,' I muttered to myself, 'you've really screwed up this time.'

'Ivy? That's your name?'

I nodded, then wished I hadn't because moving my head made me feel sick again.

'Figures,' he grunted. 'I had a girlfriend called Ivy once and she was the craziest bitch you've ever met.' He sucked on his teeth and regarded me through narrowed eyes. 'Apart from you, of course. You've already outdone her. Well done.'

Uh, thanks?

'You're a witch?' he asked.

'Yes,' I managed.

'And your boyfriend?'

I could feel Winter's familiar weight at my back. He was definitely breathing regularly but, given his lack of response, he was probably still unconscious. I weighed up the benefits of lying and decided there was no point; untruths would not aid our cause now. I needed the guard to realise we'd made an honest mistake. 'He's a witch as well.'

The guard's pupils narrowed to pinpricks. 'What does the Order want with a pet crematorium? And why would you attack me? We don't do funerals for witch familiars here, you know. We're not evil, either.'

My brain was sluggish and it took some time to get my tongue to form the right words. 'I'm sorry. I'm so sorry. We thought you were someone else. Someone really dangerous. It was a genuine mistake.'

'I've done nothing to you!' he spat. 'And look at me! I bruise easily and I'm going to be black and blue for weeks! My wife will kill me.'

'I really am sorry.' I licked my lips. 'We're looking for a murderer. A man with a bald head and a bushy black beard just like yours, who we thought might work here. He's killed seven people already. We believe he's planning to kill more. Believe me, no one is more upset than me that you're not him.'

The security guard stared at me. Something about his expression made me sit up straight. 'You know who I'm talking about,' I breathed.

'What if I do? How do I know you are who you say you are? Maybe you just have a thing against beards.'

'You know that's ridiculous, right?' I hesitated. 'Although I've always wondered whether you end up with lots of food in your beard when you eat. Do you find yourself picking out crumbs later on and having them as a snack?'

He looked me as if I were mad. Yeah, alright, but at least it was making him realise that I wasn't a dangerous witch who'd turn him into a frog and that I was just nutty. Nutty enough to mistake him for someone else.

He wiped some of the blood onto his sleeve. 'The police are coming. You can explain yourself to them.'

'And I will! But, please, you have to tell me who I'm really looking for and where I can find him. More people will die if you don't.'

He searched my face, as if seeking the truth of my words. 'You could be anyone,' he said finally. 'You could be making all this up.'

'You know I'm a witch. I cast a spell to make those ice cubes appear.'

He pursed his lips. 'Yeah, why did you do that? It was a bit weird.'

Uh… 'To cool you both off and get you to stop fighting, of course. That's not the point. The point is I could easily cast another spell now and get myself out of this situation. I could hurt you if I wanted to but I haven't done. Because I'm not a bad person. I'm on the tail of a very bad person and so is my boyfriend. We'll wait for the police if it makes you feel safe but please,' I pleaded, 'tell me what you know.'

For a moment, I thought he was going to refuse but something about my desperate begging persuaded him. Whatever it was, when he started talking I sagged against Winter's prone body in relief. Some good had to come out of this disaster.

'He doesn't work here. His family owns the place but he doesn't have much to do with it. I've only met him a couple of times. It's been a bit of a running joke among the lads that we look alike but Hal never seems to find it funny. I've only been working here for a month or so, but I've always had the impression he despises me. I assumed it was because we look similar.'

'Hal,' I pressed. 'That's his name?'

'Yeah. Hal Prescott. He lives in that swanky new building a few miles down the road. We might look alike but we live very different lives.'

'If you've only been working here for a month, who was in your job before you? Do you know?'

The guard shook his head. 'No one. I mean, you wouldn't think a crematorium would need security, would you?' He gave me a pointed look and I cringed. 'They hired me because there'd been some trouble with the furnaces. The Prescotts thought kids were maybe coming in and burning stuff. Or that maybe it was Travellers or someone, you know? They were definitely being used.' He raised his massive shoulders in a shrug. 'But until you and Blue Eyes here showed up, I'd seen nothing. No one comes here at night.'

I had a hunch that the reason Blackbeard despised him was because he was in the way, not because they resembled each other. Perhaps this was the real reason why he'd drawn out disposing of the coven's remains. He couldn't kill anyone else because now he couldn't burn their bodies without being noticed, so he had to get his kicks where he could. He would have found it easy to sneak in on his own at night before the guard was hired. Now, whether his family owned the place or not, it would be next to impossible.

Another thought occurred to me. 'You said that this place doesn't provide cremation services for familiars. Why not?'

He bared his teeth in a grin, 'Apparently they really don't like witches. In fact, I heard they think the lot of you are scum.' The guard seemed almost delighted to tell me this.

Fascinated, I had to ask the question. 'Why?'

'Dunno. No one knows.'

Hmm. Maybe they'd had a bad encounter in the past. Maybe there was a black sheep in the family who was a witch. Maybe they wanted to be witches and weren't. I chewed the inside of my cheek. Maybe it was even something to do with the fact that little Hal was a null. In the end, the motive didn't matter; finding and stopping Blackbeard did.

Behind me, Winter began stir. He groaned even louder than I had. The security guard shuffled, obviously nervous, so I leaned back my head. 'Just relax, Rafe. It's fine. We're all fine. Don't do anything silly.'

'Are you okay?'

Concussed, bleary-eyed and covered in vomit, I replied, 'I'm fine. Everything is fine. We're all calm and we're all happy. In fact—'

The door burst open and several men ran in, shouting and yelling. 'Police! Nobody move!' The nearest one jabbed a finger at me as if I were about to get up and do the cancan.

'We're tied up,' I said helpfully. 'We can't move.'

The security guard raised a hand to his head. A moment later, a police officer was on top of him, yanking his arm behind his back in a manner that looked both incredibly painful and incredibly unnatural. The guard really wasn't having a very good night.

'He's the one who called you guys,' I said, in a bid to encourage the police to let him go. Watching his takedown was making me flinch and there was every possibility I would throw up again. 'He's the good guy.' I realised what I'd just said. 'I mean, we're the good guys too. We're all good guys. There are no bad guys. This has all been a terrible misunderstanding.'

'Call the Ipsissimus,' Winter said in a loud voice which commanded attention. He certainly came across a lot more coherently than I had. 'We are here with the full knowledge of the Hallowed Order of Magical Enlightenment. We are also working with a large group of police officers on a serious matter which takes precedence over your jurisdiction.'

One of the policemen, who I took to be the one in charge because his shoes were the shiniest, gave Winter an assessing glance. Apparently deciding that he sounded credible, the officer muttered something into his walkie-talkie. This would all be sorted out in a jiffy. No harm done.

Yet another police officer entered the room. 'The owner is on his way,' he declared to no one in particular.

I immediately stiffened. Okay, that was bad. Very bad. 'Rafe,' I whispered, 'we have a problem.'

The security guard started to yell and shout, trying to free himself. All the policemen focused their attention on him. They should have known better.

Winter replied to me over the tumult. 'We're tied up on the floor of a crematorium and surrounded by angry police officers, Ivy. Not to mention that I apparently beat up an innocent man. Yes, I'd say we have a problem. Several problems.'

Actually, I thought it was the innocent man who'd beaten up Winter rather than the other way around but I decided not to mention that. 'I mean another problem. Blackbeard, the real Blackbeard, is a man called Hal Prescott. He's the crematorium owner's son and the whole family hate witches. If Blackbeard comes with his dad to see what the problem is and we're tied up like this…'

Winter sucked in a breath. 'Right.' He paused. 'Maybe he won't come. Maybe it'll just be the father.'

There was a crackle on the walkie-talkie, barely audible over the guard's continued protests. 'No confirmation yet. Hold the suspects.'

I grimaced. 'Even if it is just the owner, he'll see us and tell his family that two witches were caught breaking in. He won't even need to describe us for Blackbeard to get suspicious. If we can persuade this lot that Blackbeard is the criminal we'll be fine but I don't think there's time. I don't think they'll believe us. We need to buy ourselves an hour or two. We need the upper hand if we're going to bring Blackbeard down.'

'The Order never goes against the police, Ivy. We always do what they say, even when we don't agree with it. It's the only way the two organisations can work together.' Winter sniffed. 'But I'm not with the Order any longer. If we can free ourselves and combine our magic, we can create a sleeping spell strong enough to knock out everyone here and that'll give us time to get away. Even if Blackbeard and the owner arrive, it'll be a couple of hours before this lot come round and can answer any questions. We should have enough time to regroup and decide upon a plan of action.'

I'd created a monster. 'Or wait outside for Blackbeard to show up and go with our original plan of taking him down right here.'

'Yes,' he said drily, 'because that's working out so well this far.' Sarcastic bugger. 'Okay, let's do that.'

I felt really bad about the security guard but sleep would probably be the best thing for him. It would give him a chance to recoup his strength. I'd keep telling myself that. 'Can you wiggle free?'

Winter snorted. At least three of the police officers who were standing around waiting for orders swung their heads towards him, their eyes narrowing. 'Piece of cake.'

Two of the policemen peeled off and moved towards us. 'Then hurry.'

Winter laughed softly and I felt the bonds loosen instantly. Damn, that was good. 'On a count of three.'

'One. Two.'

The nearest policeman glared at us. 'What are you two up to?'

Together we chanted, 'Three.'

Magical power billowed up inside me, expanding outwards and suffusing the room. I felt Winter's magic mingle with mine until you could barely tell the difference between the two strands. The spell coalesced and the magic danced – and the mingled policemen dropped like flies.

'Wow,' I whispered.

Winter stood up and turned, pulling me to my feet and gazing into my eyes. 'You felt that too?'

'Yeah.' I licked my lips and we smiled at each other gleefully, as if we were Bonnie and Clyde. There was definitely a thrill in breaking the law, even if it was done with the best of intentions. I drew in a shaky breath. Then we got moving.

Taking a moment out, I checked on the hapless security guard and pulled off the policeman who was now snoring on top of him. I turned the guard carefully onto his back, adjusting his head so that he'd be comfortable and wouldn't choke on his own tongue. My eyes drifted down to his badge. Alan Hopkins. So that was his name. Sorry, mate.

'Ivy,' Winter said, 'if you're wishing that you were fast asleep like this lot, can you do it from outside when we're in place and ready for Blackbeard?'

For once the thought of sleep hadn't even occurred to me, even though my head was still pounding. I guess Winter was affecting me much as I was affecting him. I flashed him a quick smile and we darted out.

My trusty taxi was sitting exactly where I'd left it, although now it was concealed by the police cars parked haphazardly outside the crematorium. Brutus had apparently slept through the entire ruckus. I'd have thought that our spell had affected him as well, except that he let out a tiny miaow when we got inside, followed by a half-hearted demand for food. I reached back and gave him a quick scratch behind his ears and he immediately fell asleep again. Oh, to be a cat.

We didn't have to wait long. Dusk had now fallen and the headlights of the approaching vehicle could be seen for miles. Winter and I hunkered down and waited. I couldn't decide whether I wanted this to be Blackbeard – Hal Prescott – or not. It would be good to get this over and done with but I wasn't feeling my best. I had my doubts about Winter, as well. His right eye was puffing up and the skin around it was turning a vivid purple colour. He was probably in as much pain as I was. But if this really were Blackbeard, we couldn't afford to hide in the corner and lick our wounds. We would be forced to act.

'We're heroes,' I said aloud.

Winter shot me a look. 'With massive egos.'

I shrugged. 'False modesty is a waste of time. Besides, look at us. I'm covered in sick and you're covered in blood. We're both covered in bruises and could do with some serious medical attention. But we're still here and we're still going to take on Blackbeard. If we can find him.'

Winter's response was quiet. 'What other choice is there?'

The car pulled into the car park and came to a halt. 'Hush,' Winter cautioned.

I nodded and slid further down in my seat. 'Stay down, Brutus,' I said unnecessarily.

The car's engine was switched off. Although it was difficult to tell what make it was given the poor light, the car was certainly large and expensive. That engine hadn't growled, it had purred. Dead pets paid well.

Winter and I held our breath but we needn't have bothered. Only one figure got out of the car and it definitely wasn't Blackbeard. Whoever this was, they were clean shaven, with a full head of hair and a far slighter build. Daddy, then. But where was his bearded bastard of a witch-killing son?

We waited until Prescott senior vanished into the main building then I turned on the taxi engine and drove us out of there, turning left at the crossroads.

'Maybe we should have stayed,' Winter said. 'Blackbeard is bound to show up sooner or later.'

'So are more police,' I pointed out. 'Prescott isn't going to hang around and wait for that lot to wake up, is he? He's going to call in the cavalry. We need to skedaddle.'

Winter shook his head as if what we'd just done was only just starting to sink in. He passed a hand over his forehead. 'What a mess.'

I reached across and patted his arm. 'Look on the bright side. You can't get fired.'

He didn't seem entirely appeased.

I flicked on the indicator to turn right. A heartbeat later, I changed my mind. 'Do you see that?' I said.

'See what?' Winter grunted. His former life was probably still passing in front of his eyes.

'That building in front of us. It's pretty swanky, right?'

He glanced over. 'I suppose.'

'And it looks new?'

Winter peered more closely out of the window. 'Yes.'

I grinned. 'Raphael Winter, you are a very lucky man. If I weren't such a conscientious witch, we'd still be up the creek without a paddle. I've just found us a boat engine. If Mahomet won't come to the mountain…'

He was still confused. 'What on earth are you going on about?'

My grin widened. 'While you were snoozing, Alan the security guard mentioned that Blackbeard, aka Hal Prescott, lives in a swanky new apartment building. That, my friend, is a very swanky, very new apartment building. And it just happens to be a few miles from the family crematorium. Handy, huh?' I threw him a sidelong look. 'What's that gut instinct telling you now?'

Winter sat up straight and flexed his fingers. 'Ivy Wilde,' he breathed. 'I'm head over heels in love with you.'

I beamed.

Chapter Sixteen

We were on a clock; it wouldn't be long before the police were dispatched to this address. Somehow I didn't think you could send half a squadron to sleep and not expect every stone not to be turned by the police officers who were still awake. If they had any common sense, they'd come here eventually. In any case, even if time weren't of the essence, I'd lost patience with working surreptitiously. Winter obviously felt the same. We didn't even discuss the matter; we simply strolled through the front doors, ignoring the well-placed CCTV cameras and walked up to the sleepy-looking security guard at the front desk.

'Hal Prescott,' I said. 'Where is he?'

The guard blinked and stifled a yawn. Then he took in our vomity, bloody, bruisy appearances and sat up straight. 'Er, who are you?'

It was Winter who answered. 'Adeptus Exemptus Raphael Winter from the Hallowed Order of Magical Enlightenment. We need to find Hal Prescott immediately.' He leaned forward. 'It's a matter of life and death.'

Our less than salubrious appearances must have added credence to Winter's words. The guard was more than eager to help us out. 'Of course, sir,' he said. His cheeks turned bright red. 'I mean Adeptus Exceptus. Exemptus. Shit. Sorry.' He coughed. 'Shit.'

'Don't worry about it,' I said. 'Civilians often struggle when confronted by us for the first time.'

He nodded vigorously, obviously relieved that I'd

given him reason to act like a stumbling numpty, and turned to his computer. Unfortunately, his relief didn't last long. After a few frantic key taps, his brows knitted together anxiously. 'I'm afraid, Mr Prescott isn't here. He's informed us that he'll be away for the next week at least.'

A whole week? My stomach dropped. Whatever Blackbeard was planning, we could be certain that it would be catastrophic. His supposed interview as part of Clare's coven was on Tuesday; that left at least five more days for him to cause even more havoc and kill even more people.

'Do you have a mobile phone number for him?'

More key taps. The guard swallowed. 'No.'

Winter and I exchanged glances. 'Then,' he said, 'you're going to have to let us into his flat. We need to search it without further delay.'

'I can't...' The guard tugged at his collar. 'I don't think I can do that. You need a warrant.'

Winter folded his arms across his broad chest. 'You're right. It's important to stick to the letter of the law. The trouble is that lives are in danger and we don't have time to get the warrant we need.' He paused. 'Why don't you just tell us which flat belongs to Mr Prescott? We'll take things from there. Any measures we take will occur without your permission or your knowledge.'

I was impressed. Winter didn't treat the guard like an idiot and didn't deny what we were here to do. He did, however, speak with a smooth command that was difficult to ignore and his words had the clear ring of sincerity. 'If we do nothing, people *will* die,' he said softly. 'I guarantee it. You have the chance to help us stop that from happening.'

The guard swallowed. 'Okay. Yes. I can tell you which flat is his. But I can't know about you going in there, alright? I need this job.'

'All you're doing is telling us which number he lives in. That's all. No one will ever know.' Winter's voice dropped. 'Most real heroes are unsung.'

The guard gave an almost imperceptible nod of his head. 'Twenty-three,' he whispered. 'Mr Prescott lives at number twenty-three.'

'You're a brave man,' Winter said. 'Thank you.' He whirled round and headed for the stairs.

'There's a lift waiting,' I said. 'It'll be faster.'

I expected Winter to disagree but he didn't. He simply nodded and joined me, stepping inside the lift and hitting the button for the second floor. The doors closed smoothly and he turned to me. 'I lied to that guard,' he said quietly. 'It's not something I make a habit of. I'm sorry, Ivy. I don't usually pretend to be someone I'm not.'

I blinked. For a moment, I wasn't even sure what he was referring to. Then I realised he'd pretended that he was still with the Order. 'It was for the greater good, Rafe. You were right. If we can't find and stop Blackbeard, people will die. The end justifies the means. And you don't ever have to apologise to me, not for something like this.'

'I won't compromise who I am,' Winter said. 'The end does not always justify the means. Lose your morals, regardless of the reasons why, and you lose yourself.'

'You've not lost your morals. It was a tiny lie, Rafe. You *were* Adeptus Exemptus, after all.'

'It was still wrong.'

I wasn't so sure. 'We have to find Blackbeard,' I said helplessly.

The lift doors opened. 'Yes,' he said quietly. 'We do.'

He strode out of the lift with his long-legged gait,

moving even faster than he did normally. It was a struggle for me to keep up but fortunately we found number twenty-three quickly. Rather than have Winter agonise further over breaking and entering as well as lying, I jumped in and cast a rune to open Blackbeard's door. The adrenaline coursing through my veins was a little too strong, however, and the magic slammed the door open with such force that the damn thing almost fell off its hinges.

'Are you okay, Ivy?' Winter asked.

I nodded. 'Yep.'

'If you're not...'

I stepped across Blackbeard's threshold. 'I'm absolutely fine.' Then I marched in, ready to do battle.

If I were interior designer for a psychopathic murderer, I decided, I would probably aim to produce somewhere that looked exactly like this. The floors were dark tiles lined with dark grout. Slit someone's throat here and you wouldn't have to worry about staining anything. One quick mop and you'd never know that blood had been spilt. I thought of Winter's desire to scrub away at my bathroom grouting. Next time I got the chance, I would get a black Sharpie and colour it all in to look like this. Job done.

The walls, from the corridor to the living room and the bedroom beyond, were all painted in a stark white. I supposed that some people would have described the style as minimalist. To my untrained eye, it looked depressing. Coupled with the unsheathed samurai sword hanging on a wall, together with the gleaming twin knife blades hanging opposite, there was more than a pinch of the sinister.

'It's very ... clean,' I said finally, gazing round the pristine, empty surfaces. How could anyone live like this?

Winter grunted. From the expression on his face,

even he seemed to think this place was a step too far.

The kitchen was all stainless steel and more shiny black marble stuff. There wasn't so much as a kettle on display. Winter began to open drawers and cupboards but nothing seemed to take his interest. I left him to it and ambled over to a wall of smoky mirrors. There wasn't a single smear anywhere. I shook my head in amazement. If I lived here, it would take less than an hour for them to become permanently streaked with a combination of grease, dust and goodness knows what else.

It rankled that we'd been able to stroll in here so easily. Blackbeard thought very highly of himself. He obviously expected someone to look for the murdered coven members sooner or later, hence the booby traps he'd left on their doors but there had been nothing preventing our entry here. He didn't think that anyone would be smart enough to catch up to him – or maybe he didn't care. It wasn't as if there was much lying around to give us clues about what he was planning next.

Irritated by both the cleanliness and Blackbeard's apparent arrogance, I exhaled onto the mirror, steaming up as large a section as I could. While Winter's huffing from the kitchen grew louder, I used the tip of my index finger to draw a smiley face. Whatever happened, I liked the idea of Blackbeard sitting on his perfect white-leather sofa and suddenly realising that someone had been in here and marred his Zen bachelor pad with a cheeky smile.

For effect, I reached over to add two bushy eyebrows. As I did so and pressed down on the mirror, I realised that it felt loose. The mirror moved when I touched it. I knocked on the smooth surface; it definitely sounded hollow.

'Rafe!' I called. 'Something is here!'

He was by my side in an instant. 'What?'

'This mirror,' I told him. 'It's concealing something. There's definitely something behind here. It's a cabinet or a false wall.'

He stretched out his fingertips, splaying them across the glass. There was a faint clunking sound when he pressed down and he sucked in a breath. 'There must be a way to open it properly.'

I nodded. It is one thing to use magic to open a door when you can see the mechanism and understand how it works, but you can't just throw a spell at something you don't understand and expect it to do what you want. Life doesn't work like that and neither does magic.

I took a step back and looked around. 'There has to be a remote control or a button. The glass is too clean. There's no way Blackbeard uses his grubby mitts to open his bat cave. It would ruin his perfect aesthetic.'

Winter pursed his lips in agreement and we started searching. There wasn't much lying around; in theory, it shouldn't have taken long to find the secret key.

'We know his name now,' Winter said, as he delved in between the sofa seat cushions. 'You don't need to keep calling him Blackbeard.'

'Yeah,' I said. 'But Hal sounds like a friendly guy. The sort you'd invite round to a barbecue and let play with your kids. Blackbeard is an evil bastard.'

'I don't think we're likely to forget that anytime soon.'

Indeed. 'He's as calculating and clever as he is cold.' I didn't think I'd ever come across anyone who was genuinely evil before. Since meeting Winter, I'd met a whole range of plonkers, from selfish and nasty to stupid and self-centred. There had been thieves and murderers and general evil-doers. But while each of them had committed evil acts, there had been a certain method to their madness. They all had motives for doing what they did; I couldn't condone their actions but I could understand them a little. Blackbeard was different – there was a wellspring of darkness inside him. Yes, he purportedly killed Clare's coven because he hated witches but I was sure that was an excuse. The man needed to justify his actions to himself but I'd lay money on the theory that he just enjoyed killing.

With that thought bouncing around my head, I straightened up and abandoned my bid to search for a key to open Blackbeard's den. No, I didn't know how this door worked but I did know how glass worked.

I raised both hands. 'Winter?' I said calmly.

'Yes?'

'Duck.' I flicked out the rune and the glass instantly shattered into a million pieces. I have to admit that the effect was pretty amazing although the sound was bloody loud. So much for my smiley face. Oh well. I rarely did subtle – Blackbeard would definitely know we'd been here now.

Winter didn't move a muscle. 'You just broke a mirror,' he said.

'Yep.'

'A very large mirror.'

'Yep.'

'That's seven years bad luck.'

I glanced at him. 'Not according to you.'

'I might not have faith in superstitions, Ivy, but you do.' Winter's blue eyes swept across the damage. 'And both the police and Arcane Branch won't be happy about what we've done to their crime scene.'

'Neither the police nor Arcane Branch have got as close to Blackbeard as we have.' I sniffed. 'They'll just have to deal with it. And I have faith in you. That will have to be enough.' I pointed. 'Look. There's the secret door.' I stalked up and kicked it open. I didn't do that for effect – my hands were shaking so much that I didn't think I could turn the handle.

'We'll catch him,' Winter said. 'His days are already numbered.'

I just nodded and walked into the claustrophobic darkness in front of us. It was Winter's spell that lit the small room. To be honest, when I saw what Blackbeard had been concealing, I almost asked him to extinguish the light. If the flat outside was pristine, this was its natural opposite. After the bleakness of the other rooms, it almost hurt to look at it.

Every inch of wall space was covered with something. In some places, he'd pinned up yellowing news articles, all of them related to either magic, witches or the Order in some way. None of the headlines were positive. Other parts of the walls were plastered with sticky notes of all shapes, sizes and colours. Random words and numbers were scribbled on them, some as chilling reminders like 'track down strong rope' and others which made no sense whatsoever such as 'here 6731'.

There were haphazard piles of books on the floor and several plastic bags that seemed to contain clothing. In the furthest corner, there was a towering stack of ornate boxes and urns similar to the container in which we'd found Clare's ashes. Winter reached for one while I suppressed a shudder. He flipped open the lid and breathed out before showing me that it was empty.

'There are still three missing coven members,' he said. 'Their remains have to be somewhere.'

I flattened my mouth into a thin line. 'There's been no sign of their spirits yet. They might not be here.'

Winter started searching through the rest of the collection. 'Maybe there's enough of Blackbeard's null nature lingering here to hold the ghosts at bay. Or maybe he's taken them with him. We have to check, though.' His eyes met mine. 'Their ashes are all the evidence we need against him.'

You could take the witch out of the Order but you couldn't take the Order out of the witch. He was still thinking like an Arcane Branch officer. The truth was that we already knew Blackbeard was guilty and finding the rest of the coven's remains would prove nothing. It would, however, give their families some small comfort. All the same, Winter still desperately wanted to do things by the book; he really was as orderly as the Order itself. I hoped he realised sooner rather than later that he belonged with them as much as he belonged with me.

I stepped back to give him more room, inadvertently knocking over one of the book piles as I did so. I was about to kick them out of the way but one of the titles caught my eye. I knelt down and examined it. Well, that answered one question.

'Check this out,' I said. 'It's a book on pagan black spots and their potential effects. It's got to be at least a hundred years old.' I flicked through the pages. 'And there's a bookmark in the section on Wistman's Wood.'

Winter gave me a grim look. 'He's planned everything from the get go, hasn't he?'

I bit my lip. 'There's a second bookmark.' I turned the pages, sucking in a breath when I scanned through the text. 'Uffington White Horse. That's less than an hour away from Oxford.'

'It's the gigantic horse shape cut into the hillside. Is that pagan?' Winter asked. 'I thought it was just an Anglo-Saxon emblem commemorating a battle.'

'No one knows for sure. But it does say here that nearby is the spot where St George apparently killed the dragon. There's a bald patch where the dragon's blood was spilt. It's said that nothing can ever grow there.'

'Sounds pretty damned mystical to me,' he said. 'Just like Wistman's Wood.'

'Yeah.' I met his eyes. 'It can't be a coincidence that he's made a note of this place. It's so close to Oxford and the Order headquarters.'

'Look through the other books. Maybe we can get more clues about what he's planning.'

I nodded and started to crouch down. I was halfway to the floor, however, when my legs gave way completely and I ended up sprawled on my arse. Winter opened his mouth to say something and was forestalled by several loud shouts coming from further back in Blackbeard's flat.

'It took the cavalry less time than I expected to make this connection,' Winter muttered.

'Blackbeard's dad was probably worried about his son,' I said. 'Either that or he suspects him. His own flesh and blood is a mass murderer – he must have some inkling about his son's true nature. Maybe that's why he really hired the security guard.'

Winter nodded and walked to the door, his palms splayed outwards to indicate he was unarmed. Unfortunately it didn't seem to do much good; he was immediately body-slammed backwards.

'Hey!' I protested. Before I could get to my feet, however, a blank-faced, armed police officer waved a gun in my face.

'Stay down,' he snarled.

'But...'

'Secure the area!' He made some complicated gesture with his hands; if he'd been a witch, they would have conjured up an effective rune. Instead of a spell, however, another suited and booted officer appeared, yelling for me to lie face down on the ground. For a split second I was tempted to cast a spell and get rid of this lot but I knew that it was probably wiser to cooperate. That was a very big gun and I'd already been in one more fight tonight than I'd planned. There are only so many times a girl can get knocked out before she ends up back in hospital. Right now I didn't have time for that, which was a shame because hospital beds were pretty darned comfy.

There was the crunch of glass as several more officers stormed the area. Actually, forget about Blackbeard's father; this was down to breaking the mirror. Seven years' bad luck, I thought morosely. Starting right here.

We might still be in middle England but these officers were a lot warier and better trained than their counterparts at the crematorium. The first thing they did was to bind Winter's and my hands behind our backs with clever knotting that prevented our fingers from moving. Even most witches weren't that canny. I stopped admiring them when they yanked me sharply to my feet and all but dragged me back into Blackbeard's living room and flung me on his sofa. Down. Up. Down. I wasn't a yo-yo. They ought to make up their minds.

There was the faint ping of the lift opening followed by the most godawful yowling and screeching. It got louder and louder until three red-robed Arcane Branch witches appeared with Brutus in a cage.

'We have secured the familiar,' the nearest one said. This was followed by a nervous glance towards Winter, who'd been dragged over next to me. He might be tied up for the second time tonight but these witches were still scared of him. We could work with that.

Winter had obviously had the same thought. 'Adeptus Minor Green,' he said, in his best shiver-inducing voice. 'Ms Wilde and I are both here for the same reason as you – to track down the killer of the Dorset coven. This is his place of residence. We entered it expecting that—'

'Shut up.' Despite his harsh command, Green's voice still quavered. It didn't help that Brutus was throwing himself against the bars of the cage and shrieking feline misery at a level of decibels that would normally require ear protection.

'Brutus,' I said, hoping for once he'd listen to me. 'Just be quiet for now. Please?'

He paused for a moment, his yellow eyes gazing at me from behind the metal bars. 'Bitches.'

When he realised who had spoken, the burly police officer nearest me let out a high-pitched shriek that was even louder than Brutus had managed. Impressive. Brutus shut up and stared. Before things got completely out of hand, I tried to speak up. 'Look, guys, we're all on the same side here. Let's—'

'Don't say another word.'

'But—'

'I mean it,' the policeman threatened. 'Say just one word and you'll regret it.'

'Sir—'

'I told you!' he screamed in my face.

Alrighty: perhaps he was being serious about the no-talking thing. Winter nudged me with his elbow, which was pretty unnecessary. I had the message, loud and very clear.

Chapter Seventeen

There was no waterboarding or strip searches. No mention of a lawyer or even a single question. Winter, Brutus and I were simply dumped unceremoniously in a cell together and left to cool our heels.

Unfortunately, we were not alone. I'd been enjoying the spiritual peace and quiet, so it was alarming to see how many ghosts were hanging around. I guess word had got out that they had a captive audience.

'I heard,' a plump woman shouted, 'that you don't care about Grenville's list. That you're helping less worthy spirits to pass.' She put her hands on her hips. 'Well, I died before my time. Anaphylactic shock. I'm not even supposed to be dead, let alone cursed. My son was barely seven when he said he wished I'd never find any peace in death and that was only because I asked him to clean his room.'

'That was your own fault, Martha!' bellowed another woman, who had a knife sticking out of her back. My eyes were drawn unwillingly towards it. 'You deserved it.'

'Don't listen to either of them,' advised an elderly man. 'I've been stuck here for over three hundred years. Grenville's list makes perfect sense. I'm near the top. Just help me and…'

'You bastard!' The two female ghosts rounded on him. 'You only died last month! He's lying.'

I put my fingers in my ears, closed my eyes and sang, 'Lalalalalalalala.' Then I opened one eye. Damn it – they were still there although they'd stopped arguing in favour of staring at me as if I were mad. Brutus and Winter had the same expressions as the ghosts pasted on their faces.

'Look,' I said. 'I will help you out when I can. But can't you see that I can't do anything right now? I have bigger problems to worry about.'

'Bigger problems?' the plump ghost shrieked. 'Bigger than death?'

'You're already dead,' I said through gritted teeth. 'I'm sorry, but there it is. I can't change that. There are others who are still alive who might soon be dead like you if we don't stop a killer in his tracks. I will help you pass over but not today. Come back at a later date.'

'You have to promise. You have to promise to help us.'

I sighed. 'I promise.'

She pouted. 'But...'

'Let's go, Martha,' said the other woman. 'Another time.'

'Yes.'

'You won't help us today.'

'No.'

'But you will another time.'

'Yes.'

There were several grumbles but they all vanished. I breathed out and turned to Winter. 'This sucks,' I told him flatly.

He ran a hand through his hair. 'Yeah.'

'We could magic our way out of here,' I suggested.

'There are witches here. They'd stop us in heartbeat.'

Actually, they wouldn't. Both Winter and I were stronger than any of them, even in our weakened states. I picked at the drying vomit on my top and flicked it off, vaguely disgusted with myself. He was no doubt blaming our incarceration on his flagrant rule-breaking. That showed what he knew.

'If I hadn't broken that mirror, we wouldn't be here now,' I said.

'Bitch,' Brutus muttered. Just this once, I was tempted to agree with him.

'The mirror had nothing to do with it,' Winter said.

'Seven years, Rafe. Seven more years of this.' I lay down on the narrow bed and closed my eyes. 'I'm going to sleep. Wake me up in 2024.'

Winter put an arm round me. When I didn't twitch, he sat on the edge of the bed. I scooted over to give him room and he lay down. It was a tight fit but he was snuggly and warm. I grinned to myself. By comforting me, he'd stop worrying that all this was his fault. It was a win-win situation. I relaxed and took advantage of the peace and quiet.

'Food,' Brutus demanded.

'It might have escaped your notice, Brutus,' I murmured, 'but I'm not in a position to get you any food right now. You'll have to be patient.' My nostrils tickled as the smell of tuna drifted over.

'Aw,' said the irritatingly familiar tones of Tarquin, 'you two look so sweet together.'

'Food,' Brutus repeated.

Winter and I sighed simultaneously. I opened one eye. Tarquin didn't just have tuna with him. That looked like pizza. Damn him for being thoughtful.

'Food,' Brutus said, clearly hoping this was third time lucky.

I shrugged. My stomach was already growling. If you can't beat 'em, join 'em. 'Food,' I said.

Winter sat up. 'Foooooood,' he groaned.

Tarquin looked from Brutus to me to Winter. 'You know you three are really strange sometimes.' He offered a disarming smile. 'But I aim to please.' He passed through the bowl of tuna and the pizza then, as we started wolfing down the food, he jangled a set of keys. 'I'm not just here bringing you a late-night snack. I'm here to free you.' His smile grew. 'You can thank me later.'

I crammed more cheesy goodness into my mouth. Anything to avoid having to speak. Being rescued by Tarquin Villeneuve was almost more than I could bear.

'The good news is we know where Hal Prescott is. He'll be picked up before you can say "thank you very much, Tarquin darling".'

I swallowed. 'What? Where is he?'

Tarquin shook his head. 'No, you say "thank you very much, Tarquin darling" first. I am your saviour after all.'

I wiped my greasy fingers on my jeans and stood up, ambled over to him and gazed at him through the bars. 'Tarquin, if you don't tell us exactly where Blackbeard is, or what is going on, I will reach through here and throttle you.' I smiled pleasantly just to show I meant it.

He rolled his eyes. 'You're the one behind bars, Ivy. You're the one who...'

Winter stood and walked up beside me. Tarquin's voice faltered. 'Fine,' he snapped. 'The investigation team did really well. They found a book in Blackbeard's flat with a bookmark indicating that he is interested in Uffington. There's an ancient drawing of a white horse cut into a hillside there which...'

I passed a hand over my eyes. For goodness' sake. 'Yeah, yeah. We know that. How do you know where Blackbeard himself is, though?'

'Because the car registered in his name has been located at a small hotel on the outskirts of Uffington and he's already checked in as a guest.' Tarquin's voice was smug. 'We have the place surrounded. Blackbeard is ours.' He rubbed his chin. 'But I've suggested we rename him The Bearded Butcher. I think it will stick. It has a better ring to it than Blackbeard.'

'Tarquin, wait. You know you can't use magic against him, right?'

He scoffed. 'Of course! We all know that. Armed police are going to do the heavy lifting. It'll be the same team that brought you two in. They're highly talented and more than ready to save the day. With our input, of course.'

'"Our" referring to...?'

'Me. Us. The Order.' Tarquin's expression was blank. 'Who else?'

'Who else indeed?' Winter murmured.

'Tarq,' I said slowly, 'this operation is taking place over a hundred miles away.'

He bobbed his head. 'Yes.'

'But instead of being there, you're here.'

'Everyone else is afraid of you. Once I've released you and completed the paperwork, I will be joining the others in Uffington.'

I scratched my head. 'Hmmm. And how much paperwork is there?'

Winter leaned his head down towards me. 'Oh, there will be a lot,' he said. 'And you have to take great care completing it. It has to be done by hand, you see.'

I smirked. 'The Order does like everything shipshape and ticked off, don't they? You'll be sorting out that paperwork and crossing the Ts all night.'

'It won't take me that long!' Tarquin said. 'I'll still have plenty of time to make it to Uffington to help with the final arrest. You two won't. You're forbidden from going anywhere near there.'

Whether Tarquin was being kept out of the way or not, that was unwelcome news. Winter stiffened and shoved his hands into pockets, probably so we couldn't see his fists clenching. 'What do you mean,' he growled, 'we're forbidden?'

A slow grin spread across Tarquin's face. It wasn't exactly malicious; Tarquin was self-serving and wholly selfish but he didn't take pleasure in others' unhappiness per se, although he did seem to be getting a certain amount of perverse enjoyment out of this situation. I suspected that was because of my involvement rather than Winter's.

'Your reaction is not unexpected,' he declared. He reached into his pocket and, with a dramatic flourish, produced a mobile phone. He hit dial then turned the phone onto speaker, holding it up so that we could both see the screen. Apparently, we were waiting for 'Ippy' to answer.

'This is Ipsissimus Collings.'

'Ipsissimus! This is Tarquin. I'm here with Raphael Winter and Ivy Wilde. They seem somewhat perturbed by the order to stay away from Uffington.'

'Indeed,' the Ipsissimus said, sounding entirely unsurprised. 'Pass them the phone then piss off.'

Tarquin blinked. 'But…'

'Young man, you have a lot of paperwork to complete. You should probably make a start on it so you can finish it by morning.'

I didn't try to stop myself from smiling. With a flash of sulky annoyance, Tarquin passed the phone through the bars to Winter and stomped off.

Clearly not in the mood for niceties, Winter snapped, 'Is Villeneuve correct?' he demanded. 'Have we been banned from going to Uffington and confronting Blackbeard?'

'I believe,' the Ipsissimus returned calmly, 'that right now you're in a jail cell and banned from going anywhere.'

'You know what I mean.'

'The operation to bring in Hal Prescott is a joint one between the police and the Order. As you and Ms Wilde are neither, I can no longer involve you. You've caused me considerable problems by getting yourselves locked up.'

'*We* found Blackbeard,' I said, jumping in before Winter could say something he'd really regret.

'You did. And, believe me, Ms Wilde, your actions have not gone unnoted. But you both assaulted a group of police officers. You broke into a flat and destroyed property that may be key to this investigation. If it were down to me, I would maintain your involvement but my hands are tied.' He paused. 'And there's really no need to worry. Hal Prescott will be safely in custody before long. The hotel he's in is surrounded and we're being very cautious because we know he uses booby-trapped explosives. He will not be hurting anyone else.'

I looked at Winter. It was galling to be left out of the loop when we'd invested so much, but we were hurting. He could barely open his right eye. My head hurt and I hadn't gone this long without a decent night's sleep since I had colic at the tender age of one. Maybe this was a good thing.

'Are you doing this to make a point?' Winter ground out. 'That I should return to the Order then I won't be kept out of investigations?'

'You *should* return to the Order,' the Ipsissimus said frankly. 'But I am not so scheming, Raphael. You know me better than that.'

Winter's eyes flashed to mine. 'I thought I did,' he said, with more than a hint of darkness. I reached out and squeezed his arm. He still seemed determined to take my almost-death more personally than I did. 'I'm no longer so sure.'

'I'm not omnipotent. The lengths you have gone to in order to get what we needed went beyond what I can manage. I've had to pull in just about every favour I could to get the pair of you released. There's nothing more I can do. For what it's worth, the Hallowed Order of Magical Enlightenment will forever be indebted to you. And, from the bottom of my own heart, I thank you.'

'Let it go, Rafe,' I said quietly. 'They have it in hand. They'll bring Blackbeard in. By the time we get home and get cleaned up, it'll be morning.' I sighed. 'We're meeting your parents for Sunday dinner.' I was only reminding him of that for his sake, not mine.

Winter ran a hand over his face. 'Okay,' he said. 'Okay.' He hesitated. 'Tell them to be careful though. Blackbeard – Hal Prescott – is smart. Don't underestimate what he's capable of.'

'I'm still in Oxford but I'll be sure to pass that along," the Ipsissimus said. 'Go and get some rest. You both deserve it.'

Amen to that.

Chapter Eighteen

I'm not the most lithe person in the universe but I don't usually walk like a robot from an old seventies sci-fi television show either. Now, every part of me ached. I wasn't sure my legs would ever bend at the knee properly again. I had bruises in places I'd never known existed. There was a particularly colourful one tracing its way across my collarbone and up my neck, wrapping around my skin like some kind of designer scarf.

Standing next to Winter, however, I looked the picture of health. He was doing his best not to show his pain but, given the black eye and the bandages covering the worst of his cuts, that was a pointless effort. I'd taken painkillers to get rid of the worse of the throbbing pain in my skull after Winter had used his magic to assure me that my slight concussion was nothing to worry about, but they made me woozy and thick-tongued. About the only positive was that I'd had a long, hot shower so at least I no longer smelled of vomit. I was now wearing my only smart dress – a green frilly concoction that I suspected made me look like the Incredible Hulk even when I wasn't covered in bruises – while Winter had on an immaculate black suit. The pair of us looked ridiculous.

'We don't have do this,' Winter said. 'My family aren't monsters. They'll understand if we cancel.'

I grabbed Winter's hand to stop myself from running back home with a scream of delight. This was going to happen sooner or later; if I did it now, looking like I'd been in a fight with Godzilla and sounding as if I'd downed a bottle of vodka, perhaps I wouldn't be invited back. One could always hope. And I had my secret weapon. I raised a pointed eyebrow at Brutus, for once trotting by my side as if he were the most perfectly behaved cat in the world.

'It'll be fine,' I said, sounding far more confident that I was. 'I can't wait to meet your parents.'

'Liar.'

Yeah, okay. I offered him a lopsided smile and shrugged one shoulder – it hurt too much to raise both.

Winter bent his head and, ever so gently, kissed my cheek. I still felt a thrill of delight zip through me at the touch of his lips. 'Thank you, Ivy. I do appreciate this.' He smiled. 'Wait here and I'll check they're ready for us. My mother hates being surprised.'

She was going to love his bruised face then. I glanced at Brutus. 'Now remember,' I whispered. 'You don't do anything until I give you the signal. I might even *not* give you the signal at all. This might all be lovely and wonderful and flowery and sweet. But just in case, you stay on your claws.'

Brutus blinked up at me with overly innocent eyes.

'You do remember what the signal is, right?' I tugged on my right earlobe. 'When I do that, you spring into action. Got that?'

'Food.'

I counted to five in my head. 'Do this for me, Bruty baby, and you can have all the food you want. I promise. I'll even make the trip to that shop on the other side of town to get those fishy treats you like so much.'

Brutus didn't say anything else but he gave a loud purr. That was the best answer I was going to get.

Winter popped his head out of the door. 'We're all good,' he said. He held out his arm. 'You'll love my family, Ivy.'

I took his arm. Mmm. I had my doubts. If I made it

out of here without any more bruises, I'd count that as a win. I shook out my hair, drew in a deep breath and walked into Winter's ancestral home with my head held high. It couldn't be that bad.

The first thing I noticed upon crossing the threshold was the smell: old-fashioned beeswax mixed with the aroma of home-baked bread. I swallowed. The kind of person who kneaded their own dough was not the kind of person I normally had much in common with. Didn't Winter's parents know that supermarkets sold bread in handy sliced loaves?

The floor – a heavy cream carpet that my feet immediately sank into – was spotless. Winter gestured at my shoes and started taking off his own. Cool. It might ostensibly be to avoid tracking in dirt but the action made me feel more relaxed. Perhaps I should have come in my pyjamas.

There was a great deal of shiny mahogany, from the ornate banister framing the staircase to my right to an old-fashioned bureau and various side tables on my left. Yes, there was a lot of furniture but this was a big house; there was no sense of stark bleakness as there had been in Blackbeard's place, but this place didn't seem cluttered either. I thought of my own wobbly pieces, most of which had been flatpack and inevitably had several screws missing, and grinned to myself.

A couple appeared. It didn't take a genius to know who they were. The man possessed the same stiff spine that I'd often observed in Winter, coupled with a moustache which had been waxed to within an inch of its life. Although he was retired, his smartly pressed jacket still bore the medals that he must have won during his military career. The woman had the same brilliant blue eyes as Winter, together with a remarkably unlined face. Either she'd been dedicated enough to use cold cream every day since she was about three years old, or I could look forward to Winter's skin remaining soft and fresh whilst I gradually got more and more wrinkled. Then I blinked as I realised what I'd been thinking. I completely certain we were going to grow old together. Well, well, well.

Winter's mother held out her arms. 'You must be Ivy. I'm so thrilled to finally meet you. I'm Sophia. This is George.' She drew me into a tight hug which, I had to admit, was not what I'd expected. 'Raphael has told us so much about you.'

My stomach dropped. Which parts exactly? Had he told them that I was often too lazy to walk to the end of the road to buy milk, so I had an arrangement with one of the kids who lived in a nearby flat? Had he mentioned that sometimes I turned my underwear inside out so I could wear it for another day without washing it? Maybe, I thought worriedly, he'd told them about the time I'd watched five episodes of *Antiques Roadshow* in a row because I didn't know where the remote control was and I couldn't be bothered to look for it.

I forced a smile. 'All good, I hope!'

She smiled back and said nothing. Uh oh.

George, Winter's father, obviously wasn't the hugging type. I supposed I should be grateful he didn't salute; instead, he offered me his hand and, when I took it, squeezed mine until I was certain it was about to drop off. 'So,' he said, 'you're a witch.'

Retrieving my poor fingers from his grip, I managed a nod. 'Yes.'

'But you're not in the Order.'

'No.'

He regarded me with sharp eyes. 'You couldn't handle the discipline?'

'Father!' Winter said, his brow creasing.

'Something like that,' I murmured.

By my feet, Brutus let out a small miaow. George glared icily down at him. 'That is not Princess Parma Periwinkle.'

'No,' Winter said easily. 'She's off running an errand for me. She can sneak into hard-to-reach areas so I've sent her off to get some milk thistle. There's a particular strain I'm after which I think will work wonderfully in a new spell I'm developing.'

'This creature is not running an errand for you?' George asked me.

I tried to imagine what Brutus's response would be if I asked him to hunt for a particular herb in some godforsaken corner of the country. He'd probably return with a pile of stinging nettles and leave them in my bed so he could piss himself laughing when I tried to go to sleep. 'Uh no. I don't tend to use herblore much. I'm more of a rune girl.'

Winter's father looked distinctly underwhelmed.

Sophia cleared her throat. 'Let's all go and sit down, shall we? Ivy, would you like a cup of tea? Dinner won't be for another couple of hours yet.'

The words were out of my mouth before I could stop them. 'I would bloody love a cup,' I said. Then, rather belatedly, I winced. 'I mean, that would be lovely. Thank you.'

She quirked an eyebrow in a mannerism I instantly recognised. Unfortunately I couldn't tell whether she was amused or horrified because she was a lot harder to read than her son. And a whole lot scarier too. I think it was because she kept smiling at me.

We were led into what I think was a drawing room. I'd never been in a drawing room before but, now that I was standing in one, I had no doubt that is what it was. Carefully taking a seat in a high-backed chair that was considerably older than all of us in this room, I felt incredibly uncomfortable – but I still couldn't prevent myself from letting out a groan at taking the weight off my feet.

'Make yourself at home,' George said, flicking his hand in the air.

Thank goodness. I slumped back and began to raise my legs to tuck them underneath me. When I saw the expression on his face, I changed my mind. That hadn't been a literal 'make yourself at home'; I couldn't get cold pizza out of the fridge and demand to know where the television was.

I tried to ignore the fact that Winter's shoulders were shaking with silent laughter and looked round for Brutus. When I saw him poised to sharpen his claws on what looked like a very expensive chest, I sprang to my feet and grabbed him. He writhed in my arms and reached up with one paw to scratch my cheek. Fortunately, Winter was also standing and took him from me before I strangled him right then and there.

'Your familiar is … interesting,' George remarked politely.

Brutus's head shot up and he glared at him. With one twist of his body, he leapt out of Winter's arms and sauntered over to George. 'Pet,' he demanded.

Winter senior raised his eyebrows. 'Very interesting.' He leaned over and looked Brutus in the eye. 'I will pet you if you behave.'

Cat stared at man and man stared at cat. I had the uneasy feeling this was going to end badly. However, Brutus flopped onto his back and presented his belly. Winter's father did indeed reward him with a stroke. Okay, then.

Sophia bustled back in, carrying a silver tray. She set it down gently on a table. Seeing doilies and delicate china, my heart sank.

'How do you take your tea, Ivy?'

'Milk and four sugars.'

'Four sugars?' she asked, as if I wasn't sure of my own preferences.

'Yes.'

She pressed her lips together. I resisted telling her that I needed the energy after what Winter and I had been through. Given the visible bruises we were both sporting, our recent experiences were obvious but his parents had not commented on them. It made me wonder what Winter normally looked like when he showed up for formal dinners.

Sophia poured tea and passed me a cup and saucer. I generally like my tea in gigantic mugs I can wrap my hands around. This dainty little thing seemed like it would snap if I looked at it for too long and contained little more than a mouthful of tea. Great. I tried not to look too disappointed and murmured my thanks.

'I cannot believe it!' shrieked a high-pitched female voice. It shocked me so much that I jerked and spilled tea all over myself. I leapt up. It was scalding.

Sophia's eyes widened and she dashed over with a cloth. 'Is something the matter?'

The ghost glared at her. 'I'll say something's the matter! That's the best china! What are you doing giving this gerrl the best china?'

Winter watched me, fascination lighting his eyes. 'Who is it, Ivy? Who do you see?'

His mother dabbed at my front while the ghost put her hands on her hips. 'Well, that's hardly going to help, is it?' She tutted. Of course; where there was a ghost, there was bound to be tutting. 'My name is Hetty, for *his* information.'

I licked my lips. 'Uh, a woman called Hetty.'

Sophia stopped what she was doing and stared at me. 'Great-aunt Hetty?'

Winter coughed. 'Recently, Ivy has discovered that she can communicate with the dead.'

'And she's talking to Hetty?' Sophia's gaze swung from Winter back to me again. 'You're talking to *Hetty*?'

Hetty herself rolled her eyes. 'She never was the brightest gerrl.'

George looked mildly interested. 'Fascinating.'

Sophia started to back away very, very slowly. 'I don't believe it,' she whispered.

'Tell that gerrl that she should believe it. I've been haunting her for years. I know everything there is to know about her. I'll give away all her secrets.' Hetty smacked her lips with self-satisfaction. 'I know what happened at the Pickwick.'

I patted myself down to get rid of the remaining dregs of tea. 'It's lovely to meet you, Hetty. But this really isn't the time.'

'Not the time?' Hetty flounced. 'You're supposed to help me pass over, gerrl!'

'Apparently there's a queue.'

She glared at me. 'I'm practically family. I should be given special treatment.'

'Come and find me later,' I told her. I couldn't cope with the expression on Winter's mum's face for much longer. She either thought I was making all this up for some underhand reason of my own or I was someone to be avoided at all costs.

Hetty opened her mouth to speak. I drew myself up and gave her my best icy glare. 'Come and find me later,' I repeated. 'Or I will never help another ghost pass over ever again.' I almost meant it. Hetty, no longer quite the lady she was pretending to be, spat in my direction and disappeared. I breathed out. 'She's gone,' I said to no one in particular.

Sophia stared at me. 'What did she say?'

Uh… 'She wasn't very impressed that you'd given me the best china. And she called me gerrl a lot.' I made an attempt to roll my rs in the same way as Hetty.

Sophia breathed out. From the look in her eyes, she was starting to believe me. 'She did that a lot. Did she say anything else? Why is she here?'

Winter took over, briefly explaining the situation whereby ghosts wanted my help in clearing the curses that were holding them here. George, apparently already bored, nudged Brutus out of the way and got up to pour his own tea.

'I never met the woman,' he said to me in a shrugged aside. 'She died before I came on the scene.' He seemed unperturbed by all this. Maybe that was what came of a lifetime in the army; after a while nothing shocked you any more.

Sophia looked back at me. 'Did she say anything else?'

I wondered if she really wanted to know. I shrugged. It was hard to believe that Winter's mother could have any skeletons in her closet to worry about. 'She said she knew your secrets and all about Pickwick.' I shrugged. 'That was about it.'

Sophia's brow creased. 'Pickwick? I don't have the faintest idea what that is.'

George chuckled. 'It's not a what. It's a where.'

She shook her head. 'I still don't…' Her expression changed. 'Oh.' She sneaked a look at Winter.

'What?' he asked. 'What's Pickwick?'

'The Pickwick Inn to be precise,' George boomed, while his wife started blushing. 'I was on leave. Only had a few days before I was due out again and we were determined to make the most of it, weren't we, dear?'

Sophia choked slightly. 'I don't think this is the best time for this conversation. Maybe I should get out the baby photos.' She gave me a desperate glance. 'You'd like to see those, wouldn't you? I have a wonderful photo of Raphael in the most adorable little dungarees—'

'You were conceived there,' George said, choosing not to hear a single word that Sophia had said. She briefly closed her eyes while Winter's mouth dropped open. 'We weren't quite married at the time so we checked in as Mr and Mrs Smith. We thought we were being very clever.' He glanced at me. 'Those were the times we lived in. Things are much better for lovebirds like you two these days. It's a very different world.' His eyes dropped to my stomach. 'When is your baby due?'

Sophia gasped in horror while Winter began to cough. Even Brutus seemed to be laughing his feline head off. I didn't smile, however; I just stared at him.

'Didn't mean to offend you,' George said. A little voice in the back of my head told me he was telling the truth. Whatever. The chill was still descending down my spine as I thought about what he'd said.

I reached into my pocket and took out my phone. Very slowly, I found the number I needed and held the phone to my ear. George glanced askance at Winter. 'Is she calling a cab already? We've not even sat down to our starters and your mother's got her famous Yorkshire puddings ready for the mains.'

Winter finally managed to stop coughing. Something about my expression must have alerted him to the seriousness of the situation because he suddenly looked concerned. 'Ivy?' he asked.

I shook my head at him as Tarquin answered. 'Tarq,' I said. 'I need you to tell me one thing.'

'Ivy, darling! How are you? Are you busy? Because I'm still trying to finish off that paperwork and there's no movement yet with our murderer, so there might still be time for me to hoof it over there before the fireworks begin.'

'Has anyone actually seen him?'

'You mean Hal Prescott? No. Not since that initial sighting yesterday. He knows he's under surveillance, though, and that he can't go anywhere. The entire hotel is surrounded. He's in his room. I think the bomb squad is preparing to go in but—'

I interrupted him. 'Under what name did he check into the hotel?'

'Pardon?'

I tapped my foot. Winter stilled completely and watched me. 'The hotel in Uffington,' I repeated. 'What name did he register when he checked in?'

'Hal Prescott, of course. What other name would he use?'

I swallowed. 'I need you to double check. Are you absolutely sure he used his real name?'

'Yes,' he said, sounding hurt. 'I have the paperwork right here. He checked in yesterday morning at 11.32am. He…'

I hung up the phone and looked at Winter. 'Blackbeard is not in Uffington. If he was, he'd have used an assumed name like he did last time. He's still a step ahead of us and he's still toying with us. He's set us up, Rafe. It's the only explanation.'

Winter's blue eyes met mine. 'If he's not there, there's only one place he's likely to be.'

I nodded. 'The Order.'

Winter made for the door. 'Mum, Dad, thanks for the tea. We have to go.'

'Come on, Brutus!' I yelled, running after Winter. Given my limbs were still stiff and unyielding that wasn't a particularly easy feat.

Brutus let out a yowl. 'Mouse!'

It was our secret, pre-arranged signal designed to cause havoc and offer me an escape. His timing sucked. 'Not now, Brutus!' I yelled over my shoulder.

There was a faint mutter, 'Bitch,' then he came careening out after us. We had to get back to Oxford. Right now.

Chapter Nineteen

While I drove, Winter called just about everyone he knew. Unfortunately half of his ex-colleagues were already in Uffington and had their phones turned off so they didn't get distracted. The other half proved equally elusive. It seemed that no matter how hard Winter tried to reach them on the phone, they were screening his calls; he was either persona non grata or they were incredibly busy. Truthfully, either was possible. It was a requirement that all phones were checked in at the front of every Order building to avoid untoward accidents caused by magic and technology mixing when they shouldn't. It was a highly unlikely scenario but, if they did mingle, the ensuing explosions and catastrophic disasters would make Blackbeard's efforts to spread horror look like a five year old dressing up for Halloween.

'Phone the Ipsissimus,' I said, with my foot down to the floor. 'If his phone is with him, he'll take your call. He can't wait for you to make up your mind and go back to the Order.'

Winter's mouth flattened. 'He was the first person I tried.'

Oh. Well, that sucked. I threw out names, one after another. Winter left messages all over the place but there wasn't a soul picking up. When Eve didn't answer, it was clear that everyone we knew in the Order was either at Uffington or buried in meetings. Winter even tried Tarquin. His phone rang but he didn't pick up; that was probably my fault for hanging up on him mid-sentence earlier.

It was clearly time to take drastic action. 'Take my phone,' I said. 'Call Iqbal.'

'He's not in the Order, Ivy. He's not even a witch.'

'No,' I said. 'But he can get to the damn Order and find out what's happening.'

'Okay.' Winter dialled and I waited with bated breath. When Winter started speaking, my body sagged with relief. Finally someone was answering their damned phone.

'He's in Manchester,' Winter said. 'He's even further away than we are.'

I let out a strangled scream. I never should have broken that bloody mirror. There had to be some way of contacting the bloody Order, even if we had to set signal fires or send out carrier pigeons. There had to be a bloody way.

'Try the magic hotline,' I said finally. 'You'll be able to get through to someone on that number.' It was a helpline designed for non-witches to use when they required magical intervention. It was notoriously inefficient but we were running out of options.

'Good idea.' He nodded and found the number. After a moment or two, he swore violently.

'What's wrong?'

He turned the phone onto speaker. A tinny voice chimed out: '...press three if you believe you have triggered an omen. Press four if you have discovered a family member has magical abilities. Press five if...'

I passed a hand over my forehead. Good grief. 'Screw that,' I said. 'Call the police. Tell them it's an emergency and get them to the Order.'

Out of the corner of my eye, I saw Winter's expression grow even grimmer. 'They won't go. It won't matter what I say to them, the police won't interfere with anything that happens on Order grounds without direct orders from the Ipsissimus.'

'So pretend to be him! He won't mind! Not given the circumstances, anyway.'

'There's a code word. Only the Ipsissimus knows it.'

Bloody hell. Order geeks didn't half like making life difficult for themselves. Plonkers.

Winter pressed nine. Apparently this was for emergencies, although a few beats later the same recorded voice happily informed us that we were thirteenth in the queue but that our call was being taken very seriously. The melody for *I Put A Spell On You* kicked into action.

'Thirteenth,' I muttered under my breath. 'Of course we are.'

Winter opened his mouth, ready to tell me yet again that my superstition fears were nonsense, but clearly thought better of if it. No wonder, given our current predicament. Instead, he switched subjects while I continued to speed back down the motorway towards Oxford. Three speed cameras had already flashed us; that wouldn't go down well for my career as a taxi driver. I sighed. Whatever.

'What made you check?' he asked. 'About what name he'd registered under at the hotel?'

I ignored the angry gesture from the motorcyclist in the lane next to me as I overtook him and answered. 'It was always too easy. It's been niggling away at me that we know how clever Blackbeard is. We know what he's achieved so far. Would he really allow himself to be surrounded by both police and witches?' The heavy weight that had settled across my shoulders when I hung up on Tarquin increased. 'I should have thought of it earlier. I should have asked about it earlier.'

'Less than twenty-four hours ago, you were lying unconscious on the floor of a pet crematorium. Not to mention the fact that you're still recovering from Scotland.'

'I can't use either of those as an excuse.'

Winter looked at me sternly. 'This is not a one-man band, Ivy. It's not even a duet. There are hundreds of people involved in this operation. It's not your fault if we all believed he was in Uffington.'

I bit my lip. 'It feels like it is.'

The taxi's dashboard flashed an orange warning light. Arse. 'We need petrol,' I hissed in irritation.

'There's a service station coming up. Don't worry,' Winter said. 'We're getting closer to Oxford. We'll be there soon.'

'Let's just hope it'll be soon enough.'

The song still chiming out of Winter's phone came to an abrupt halt and the recorded voice broke in again. 'Your call is very important to us. You are now number fourteen in the queue.'

My knuckles turned white around the steering wheel. Throwing the phone out of the window would really not be helpful right now.

I slowed down, indicating left to pull off the motorway. At least the service station wasn't too busy and there wasn't a queue at the fuel pumps. As soon as I stopped the taxi, I leapt out to fill it up. There were still another sixty miles to go until we reached Oxford and the Order Headquarters. It was barely midday on a Sunday; the roads would be quiet. But we had no idea what Blackbeard was planning, or when he was going to try and pull it off.

From the other side of the forecourt, a man in top hat and tails raised a hand in greeting. I rolled my eyes and pretended not to see him I really didn't have time for another damn ghost, not right now. They could have my full attention, such as it was, when Blackbeard was out of the way. Until then, they'd have to wait.

'Coooeeee!'

I stared at the pump, willing the numbers to move faster and for my tank to fill just that little bit quicker. Another twenty seconds and we'd be ready to go again. Come on. Come on.

'You're Ivy, right?'

Tralalalalala. The petrol finally stopped flowing. I hastily re-hooked the hose and put the taxi's fuel cap back on.

'Hello?'

I can't hear you. I reached into my back pocket to pull out my purse to pay and strode towards the main booth.

'Clare Rees asked me to find you.'

Arse. I halted abruptly, causing the person behind me to smack into my back. I turned and glared at her, as if it were her fault that we'd collided, then looked at the ghost. 'Is there a problem?'

'No, no!' he trilled. 'Quite the opposite, in fact.'

I gritted my teeth. If Clare had sent a fellow phantom here simply to say hello, I'd kill her whether she was a ghost already or not. 'Then, why,' I asked, 'are you here?'

'Well,' he said, flipping his white silk scarf over his shoulder and considering the question, 'I'm not entirely sure. I must say, I'm very glad to be here though. I perished on the *Titanic* so I could have ended up either in New York or here.' He shuddered. 'Or at the bottom of the ocean. Can you imagine having to haunt a bunch of fish for the rest of eternity?'

I stared at him then I began to turn away. Sod this malarkey.

'Oh,' he said. 'You mean *here* as in this place. Whatever it is. I'm looking for you because Clare Rees wants you to know that the rest of her coven have appeared.'

I spun back round then immediately regretted it as I almost toppled over. I definitely needed a holiday to regain my equilibrium. I'd had three days' hard graft. That was more than enough for this month. Or this year.

'Ivy!' Winter called from the car. He tapped his watch and I nodded to show I understood.

'Give me a minute. Can you pay for the petrol? I need to talk to this guy.' I gestured at the overdressed spectre.

Unfortunately, a man who was most definitely not dead – but who looked like he had the sort of hangover that made you wish you were dead – passed in front of me and frowned blearily. 'What? Were you at Jill's party? Because what happened with that bush wasn't my fault.'

'I wasn't talking to you,' I said.

He glanced over his shoulder. There was no one there apart from Mr Titanic who, of course, my new acquaintance couldn't see.

I rolled my eyes. 'Just piss off.' Politeness was all very well when you didn't have dead people and mass murderers and potential Order destruction on your plate at the same time. I could see him thinking about retorting but in the end the hangover won out and he continued on his way. It was probably just as well.

I returned my full attention to the ghost. 'Where are they?' I asked. 'Where are the other coven members?'

'Visiting their families, I believe.' He sniffed. 'The newly dead often find it hard to let go when they realise they're no longer physically viable.'

'I meant where are their remains?'

His eyebrows lifted. 'Oh yes. Apparently I'm to tell you that they're in a hotel room in a place called Uffington. There's a lot of activity going on outside. Something to do with magic? Or police?' He shrugged. 'I don't really know.'

My stomach sank. 'Is that it?'

'Yes.'

'Thank you.'

He bowed. 'It was my pleasure, my dear. Toodle pip.' He vanished.

I returned to the car at the same time as Winter. 'All paid,' he said. 'Was that another ghost?'

I nodded grimly and told him what Mr Titanic had said. Winter's expression grew even bleaker while his blue eyes darkened. 'It's confirmed then. They wouldn't have appeared if Blackbeard was in the vicinity. His null nature would have prevented it. He's definitely not in Uffington but he wants us to think he is.'

I turned on the engine. I thought I'd been driving too fast before; that was nothing compared to what I was about to do.

***

I half expected to arrive at the Order headquarters and find a scene of bloody carnage. We'd kept the radio on as we drove on the off-chance that a breaking news bulletin would tell us everything we didn't want to know, but there was nothing. Abandoning all sense of propriety or sanity, I abandoned the taxi in the middle of the road and jumped out.

'Stay with the car, Brutus,' I ordered. This wasn't the time to have him loose on a magical campus. We had enough to worry about as it was. Fortunately, he simply yawned in response and curled up to sleep in the back seat. Thank goodness for small mercies.

Focusing on the nearest group of witches, I grabbed a

red-robed Neophyte and pulled her to the side before shaking her. 'What's going on? What's wrong?'

'Huh?'

'Have you seen a man with a black beard and a bald head anywhere near here?'

Her jaw hung gormlessly as she tried to work out who I was and what I really wanted. The relief on her face when she spotted Winter was almost palpable. 'Adeptus Exemptus!'

'Ivy,' Winter said, 'let go of the innocent Neophyte. She clearly doesn't know anything.' I bared my teeth and she jumped but I did as he asked. 'I'm sorry,' Winter continued with a professional smile. Now we were back at the Order, he'd automatically slipped back into serious witch mode.

She gave him a fawning glance as if he'd just rescued her from a wildebeest. 'I'm Lily. You won't remember me,' she said, 'but we've met before. It was only once during orientation, and there were lots of other Neophytes in the same group, but it was a real honour for me.'

Winter smiled. 'Lily, of course I remember. You're the girl from Devon who likes fish and is looking forward to learning more about herblore.'

Her cheeks turned bright pink. Damn him and his almost perfect memory. I tapped my foot impatiently. Did we seriously have time for this crap?

'Tell me, Lily,' Winter said, leaning in towards her. 'Have you noticed anything out of the ordinary about the Order today? It's very important. Anything you've seen will be helpful.'

'Uh…' She blinked rapidly, obviously desperate to help her hero. 'There are a lot of Arcane Branch witches absent.'

Winter nodded quickly. 'Anything else?'

Her brow furrowed as she tried to think. This was a

waste of time. 'The cafeteria in the north quarter has green jelly instead of red. I don't know why.'

I huffed and rolled my eyes. They ignored me.

'And have you seen the man Ivy described? He's quite distinctive. A very large build, a big bushy black beard, and an earring with a skull in it.'

She desperately wanted to say yes but in the end she felt compelled to tell the truth. 'No.'

'How about your friends over there?' he asked gently, pointing towards the rest of the Neophytes who were goggling at us.

'I'll go ask.' She turned tail and jogged away.

'You can stop that,' Winter said to me in an undertone. 'I learnt those skills from you.'

'Skills?' I scoffed. 'Getting young women to all but drop their knickers at one flash of your baby blues? That's not one of *my* skills.'

'I meant being nice to people to get them to tell us what they know.'

I crossed my arms. 'I don't think Lily knows anything.'

'Wide-eyed Neophytes have wide eyes. They see more than you think.' He gestured around. 'There's nothing wrong here. No one is screaming. There is no blood.'

'Just because Blackbeard's not acted yet doesn't mean he won't.'

'I know that.' Winter touched my arm. 'Don't let the stress get to you.'

My mouth twitched, ready to continue arguing, but I forced myself to relax. Winter was right: I'd been so worked up about what we were going to see when we arrived that seeing nothing had amped up the pressure inside me. I breathed out. Breathing was good.

Lily ran back over. 'No. No one's seen a thing.'

'Thank you,' he said. 'It's really appreciated. Ivy and I are going to see the Ipsissimus now but I need you to pass the word round. If anyone sees the man I described, they are not to approach him. They must come and find us as quickly as possible. Can I trust you to do this?'

Lily pulled her shoulders back. 'Yes.' Her eyes shone. 'Yes, you can. I won't let you down.' She half curtsied and sped away once more.

'Okay,' I conceded grudgingly. 'She's going to bend over backwards to do your bidding. That was actually quite smart.'

Winter gave me a fleeting smile. 'I am actually quite smart.' Then his expression sobered. 'But perhaps not as smart as Blackbeard. Let's get to the Ipsissimus now. He'll be able to prevent this from happening.'

I sighed. Yeah. Whatever 'this' was.

'I'll tell you one thing,' Winter said, as we marched towards the main building where the Ipsissimus hung out. 'I really can't believe they're selling green jelly instead of red.'

I glanced at him. 'Did you just crack a joke whilst under extreme pressure?'

'I did.' He paused. 'Did it work?'

'Nope.' I gave him a quick kiss on the cheek. 'But I do love you for it.'

Chapter Twenty

About three seconds after we entered, a security guard strode up to us. 'Adeptus Exemptus Winter, Ipsissimus Collings told us that if you appeared we were to inform him immediately and ask you to wait to be shown up to his office.' His tone was warm and respectful. It certainly made a change. 'Unfortunately, he's not here at the moment but we can try to locate him for you. Why don't you come with me and I'll show you to a waiting area?'

'We need to speak to him as soon as possible,' Winter said, frowning.

'We'll do our best to find him quickly.' The guard led us up the first flight of stairs and pointed towards a narrow bench before twisting round to hopefully do as he'd promised. The bench was situated directly in front of Grenville's portrait. Well, well, well; Ipsissimus Collings was either having a joke or being incredibly respectful. I was hard placed to say which.

Rather than sit down, I tapped my foot. 'We should just barge our way up to his office and find him.'

'Yes,' Winter agreed. 'Except you're not in the Order and my privileges have been revoked. We can't ascend any further than this floor. The wards will stop us.'

I tilted my head and a tiny smile crossed my face. He should have learnt my ways by now. 'I've got a few spells up my sleeve. I reckon I can break the wards long enough for us to get inside.'

For a moment Winter didn't speak then he ran a hand through his hair and exhaled loudly. 'You're not even exaggerating, are you?'

I shrugged. 'Given the lifestyle I lead now that you're always around, it seemed prudent to brush up on my skills.'

'Your skills of breaking into the most highly secured magical rooms in the country?'

'Yep.'

Winter shook his head. 'Sometimes I'm really glad we're on the same side, Ivy. Let's keep that as a last resort, shall we? The Ipsissimus might be round the corner and the last thing we want is for you to knock yourself out by performing a few difficult spells.'

Grenville's face poked out from his portrait. The effect was decidedly weird, like a strange 3D picture where the creepy eyes followed you wherever you went. 'He's not round the corner,' he chirped. 'Collings, I mean. He's really upstairs in his study.' His eyes lost focus for a moment. 'It used to be my study, you know.'

I frowned. 'Eh?'

'Pardon.'

'You're excused.'

Grenville tutted. 'No. *You* should say pardon. Not *eh*. Eh is not even a word.'

Yeah, yeah. I brushed away Grenville's censure and focused on what he was saying. 'What do you mean?' I asked. 'The Ipsissimus is really in his study? The one upstairs? You mean he's hiding from us?'

Winter's head turned sharply towards me and he glowered.

Grenville pretended to look innocent but it didn't work. 'All I'm telling you is the truth. I wouldn't lie and damage my chance of crossing over to the other side, would I? I need you on my side.'

'You would happily lie if you were still annoyed at me for breaking protocol,' I said. 'Are the other ghosties talking to you again?'

His lip curled. 'They're coming around. Anyway, don't concern yourself with me. Go and see Collings.'

My shoulder blades twitched. Since when had Grenville cared about the living? 'What's going on?' I asked suspiciously.

He threw his hands up in exasperation. 'I want you to stop faffing around with this killer fellow and start doing what you promised. Honestly, I never would have started you down this track if I thought you'd spend this much time over it. He's only one man.'

'Who's only killed seven witches and is trying to kill several more.'

Grenville looked away. 'Just sort it out,' he mumbled. 'If you want to pass through the wards on the upper floors, the skeleton password is *primogenitus ducis*. Just don't tell anyone that I told you.'

My eyebrows flew up. 'Skeleton password?'

'It's not a corpse,' he said. 'There's no empty eye-socketed skull. It's like a skeleton key that—'

I held up my hand. 'I know what a skeleton key is. Are you saying that this password will let me pass through any ward I choose?'

'Yes.'

'Cool,' I breathed out. 'Thanks, Grenville.' I grabbed Winter's arm and tugged at his sleeve. 'Come on.'

'A skeleton password?' Winter asked.

'Apparently so.' I paused. Maybe I'd keep old Grenville around for a while; he clearly had his uses. 'And apparently the Ipsissimus is actually in his study, despite what that guard said. It doesn't make any sense for him to hide from us.'

'Unless,' Winter pointed out, 'he thinks we're here to petition him to be allowed to go to Uffington.'

I wrinkled my nose. 'Yeah, but he wouldn't be afraid

of saying no. He's not the easily intimidated type.' We reached the next set of stairs and the first ward pushed against my skin. I muttered the skeleton password, the pressure lifted and we passed unimpeded.

'Let's not jump to conclusions,' Winter advised. 'Although maybe the Ipsissimus has changed his mind about inviting me back in now that I'm responsible for beating up an innocent man.'

'You're beating yourself up more than you beat him up,' I said. 'Come on, let's get a move on. Whatever Collings's reasons are for skulking in the shadows, what Blackbeard is up to is more important.'

Winter and I exchanged looks. 'Indeed,' he said. 'Indeed.'

***

We made it all the way to the Ipsissimus's study without having to slow down. No one stopped us – in fact, no one even saw us. Not for the first time, it occurred to me that the Hallowed Order of Magical Enlightenment relied far too heavily on magic to keep itself safe. All witches did. No wonder a null like Blackbeard could cause so much chaos.

I had to admit that, vexing as all these ghosts were, they were proving useful. They ought to be careful; they were in danger of talking me out of helping them to leave their current state of limbo for whatever lay beyond.

The Ipsissimus's door was firmly closed. Winter strode up to it and knocked smartly on the wood. We waited for a few beats but heard nothing. Maybe Grenville had been lying. There was only one way to find out.

Ignoring Winter's sharp intake of breath, I reached for the doorknob and twisted it. 'It's not locked.' I pushed the door open all the way and peered inside.

The study was dim. Considering the cold sunshine

outside, the closed curtains and the lack of a single light, there wasn't much to suggest that the Ipsissimus was inside. Unless he were a vampire, of course.

'Knock knock,' I called.

There was no answer. Winter's expression was studiously blank but I reckoned he was feeling the same trepidation that I was. Something wasn't right. That darned gut instinct was kicking in again.

Quashing down the butterflies that were flapping around in my stomach, I stepped over the threshold. Nothing happened. I still couldn't see the Ipsissimus. As befitted his station, his study was large but he definitely wasn't in here. Not unless he was hiding underneath his desk. I bent down and checked, just to be sure. Nope, no one there.

'Bloody Grenville,' I muttered under my breath. The plonker was probably trying to get his revenge on me for not sticking to his rules. 'Where is the Ipsissimus likely to be if he's not here?'

'I don't know,' Winter said. 'He's not in Uffington and he's not here.' He checked his watch. 'It's too late for him to be doing his daily rounds of each Order department. He could be anywhere.'

'It's a Sunday,' I pointed out. 'Wouldn't he be at home?'

'With his feet up and a mug of hot cocoa?' Winter snorted.

'That's what ordinary people do, Rafe. They relax in their own homes. It's not weird.'

Winter picked up a jar of herbs and unscrewed the lid, giving it a quick sniff. 'It is if you're Ipsissimus.'

'Delegation is a beautiful thing.'

I almost fell over when Winter agreed with me. 'You're right. It's important to accede responsibility to others. They will have different points of view and different perspectives – and everyone needs a break.' At my expression he gave a short laugh. 'Not your kind of monthly sabbatical, Ivy. I mean a day off from time to time.'

The Ipsissimus appeared in the doorway with an odd expression on his face. 'When my wife was alive, I took more holidays and I believe I was a better leader for it.' He smiled sadly. 'Maybe that was her influence rather than the time away from this place. But in any case, the boy understands that you cannot work all the time, no matter how much you might love it. It's simply not healthy.' He held my gaze. 'Thank you for that, Ivy. I think he could only learn it from you.'

I actually blushed. 'Well, working somewhere like the Order has its benefits too. For all that I moan about it, it does a lot of good. It's a vital organisation.'

A faint smile crossed the Ipsissimus's face. 'I'm glad you think so. It's important that you do.'

Winter coughed slightly. 'Ivy, would it bother you if I came back?' he asked. 'If I took the Ipsissimus up on his offer? Just say the word if it would and I won't mention it ever again. There are plenty of other places I can work. There's still plenty of good we can do together with the Hallowed Order of Magical Enlightenment.'

I turned and beamed at him. 'I've not been paying lip-service to this place, Rafe. I'll be really happy if you decide to return because I know how much you love working here. But it's not down to me. This is your decision.' I paused. 'I'll expect you to have days off that we can spend together,' I added with a wag of my index finger. 'But I do understand that you want to be here and that it's as much a part of your life as I am.'

His expression softened. 'I can't persuade you to join me?'

I opened my mouth to answer when there was a

sudden loud thump from the end of the corridor. All three of us turned towards the noise.

'Stay here,' Winter said grimly. 'I'll check it out.' He marched past me, passing through the body of Ipsissimus and out the other side before disappearing from sight.

My legs suddenly felt like jelly and I felt my knees give way. I collapsed onto the floor. 'No,' I whispered.

Ipsissimus Collings glided over to me and reached down with an outstretched hand. 'You knew it the moment I appeared, Ivy,' he said. 'You just didn't want to believe it.' He glanced at his hand ruefully and withdrew it. 'It's a very strange sensation,' he said, 'no longer being corporeal.'

'I ... you...' I squeezed my eyes shut. This couldn't be happening. 'We need you.'

'Tough.'

I still couldn't look at him. 'How did this happen?'

'Blackbeard is not in Uffington.'

Oh God. Even though I'd already known that, my stomach still dropped. 'He ... he ... killed you?'

'Yes. Don't worry, it was quick.' Somehow I knew he was lying when he said that. His voice changed. 'Now open your eyes and listen to me. I don't have long. It's already taking everything I have to remain on this plane but this is important.'

I swallowed hard and did as he asked before struggling to my feet. He was the one who was dead, after all; his problems were far greater than mine. 'Go on,' I said with a catch in my voice.

'The paperwork for Raphael to rejoin the Order is in the top drawer of my desk. I signed it weeks ago. It's all ready to go. He just needs to sign it. It is imperative he does this before my body is discovered. Blackbeard has clearly abandoned his plan to cremate his victims. He has hidden my body but it won't stay that way for long. This time he wants everyone to know what he's done. Beyond that, I cannot speak for his motives or his reasoning. You will need to ascertain those for yourselves and find him before he can do even more damage. The Order is everything, Ivy. It must survive.'

My mouth was parched dry. 'It will. Of course it will.'

'You remember the conversation we had in Scotland about what would happen if I were to die? About the chaos that would ensue?'

Shit. It was the reason why I'd confronted Alistair the teenage necromancer instead of the Ipsissimus doing it. There were too many Order witches with too much ambition and too many hidden agendas for peace to ensue. 'Yes.'

'The events in Scotland prompted me to take action to ensure that will not happen. It was something I should have done long ago and which I have long regretted I did not plan for. I have named my successor and he will do the Order proud. He will not let it falter and he will be a unifying force. He will be accepted as the new Ipsissimus,' he paused, 'but only if he is already back as an Order witch. The contract I've prepared promotes him to Third Level. He hasn't passed the examinations but, in his case, they are a mere formality.' His voice grew stern. 'However, if his return is not acknowledged before my death is discovered, the dissenters will find reason to keep him out and the in-fighting will start. It will continue for years, maybe even decades.'

'Rafe,' I whispered. 'You've named Rafe.' So the Ipsissimus had always expect Winter to return to the fold. Truthfully, so had I.

'Yes. He was not ready before but he is ready now. He will need you by his side to guide and support him. Your role will perhaps be even more important than his in the months to come.'

I hoped he was just saying that because he thought I needed my ego massaged. I was more than happy to be the nonentity in the background. Yes, please, sign me up for sofa duty. I was not the Caesar's wife type especially when, deep down, I knew that Winter was the perfect person for the role of Ipsissimus. He made mistakes but he'd learnt to acknowledge them; he didn't cut corners. He had the dedication and the integrity; he'd be brilliant. My expression twisted.

'What's the problem?' the Ipsissimus asked.

'Nothing.' I couldn't tell him that it had just occurred to me that my boyfriend would be the geekiest of all the Order geeks. 'It's all fine. Apart from the part where you're dead, of course.'

A spasm lurched through the Ipsissimus's body. 'I can't deny the lure of the other side for much longer. Make sure Raphael signs those papers. Make sure others see them before I am found.'

His shape was beginning to falter and become transparent, and there was a bright glow surrounding him that was difficult to look at.

'Wait!' This couldn't be it. He couldn't leave already. 'Where are you? Where's your body?'

'In a shed towards the back of the Herblore Department. He dragged me there.' A beatific smile crossed his face and his gaze rested on a spot seemingly far away. 'Goodbye, Ivy.'

'But what about…?' The light brightened and I was forced to shield my eyes. I yelled, 'Wait! Don't go!' Even as I said the words, I knew they were pointless.

When I could finally see again, he'd gone. Winter was back in the room, rushing to my side. 'What's wrong? What's happened? Ivy!'

I stared at him dully. 'The Ipsissimus,' I said. 'The

Ipsissimus is dead.'

The colour drained from Winter's face. Behind him, I spotted Philip Maidmont, his hand covering his mouth in horror.

'It was Blackbeard,' I said. 'Somehow Blackbeard found him and killed him.' My voice was quiet but surprisingly steady. I drew in a ragged breath. 'The Ipsissimus has gone and his spirit has already passed over. As for Blackbeard, I don't know where he is.' But I did know that nothing would ever be the same again.

Chapter Twenty-One

What I wanted to do was to throw myself into Winter's arms, burrow into his chest and cry. What I did was shake myself and head directly for the Ipsissimus's desk.

Maidmont and Winter stared at me dumbly. I yanked open the top drawer and found the scrolled contract lying on the top of the papers inside. I picked it up between my finger and thumb, afraid that I might damage it, then held it out to Winter.

He looked at me as if I were holding a poisonous snake. 'What is that?'

'Your contract,' I said simply. 'You have to sign it. We have to take it to HR right now and get you reinstated.'

'The Ipsissimus has just died, Ivy. Blackbeard is still on the loose. I hardly think my employment status is a high priority.'

'Right now,' I said fiercely, 'it's the highest possible priority.'

It was Maidmont who understood first. Dawning comprehension lit his face and he began to nod vigorously. Maybe Ipsissimus Collings had already given the quiet librarian some indication of what he'd been planning. 'Yes,' he breathed. 'Yes. You have to sign it now. I'll witness it.' He reached into the pocket of his robes and drew out a fountain pen. 'This is my lucky pen. Use this one.'

Only a librarian would have a lucky pen. I smiled sadly at him. 'Thank you.'

Winter still didn't get it. 'We have to find the

Ipsissimus. His body, at least. We have to find Blackbeard.'

I grimaced. 'The fact that I could talk to the Ipsissimus means that Blackbeard probably isn't anywhere near here. Not now. Maybe killing the Ipsissimus was his grand plan all along and now he's achieved it, he'll go to ground.' That was about as likely as me taking learning to play the harp. There was no way Blackbeard was done yet but I needed Winter to focus on the scroll. I pressed it into his hands. 'Listen to me,' I said softly. 'This is what the Ipsissimus wanted. He hung on especially for this when the other side was already dragging him away. He's signed your contract. He's promoted you to Third Level. And, Rafe,' I licked my lips, 'he's named you as his successor.'

For a long moment Winter didn't react. It was only because of the faint narrowing of his eyes that I knew he'd even heard me. 'No,' he said eventually.

'This is it, Raphael Winter,' I said sternly. 'This is where you make your mark. You step up and take the responsibility that is being handed to you. You're the best person for the job. You're the *only* person for the job. You have to do this.'

'No.' He met my eyes. 'If this were you, you'd run away screaming.'

'But it's not me. We're different people.'

From the doorway there was a tiny miaow then Brutus sauntered in. He slunk round Winter's legs before plonking himself directly in front of him. I frowned. How on earth had he managed to pass through the wards on his own?

'It is only natural,' Brutus said, while my heart skipped several beats and my jaw dropped, 'to feel intimidated by complex situations where the course of one's life is about to be decided. I had to undergo similar soul-searching when I met Ivy for the first time. I possessed deep-seated doubts. She has questionable hygiene. Her hair makes her look as if she's a close relation to Albert Einstein but without any of the brain cells to match. She likes to pretend that her work ethic is weak and her morals are non-existent. The truth is, of course, that the Ivy she presents to the world is very different to the real Ivy. Only very special beings recognise her for who she is inside. I am one of those beings. You are another. You see the truth of her. And you see the truth of the Order.'

In the background, Philip Maidmont started to raise a hand as if to indicate that he too believed I wasn't a complete waste of space. Brutus narrowed his eyes at him and he changed his mind abruptly and brought his hand down again.

I couldn't move. Or speak. What exactly was going on with my damned cat? Had he been possessed by one of those blasted ghosts?

Brutus wasn't finished. 'You, Raphael Winter, have the ability to be Ipsissimus. You can be the leader these witches deserve. Under your guidance, they will enjoy heady heights. Magic will never be the same again and the whole country will benefit from what you can provide. I shall be by your side, offering the support you require to be successful. Ivy will also be there. I imagine that fluffy floof you call a familiar will want to stick around as well.' He sniffed. 'But I wouldn't listen to her too often. She enjoys that tuna-flavoured gloop out of the blue packets. No cat in their right mind enjoys that filth.'

Brutus licked his paw and began to wash his face before pausing to speak once again. 'Of course, if you'd rather abandon the Hallowed Order of Magical Enlightenment to chaotic bureaucracy, and you would enjoy seeing them descend into obscurity for the rest of eternity, by all means don't become Ipsissimus. I am sure you can develop a nice new career of your own by creating new grout cleaners.'

Nobody moved. Then, very slowly, Winter unfurled the scroll. He held out his palm towards Maidmont who dropped his lucky pen into it. Winter walked over to the Ipsissimus's desk and sat down, poised to sign.

'I can't do this without you.' His voice was so quiet that I had to strain to hear him. Both Maidmont and Brutus studiously looked away.

I met his eyes. 'I'm not going anywhere,' I told him. 'I'll be that dead weight holding you down. The ball and chain tied to your ankle. The bad smell that follows you everywhere you go.'

Winter suddenly flashed me a smile. It was so fleeting I almost missed it. 'Thank goodness.'

'But don't expect me to make you packed lunches or fold your socks just because you'll be a magical bigwig and I'll be a lowly taxi driver,' I grumbled.

'*The*,' Winter said. 'I'll be *the* magical bigwig.' He paused. 'Do you even know how to fold socks?'

Ha bloody ha. I gave him my very best glare and turned to Brutus. 'You shit,' I said.

'Food.'

'Have you been hiding that vocabulary all this time?'

Brutus blinked. 'Food.'

'You know I could give you up and find myself another familiar if I wanted to?'

'Food.'

I sighed; I was clearly never going to win this conversation. 'Stay here,' I said eventually. 'I'll bring you food later. Keep an eye out in case Blackbeard shows up and come and tell me if he does. Do not do anything stupid like approach him.'

Winter nodded in agreement. 'The Ipsissimus wasn't

the only powerful witch with a room up here. It's possible that others might be targeted.'

'I'm sure Blackbeard is lying low,' I said. 'But I'll talk to Grenville and see what he's noticed. You need to go and sort out your paperwork. Ipsissimus Collings might be discovered at any moment.'

'Brutus is not the only one who shouldn't do anything stupid like approach Blackbeard.'

'Please,' I scoffed. 'I've already had one stint as a martyr. I have no desire for another.' Then, before Winter could say anything else, I continued. 'Let's get a move on while we still can.'

***

On our way back down the stairs, Grenville's face poked out of his portrait. He looked slightly nervous.

'You should have told me,' I said, gesturing to Winter and Maidmont to go on ahead. 'It would have been nice to have some warning about what had happened.'

'I will not apologise for that,' Grenville said stiffly. 'It was not my place to inform you. Besides, old Collings is a lucky man. He was able to pass to the next plane. There are not many people who have enjoyed his position who have also escaped eternal curses.' It was impossible to miss the envy in his voice.

'I will help you,' I said. 'I promise I will. I'll do everything I said I would. But I have to deal with the living right now.'

I watched as Maidmont and Winter crossed the lobby, heading for HR. The pair of them would ensure that Winter's return was notarised and time-stamped. In a couple of hours, assuming the Ipsissimus's death remained concealed, Maidmont would walk into the small shed where the great man had breathed his last and 'discover' his body. That's when all hell would break loose. At least with Winter formally named as successor, the hell would be containable.

Grenville cleared his throat, ensuring my attention returned to him and him alone. 'You need something from me.'

I smiled humourlessly. Grenville had been Ipsissimus for a reason. He might be as irritable as he was irritating but he certainly wasn't stupid. 'The man who killed Ipsissimus Collings…' I bunched up my fists. I'd managed to keep my emotions under wraps until now but it was becoming impossible and I could hear my own voice shaking with rage. 'The bastard who did this … he's a null. If you go near him, you'll vanish. You won't exist here and you won't exist on another plane. You'll just be … nothing. It's not long term. As soon as he's moved away, you'll return.'

Grenville frowned. 'That's a shame. I quite like the idea of not existing. Existence can get remarkably tiresome, you know.' He sighed. 'But yes, I have heard of nulls before. I understand the concept.'

Good. 'Get in touch with as many spirits as you can. Send them out across the campus. Blackbeard is here somewhere. I have no idea what kind of range his null nature provides but when ghosts start disappearing, you know you're getting close. Find out which area he is in and tell me. He's killed the Ipsissimus but I don't believe for a second that he's finished. While Winter is ensuring the safety of the Hallowed Order of Magical Enlightenment, I'm going to be ensuring Winter's safety.'

'How exactly?'

'By sending that bastard to the fires of hell,' I said. I didn't know how yet but I would do all that I could to achieve it.

'Good plan,' Grenville said.

Yep. Planning to that kind of depth and detail had always been my forte.

***

As I walked through the Order, I kept catching snippets of conversation. They all followed the same pattern.

'You'll never guess what?'

'Tell me!'

'Adeptus Exemptus Winter has returned. He's back for good!'

'Thank goodness. We were lost without him.' I'm paraphrasing slightly but that was definitely the gist. I kept my head down as I walked. I was either going to be blamed for his departure or congratulated for his return – I didn't really care which. What I did care about was not being interrupted. Whatever Blackbeard was planning, it was bound to be bloody. It was imperative I found him and stopped him before anyone else got hurt.

'Ivy!'

Arse. I turned and spotted Eve jogging towards me. She caught up and gave me a quick hug. 'Is it true? Is Winter really back? It's all over campus. Tell me it's not just a rumour. Tell me he's not just here for a visit.'

'Yeah, he's back. For good. Listen, Eve, I really have to go.'

She beamed. She wasn't hearing me properly. 'That's wonderful news!' Then her smile vanished. 'Are you okay that he's back?'

'I'm in love with him, Eve. Whatever makes him happy makes me happy. As long as his happy doesn't involve throwing water over me to wake me up or making me go jogging. You get what I mean.' She nodded vigorously. 'Now,' I continued, 'I really have to go.'

She finally seemed to realise that I was serious. Her

smile dropped and her gaze grew anxious. 'What's going on?'

I looked at her assessingly. Eve was in Arcane Branch; she knew how to maintain a level head. 'There's a serial-killing null on campus. He's already killed the Ipsissimus and there's no doubt that he's here to kill others. The more witches the better, as far as he's concerned. We have to find him and stop him but we can't use magic against him. I have a bunch of ghosts on the look out for him but it's difficult because they tend to vanish whenever he is in the vicinity.'

She blinked. 'Uh…but…'

'Everyone thinks he's in Uffington. He's not.'

'You're talking about Hal Prescott. The Bearded Butcher.'

Bloody Tarquin Villeneuve. 'Blackbeard. Yeah. Whatever. He's here and we need to find him before he kills anyone else.'

'They wouldn't let me go,' she said, the colour draining out of her face. 'They only wanted the experienced witches to go to Uffington. The only ones left are people like me who don't know what they're doing.'

'Don't be ridiculous,' I snapped, marching off again, my gaze swinging around desperately for any glimpse of Blackbeard. Eve had no trouble keeping up with me with her long-legged stride. 'You know exactly what you're doing. Find the bad guy. Stop the bad guy. Don't use magic. It's pretty simple.'

'Ivy,' she whispered, 'if we can't use magic, how can we stop him?'

I opened my mouth to answer her, just as the familiar figure of Lily came flying round the corner, her arms flapping wildly. As she ran, three other figures popped into existence beside her, fleeing even faster than she was. She zipped past both Eve and I without a second glance. Of course – she was looking for Winter, not me. He was the one she trusted; I didn't even register in her field of vision.

Fortunately the dead had more respect. All three ghosts came careening to a halt. 'You're her,' one gasped. 'He must be over there!'

'It was the strangest thing,' said another. 'I was walking along minding my own business and keeping an eye out, then everything went black.'

'You reappeared in the same spot?' I demanded.

I felt rather than saw Eve staring at me. 'Are you talking to one of them? Are you talking to a ghost?'

We all ignored her. The ghost nodded. 'Yes. I was beside the fountain. When I returned I was still there.'

'Blackbeard is on the move.' I grimaced. It was a long time since I'd been here and my knowledge of the Order campus layout wasn't as up to date as it should have been. 'What's beyond the fountain, Eve?'

Eve's hand went up to her mouth and she stared at me in horror.

'What? What is it?' I tamped down the temptation to shake her as hard as I could.

'The crèche,' she said. 'Witches who have kids can leave them there during the day. It's the only building past that point.'

I felt ill. It made a sick kind of sense – if you were Blackbeard. Lop off the head then move on to the future. Destroy the next generation of witches and you'd destroy the Order for good. I swallowed. And then I began to run.

***

Even with the sound of the cascading water from the fountain and the distance between Eve and me and the crèche, it was obvious that something was terribly wrong. The screams and shouts said it all. You'd have had to be truly evil not to have felt terrified by the sounds that were renting the air.

I sprinted as fast as I could but Eve quickly overtook me. She pelted straight ahead while I was left gasping. Maybe I ought to join the gym once all this was over and done with. Then I shook myself. The fear and trepidation were clearly getting to me. Every time I was in a life-or-death situation, I started to think I should lead a healthier lifestyle. The trick was to start avoiding life-or-death situations. With that in the forefront of my mind, I put on an extra spurt and rounded the corner just as Eve flung herself towards Blackbeard and leapt onto his back. Four witches, all of whom must have been crèche workers, flung repeated streams of magic attacks in his direction.

He laughed and tried to shake off Eve. 'Do your worst, witches,' he bellowed. 'You can't hurt me!' He spun round and I spotted the long, shining blade in his hands. That was probably the same one he'd used to kill Clare and the rest of her coven. It was probably the same one he'd used to kill the Ipsissimus.

Eve shrieked like an Amazon warrior and curved her head down, biting his ear. Blood spurted everywhere. Unfortunately, it only enraged Blackbeard and didn't slow him down in the slightest. He thrust the blade upwards, narrowly avoiding sliding it straight through Eve's neck. She swung to one side. Terrified that he'd succeed if he tried the manoeuvre a second time, I ran towards them.

I gestured frantically to the four crèche witches. They got the message and used the momentary distraction to vanish back indoors and look after their charges. They'd probably already realised that magic wasn't going to work here. While I charged at Blackbeard to try and help Eve, a window opened and various objects were thrown out. Somehow I didn't think a plastic toy elephant was going to be much of a weapon; neither was the breast pump much use. The milk bottle, however…

I switched direction and darted over to snatch it up just as Blackbeard finally threw off Eve. Her body smacked into the wall of the crèche and she slumped down like a broken doll. Shit. He turned towards her, blade raised, obviously ready to finish her off.

I yelled and twisted off the bottle top. 'Have some boiling water,' I shrieked, throwing the milk at him.

Blackbeard raised his hand to shield his eyes; he didn't know the liquid was barely lukewarm. When he realised he'd been fooled, he snarled and abandoned his bid to kill Eve in favour of facing this new threat. Me.

He swiped the blade forward. Surprise, surprise, I wasn't fast enough to dodge it and it sliced through my arm. I cried out involuntarily. Blackbeard's eyes widened as he recognised me. A small, dull voice nibbled at the back of my mind: use this, Ivy. You can use this.

I threw myself to the ground, collapsing onto my knees in front of him. 'I'm not a witch!' I wailed. 'Don't kill me! I can't use magic at all!'

Blackbeard paused, the knife held aloft. He frowned at me as if trying to decide what to do. Then he lowered his arms and glanced around. Eve was out cold and the crèche witches had vanished. To all intents and purposes, it was just him and me.

'You might not be a witch,' he spat, 'but you sleep with witches. You are here with witches. As a collaborator, you are as bad as they are. Worse even.'

'It's not my fault,' I babbled. 'I'm not smart. I don't have any special skills. I'm just a taxi driver. I thought hanging around witches would make my life better. Instead it's much, much worse. Now I'm stuck with them and I don't know how to escape.' I grabbed hold of his trouser legs. 'You can help me.'

He kicked me away. 'You're lying.'

'I'm not!' I held up my hands. 'My ID is in my pocket.' I pulled it out and tossed it over to him. 'See?' I said. 'I'm a taxi driver. I'm like you. I'm not a witch, I don't want to be a witch. I think they bewitched me because they wanted a chauffeur. I'm no other use to them. But…' my voice dropped '…I think they want to use me in some of their spells. Black magic stuff. They want my blood. They want to do evil things.'

When it came to killing and planning for killing, Blackbeard was a clever man but even clever men have blind spots. Prejudice can blind even the smartest fool and Blackbeard's prejudice was against witches. All I needed was to cast some doubt; all I needed was to gain some time.

He shook his large head. 'I'm sorry,' he said. 'But I can't trust that you're telling the truth.'

'You know I'm not a witch,' I pleaded. 'You know from my ID that I'm just a taxi driver. I don't know what else I can do to prove that I'm not like them.'

'Tough. I've already let you escape once. I was kind then but I can't afford to be kind now. You had your chance.'

I sagged. 'Fine,' I whispered. 'In truth, anything will be better than remaining here with these bastards. But … are we the same? Do we hate them in the same way? Is that why you're killing them?' I kept my head low and subdued my body language. I was already defeated; I was already prepared to die.

'All witches are evil. All witches are unnatural.' Blackbeard said the words as if by rote. He'd been taught to believe this. More fool him.

'Why did you kill the coven?' I asked. 'Why not come straight here first? Raphael, the witch I was with on Dartmoor? He learned about you because you destroyed that coven. Without their deaths, no one would have known you existed. Why them?'

He gave me a blank look. 'They were there and I needed the practice. I had to know if I was capable of murder. Not everyone is.' He rubbed his ear where Eve had bitten it, then pulled his hands away and gazed at the blood as if seeing it for the first time. 'It's a lot easier than I thought it would be. I knew that having ended them, I could end anyone.' He raised his massive shoulders in a shrug, as if surprised by himself and his ability to kill, in the same way that I would be surprised if I discovered some money wedged underneath a sofa cushion. 'How did the witch find out about them anyway?'

Ah ha. Maybe I'd piqued his curiosity. A glimmer of hope rippled through me. I had to manage this properly; I had to give a good enough answer to keep him talking. The closer I stayed to the truth, the more believable I'd be. 'I told you. Some kind of black magic. I think…' I hesitated. 'I think he's been talking to corpses and they talk back.'

'Unnatural,' Blackbeard muttered.

Tell me about it. 'Why didn't you just burn all their bodies at once? Why not get rid of them in one go?'

He checked his watch. 'How many questions are you planning on asking?' His voice wasn't irritated, just curious as if he wanted to be sure he could adjust his schedule if necessary. At that point I realised that he wanted to talk; he was desperate to share his exploits with someone who would listen. He'd spent so long hiding his actions that all he wanted to do now was to spill his secrets to the world. And the more I could delay him, the better chance I had.

'Only a few more,' I said. 'I just want to understand.'

He nodded. 'Well,' he said, 'it's kind of hard to burn

seven bodies in one go. They don't burn quickly and I had limited time each night to do it. I had to keep them in my flat until I could transport them to the crematorium without anyone noticing. And the longer I had to wait, the more I realised I enjoyed it.' He bared his teeth. 'Anticipation is a wonderful thing. It's usually a greater pleasure than the end result. So I drew out disposing of the ashes in the same way.' He smiled. Chillingly, it was a genuine smile, filled with joy. 'It was a lot of fun. And each time I got rid of the ash, the feeling built up here.' He thumped his chest. 'The need. The desire.'

'The desire to kill?'

His eyes glowed. He thought I understood, that I 'got' him. I'd get him alright, just not in the way he thought. 'That's it exactly.'

'You planned everything so well,' I said. 'The secret room in your flat was a stroke of genius.'

'I had to be in control, to make sure that when those bastards came after me they did it on my terms. Not on theirs.' His face twisted. 'This was Plan B, though. Plan A was even better but I had to change it because of you. You knew I'd killed that coven so I had to alter everything.'

I tried to keep my expression blank. All those media embargoes and all that tiptoeing around – and I'd already given the game away when I met Blackbeard in the pub car park. Eve was unconscious. Perhaps I'd manage to keep that little titbit to myself.

'Uh, sorry,' I stammered.

He shrugged. 'It's good to be tested. And I always had my Plan B ready. That's why I had that fake glass wall made. I wasn't sure anyone would be smart enough to spot it was a fake but I hoped they would. Then they'd follow my fake trail and I'd be safe to do what I wanted.' He gestured round. 'As you see.'

'Fake glass?' I asked. 'Not mirror?'

'Real mirrored glass is costly and difficult to break.' He stroked his beard. 'The stuff I had was the same as they use in films for actors so they don't get hurt when they jump through windows.' He sounded very proud.

If it wasn't a real mirror that I'd broken in Blackbeard's flat, I didn't have seven years' bad luck coming my way. This day was looking better and better. 'Thanks,' I said, meaning it. 'I appreciate knowing that.'

'You're welcome.'

A mass murderer with manners. I swallowed. 'There is one thing I should mention,' I said. 'One thing that leaves you a little bit screwed.'

He raised his black, bushy eyebrows. 'What's that?'

'I lied. I'm a witch.' I smiled. 'I'm a witchy witch with witch blood running through my veins and magic in my soul.'

Apparently I was a better liar than I thought. 'No, you're not,' Blackbeard said. 'If you were a witch, you'd have tried to bespell me the first time we met.'

It was my turn to shrug. 'I had my reasons for avoiding magic back then. And I have to avoid it now, of course, because it won't affect you. This will though.' And I reached up with both hands and yanked on his beard as hard as I could.

He screamed: apparently trying to rip off someone's chin really hurts. I held on with left hand, avoiding the swinging knife, and let go with my right hand so I could reach upwards. I jabbed two fingers into his eyes, jamming them into his eye sockets. I didn't blind him permanently – he jerked away too quickly for that – but he wouldn't be able to see much for the next few minutes. There was still hope.

He flailed around, still clinging on to that damned blade. Until I got him to drop it, we were all in danger. I danced round, lunging for his hands and trying to grab the knife handle so I could wrestle it from him. Blinded as he was, he still worked out what I was doing and slashed the weapon at me again, this time managing to cut my cheek. I yelped. Then Blackbeard's free hand snaked out, grabbed a hank of my hair and dragged me over.

'You little bitch,' he hissed. 'You thought you could fool me? You thought you could best me? I might well die this day but I'm going to take you with me. And as many of your little witch friends as I can manage.'

There was a loud thud. For a moment, Blackbeard stood stock still then he keeled over, knocking me to the ground in the process. Behind him stood Tarquin, holding a bloodied rock in both hands.

'I did it,' he breathed. 'I'm a hero.' He looked at me with what was supposed to be a disarming smile. 'I saved your life and saved the day.'

Arsing hell. I scrambled away from both Blackbeard and Tarquin and rolled over. Maybe that damned glass had been a real mirror after all.

'I saved everyone!' Tarquin shouted. 'I killed the serial killer!'

I lay on my back, panting like a dog. From the wall of the crèche, I heard Eve groan. 'What the hell?' she said. 'What happened?'

'I won!' Tarquin shouted. 'I'm the best!'

Warm, sticky blood coated my skin where Blackbeard had cut me but I could already feel it congealing. I was going to live. More importantly, so would everyone else. Although maybe I could still grab hold of Blackbeard's knife and slide it into Tarquin's ribs when no one was looking.

A shadow fell across my face and I squinted upwards. When I saw Winter's familiar sapphire eyes frowning down at me, I gave him as wide a grin as I could manage. 'Ipsissimus Winter,' I said. 'How lovely to see you. I would get up but I'm not sure my legs can hold my weight.'

He put his hands on his hips. 'You bloody idiot. What the hell did you think you were doing taking on Blackbeard single-handed?'

'Eve helped. I wasn't on my own.' From the side, Tarquin continued to crow. 'Besides, the real hero is over there.'

Winter rolled his eyes and snorted. 'Dragging Eve into your foolish schemes is not likely to help your cause. At the rate you keep flinging yourself into danger's path, I'm going to have tie you up to keep you out of harm's way.'

'I'm sure we've had this conversation before,' I said. 'I quite like being tied up. You must have spotted my furry handcuffs by now, Rafe.' I wasn't lying; it was a lot of fun abandoning yourself to someone else. Especially if they were Raphael Winter and they were going to do all the hard work. So to speak.

Winter sighed but there was a glint in his eyes at my words. Then he looked around soberly. 'You shouldn't have done this. It's not your job to save me, Ivy.'

'It wasn't Ivy who saved you. It was me!'

Before Tarquin received a sharp slap, someone had the sense to pull him away. I breathed out and raised myself onto my elbows. 'Someone's got to try and rescue you, Rafe. Especially with all these young witch women throwing themselves at you like you're some kind of rock hero. I need to stamp my mark. Unfortunately, Tarquin beat me to it.'

A look of exasperation crossed Winter's face. 'Can you stand up?'

I pretended to make the effort. 'Oh,' I groaned. 'I

don't think so. You'll have to carry me.'

'Fireman's lift it is, then.'

Whoa. 'I'm getting up! Bloody hell.' I used his hand to bring myself upright. Then I looked around; there was a great deal of blood. And mess. 'The Order aren't going to bill me for this, are they?'

'Don't worry,' he said drily. 'We have insurance.'

Just as well. I stumbled slightly, falling against him. Maybe I did need some help. 'Ipsissimus Collings,' I began.

'We've found him.' Winter's voice was grim. 'He put up a hell of a fight.'

I bit the inside of my cheek to keep the tears at bay. It almost worked. 'He was a good man.'

Winter nodded. He didn't say anything but I knew it was only because he couldn't trust himself to speak. I put a hand on his arm and squeezed.

The air in front of me shimmered and Clare's face appeared, although it was remarkably transparent. Just like Ipsissimus Collings before her, she was already being called away. Her time here was up. Funnily enough, she didn't look in the least bit sorry about it.

'Thank you, Ivy.' She turned her face and glanced away as if someone was shouting her name. A smile spread across her face. 'I have to go but I had to say thank you. All of us thank you.'

'You're very welcome,' I whispered. 'I'll make sure no one forgets you or the rest of your coven.'

She blew me a kiss then there was the now familiar flash of bright light. The witches around us gasped. Even Tarquin fell momentarily silent.

'And just like that,' I said quietly, 'she was gone.'

There was a loud snort. 'How many times do I have to tell you, woman? There's a queue! We need to be orderly about this!'

I smiled at Ipsissimus Grenville. 'Would you like me to help you now? You can pass over next. You've been here for long enough.'

His eyes widened fractionally then he wrung his hands and looked away. 'I would like that.' He sighed. 'But I will stay until all the others are taken care of.'

I raised an eyebrow. 'All of them? That could take years.'

'Yes.' He nodded to himself. 'But you'll do it. We both know you will. I have full trust in you.' I blinked. 'Besides,' he continued, 'you'll probably need my help.'

'You're not going to let me get any peace, are you?'

Grenville roared. 'My dear! Peace is for wimps!'

'I'm a wimp,' I pointed out.

Winter pressed his lips against my temple. 'No, you're not.'

'I'm not like you,' I protested. 'I'm not even like Tarquin.'

'Thank goodness,' he murmured. 'Besides, we all know you're much better.'

Arse. At this rate everyone would know all of my secrets. I'd have to work harder at being lazier. Much, much harder.

Epilogue

There was a shaft of sunlight hitting the bedroom floor. At this time of day, Brutus always found it something of a dilemma. Was it better to lie in the shade but on the comfort of the bed, or to lie in the sun but on the hardness of the floor? Both spots had a lot of merit and it was a difficult choice. However, this was the sort of problem he enjoyed toying with; lately, there had been challenges of far larger import – none of which he had appreciated in the slightest.

He'd just about made the decision to choose the sunshine when the door opened and a witch walked in. Excellent. Brutus immediately flopped onto his back and rolled around in the manner that humans seemed to adore. The witch crouched down and gave him a fuss, just as Brutus wanted. He could definitely get used to this kind of lifestyle. The more minions at his beck and call, the better.

Then the witch went back to the door and heaved in a vacuum monster. Brutus shot a wistful glance at the sunbeam and skedaddled. Ivy might enjoy someone else cleaning the house on a daily basis but did they have to do it every damn day? He missed having dust bunnies to chase after, and he was no match for the vacuum monster, much as he tried to kill it when it was sleeping in the cupboard.

With some regret, Brutus abandoned the bedroom and padded off in search of another place. He was tempted to head for the garden; not only would there be plenty more sunny warm spots where he could curl up, there might be the added bonus of birds. He was feeling slightly peckish. Unfortunately, he was also fairly certain that he'd seen Princess Parma Periwinkle stroll in that direction. That was all very well but if she was running an errand for the man, she'd no doubt try to draw him into her plans.

Brutus had long since decided that work was a beast better left to others. There was a reason he had attached himself to Ivy, after all. It had taken a lot of training to make her even remotely adequate as his witch, and she still had a long way to go, but Brutus remained optimistic. If he couldn't claw her into shape, no one could.

He wound away from the residence and out towards the main Order buildings. There was always fun to be had with the red robes. Initially he'd considered demanding a diamond-studded collar so that everyone would know who he was but collars tended to chafe. Anyway, within three days everyone knew him. If you wanted to remain scratch free, you either carried fishy treats or you stayed far away from Brutus – unless you were particularly dumb. Some humans couldn't be trained, no matter how hard you tried. The floppy-yellow-haired one heading towards him right now was a case in point.

'Brutus!' Tarquin nudged his companion, who was already doing the smart thing and backing away. 'You know whose familiar this is, of course. We were childhood sweethearts but I was bit too much for her. She couldn't keep up with my pace so we decided to split up. She was upset about it, of course, Cried for weeks, but it was for the best. There are no hard feelings on my part. I even saved her life when I saved the Order. Between you and me, she'd leave Ipsissimus Winter in a heartbeat if I told her I'd take her back but I wouldn't do that to him. That's the kind of good guy I am.'

Tarquin crouched down. Brutus purred and knocked against his hands then leapt up into his arms. It was only when Tarquin had straightened back up again with an overly wide smile that Brutus acted, slashing out one paw and scratching him across his eyelid. Tarquin shrieked and dropped him. 'You little furry bastard!'

'You big slimy bitch,' Brutus answered. He flicked his tail and continued on his way.

He paused in front of the library, debating whether to enter. The skinny, nervous one was quite adept at petting, not that you'd expect it to look at him, but he often got distracted by witches asking questions or by old books which caught his eye. Brutus liked the man but he wasn't playing second fiddle to a pile of papers. Not for anyone.

In the end, he continued towards the study. The man would be delighted to see him. One day those other witches would create a warding spell that would keep Brutus out – but Brutus doubted that day would be today.

***

When he reached the man's office, the door was closed. Brutus sniffed. Doors were made to be open; that was their raison d'être. Fortunately this one did its job, swinging backwards so that the tall, fit female could exit.

'Thank you, Eve,' the man said. 'Will you be round later for dinner?'

She paused at the threshold. 'Is Ivy cooking?'

There was a faint snort. 'No.'

'I could cook if I wanted to!' Ivy yelled. 'I have a microwave, you know. I'm just not going to be cooking tonight.'

Eve smiled. 'Then, yes, I'd love to pop round.' She glanced down. 'Hey Brutus.' She reached down and scratched him under his chin then sneaked a hand into her pocket and pulled out a crunchy biscuit. She placed her finger to her lips and Brutus nodded. He wasn't an idiot;

he was far more likely to get treats from others if he didn't boast about the ones he'd already had. He snaffled it surreptitiously then made his way in.

Goody. The computer was on. Since becoming Ipsissimus, the man had designated certain areas to be magic free so that technology could be utilised and the Order could become more efficient. There had been some grumblings but the zones were clearly demarcated and there had been no explosions of any sort. Bit by bit, even the worst of the naysayers were beginning to admit that the new blood and new ideas which Ipsissimus Winter brought to the Order could be advantageous. Brutus thoroughly agreed; he leapt onto the desk and sat down on the keyboard. It was always warm and tingly, even if it did make an annoying beeping sound when he jumped onto it.

Ivy leaned down and nudged him off. He scowled. 'Bitch.' Then he immediately returned to the same spot.

She sighed. 'Why can't we have a normal conversation?' she asked. 'I know you're capable of it. What have you been up today, Brutus?'

'Food.'

She rolled her eyes. 'Come on,' she coaxed.

Absolutely not. This was why he'd avoided long sentences around her before. She'd want to talk; she'd want him to talk. They'd both lose out on valuable sleeping and eating time. You'd think that Ivy, of all people, would understand that but she didn't truly understand what it meant to be lazy, not like a cat did. It was an art form; it required dedication that even humans like Ivy weren't capable of.

The man smiled indulgently and focused on Ivy. 'I have a proposition for you.'

Brutus perked up. That sounded interesting.

'A new job.'

Wait a minute.

Ivy seemed to think the same. 'Hang on,' she said. 'Kind of you as it is to think of me, Ipsissimus Winter, I would hate for you to be accused of nepotism. It's probably far better if I don't have a job. I'm really quite busy already.'

Good girl.

The man held up a finger. 'Hear me out. Your title will be Global Phantom Solutions and Assurance Strategist.'

Ivy paused. 'That's a very long title.'

'It is.'

'I thought you said that the more complicated the job title, the less there is to do.'

He tapped the corner of his mouth. 'I did say that, didn't I?'

Ivy grinned. 'Do I get my own office?'

'If you need one.'

'I *am* the only person who can talk to ghosts,' she mused. 'I will be providing an important service. Can I have some staff to work with me? There'll be errands to run and curses to cancel, after all.'

'I'm sure we can work something out.'

Brutus tutted. Ivy obviously couldn't see what the man was doing. It was basic manipulation; before she could say Global Phantom Solutions and Assurance Strategist, she'd be working several hours a day. Well, she'd only have herself to blame.

Brutus got up and headed for the door. It wasn't as much fun here as he'd thought it would be. 'Open.' When neither human sprang into action, he growled and tried again. 'Open.' Then, for good measure, he reached up and started clawing at the door's surface. One long good rake along that wood and the man opened the door for him. Brutus slunk out and the door closed behind him.

He took a few steps down the corridor then paused. Actually, this was a bad idea. If he left them alone now, there was no knowing what Ivy would find herself agreeing to. He had to protect her from herself. He twisted back again and sat in front of the door, albeit now on the wrong side. 'Open.' No answer. 'Open.'

Still no answer. Yet again he was forced to resort to scratching. The door swung open but neither the man nor Ivy were looking at him. Their faces were glued to each other's. It looked remarkably uncomfortable, not to mention unhygienic. The man kicked the door shut and Brutus had to rush forward to avoid his tail getting trapped. He wasn't going to sit here all day while those two locked their lips together. How utterly ridiculous.

He turned back to the door. If they just left the damn thing open they wouldn't have this problem.

'Have I told you,' the man said, 'that I love you?'

'Not today,' Ivy breathed back. 'And I'm sure I've already said it to you three times.'

'I have a lot of catching up to do then.'

'You certainly do, Ipsissimus Winter.'

Brutus rolled his eyes. Fine. He'd wait until they were done but he was expecting some damn good treats for his patience. He bloody deserved them. He hunkered down and curled up, wrapping his tail round him. There were important naps to be taken.

Thank you so much for reading Star Witch! I really hope you enjoyed it. It would mean a huge amount if you could leave a review – any and all feedback is so very, very welcome and hugely important for independent authors like myself.

Find out more about me and my books, as well as the chance to sign up for my newsletter at
http://helenharper.co.uk

Acknowledgments

In 2016, I was lucky enough to be able to travel from Malaysia to the USA to attend a conference – and have a holiday. My best friend came along with me and, as we wandered out of a workshop, she remarked that it would be a great idea to have a series where the main character was very lazy. From that germ of an idea, Ivy Wilde was born. I had to partake in considerable research – lying on my sofa and binge watching television is a dirty job but someone had to do it. However, there are a whole host of other people who have helped to bring Adrianna's idea alive.

Huge thanks must go to Karen Holmes from 2QT for her sterling editing, as well as to Clarissa Yeo for her wonderful covers. For this series she mocked not one but two different sets which Facebook followers then voted on. If that was you, then thank you so much for your input! I have to also thank all my family and friends for their continued invaluable support. Without them, none of this would ever be possible.

Finally, a special mention has to go to Scout, Mavis and Lara – three cranky Malaysian cats who have provided no end of inspiration for Brutus. If they could talk, I have no doubt about what they would say. Most of it would indeed involve foooooooood.

About the Author

After teaching English literature in the UK, Japan and Malaysia, Helen Harper left behind the world of education following the worldwide success of her Blood Destiny series of books. She is a professional member of the Alliance of Independent Authors and writes full time, thanking her lucky stars every day that's she lucky enough to do so!

Helen has always been a book lover, devouring science fiction and fantasy tales when she was a child growing up in Scotland.

She currently lives in Devon in the UK with far too many cats – not to mention the dragons, fairies, demons, wizards and vampires that seem to keep appearing from nowhere.

You can find out more - and learn how to get a FREE copy of Corrigan Fire - by visiting Helen's website:
http://helenharper.co.uk

Other titles by Helen Harper

The complete *Blood Destiny* series

>Bloodfire

>Bloodmagic

>Bloodrage

>Blood Politics

>Bloodlust

>Blood Destiny Box Set (The complete series: Books 1 – 5)

Also
- Corrigan Fire
- Corrigan Magic
- Corrigan Rage
- Corrigan Politics
- Corrigan Lust

The complete *Bo Blackman* series

Dire Straits

New Order

High Stakes

Red Angel

Vigilante Vampire

Dark Tomorrow

The complete *Highland Magic* series
Gifted Thief
Honour Bound
Veiled Threat
Last Wish

The complete *Dreamweaver* series

Night Shade

Night Terrors

Night Lights

Olympiana stand - alone

Eros

SPIRIT WITCH

Printed in Great Britain
by Amazon